Shadowed is feast of intrigue, roma[...]
on a platter of fresh descriptions! I [...] this book, curled up
by the fire, poker in hand—just in case. It feels that real.

—CINDY SIGLER DAGNAN
AUTHOR OF *HOT CHOCOLATE FOR COUPLES* AND
WHO GOT PEANUT BUTTER ON MY DAILY PLANNER
WWW.CINDYDAGNAN.COM

Shadowed is Kariss's best novel yet. When the smoke clears, two
people discover the heartbeat of love is birthed in betrayal, tragedy,
and faith.

—DIANN MILLS
AUTHOR OF *FIREWALL* AND
DOUBLE CROSS
WWW.DIANNMILLS.COM

Lynch brings us a follow-up tale that is bolder and bigger than the
first as she takes us deeper into the lives of her characters and adds
an immensely satisfying tickle of suspense. Another well-rounded
story that has something for every reader, and a darn fine job in
telling it too.

—HEATHER JAMES
AUTHOR OF *UNHOLY HUNGER* AND
HANDS OF DARKNESS

Once again Kariss provides readers with a thrilling book show-
casing a love-struck couple with God at the center of the lives and
struggles. This one is packed with action and seemingly devas-
tating events that test and build faith. Exposing a warrior's heart
for God, his country, and his woman, *Shadowed* brings readers
into the storm of service, sacrifice, passion, and love.

—NAVY SEAL

An action-packed salute to Navy SEALs and their families. Danger, secrets, and bold acts of courage are balanced by playful humor and sweet romance. Kariss Lynch offers it all.

—CANDACE CALVERT
BEST-SELLING AUTHOR OF THE GRACE MEDICAL SERIES
AND *BY YOUR SIDE*
WWW.CANDACECALVERT.COM

Shadowed is a thrill ride of intrigue and romance from beginning to end. Kariss Lynch manages to balance tenderness and courage with the perfect amount of suspense. I fell in love with Nick and Kaylan because they're real and imperfect, not to mention the fact that Nick had me swooning through to the last sentence. *Shadowed* is sure to satisfy romance and suspense lovers everywhere!

—AMY K. SORRELLS
AWARD-WINNING AUTHOR OF *HOW SWEET THE SOUND*
AND *THEN SINGS MY SOUL*
AMYSORRELLS.WORDPRESS.COM

HEART OF A WARRIOR SERIES / BOOK TWO

Shadowed

KARISS LYNCH

REALMS

Most Charisma House Book Group products are available at special quantity discounts for bulk purchase for sales promotions, premiums, fund-raising, and educational needs. For details, write Charisma House Book Group, 600 Rinehart Road, Lake Mary, Florida 32746, or telephone (407) 333-0600.

Shadowed by Kariss Lynch
Published by Realms
Charisma Media/Charisma House Book Group
600 Rinehart Road
Lake Mary, Florida 32746
www.charismahouse.com

Scripture quotations are from the King James Version of the Bible.

Cover design by Lisa Rae McClure
Design Director: Justin Evans

Visit the author's website at www.karisslynch.com.

Library of Congress Cataloging-in-Publication Data:
Lynch, Kariss.
   Shadowed / Kariss Lynch. -- First edition.
      pages cm. -- (Heart of a warrior ; book 2)
      ISBN 978-1-62998-006-5 (paperback) -- ISBN 978-1-62998-007-2 (e-book)
   I. Title.
   PS3612.Y37S526 2015
   813'.6--dc23
                                        2014034344

15 16 17 18 19 — 9 8 7 6 5 4 3 2
Printed in the United States of America

To the Lynch Mob and Brandon Bunch,
for teaching me the importance of family

For the strength of the Pack is the Wolf,
and the strength of the Wolf is the Pack.
—RUDYARD KIPLING,
"THE LAW OF THE JUNGLE"

PROLOGUE

THE SMELL OF lilacs and sea spray hovered in the room. Janus's eyes traveled around the bright space, taking in the dance pictures and shots of Kaylan and a blonde girl. Kaylan was pretty; she'd give her that. Her auburn hair hung in loose waves, a smattering of light freckles dotted her nose, and her eyes glowed as green as a forest.

No wonder she'd captivated Nick.

The room appeared organized in its disorganization. The cream comforter lay thrown over the bed haphazardly dotted with purple throw pillows. Each drawer in the desk seemed scattered, yet categorized—notes in one, office supplies in another—the mark of someone attempting neatness but failing in the rush of life. Janus grimaced. How would Kaylan ever keep up with a home?

Nick could do better.

Then she found it. A picture of Nick and Kaylan on the beach, laughing and covered in sand. Janus's mouth pulled in a tight line. Too bad she had to ruin his happiness.

From what she could tell, Nick Carmichael pursued a task with tenacity and demonstrated a drive for justice unlike anything she'd ever seen. She flipped the frame over and deftly lifted the photo from the glass, leaving behind the generic piece of paper with smiling faces. Nick would soon know she'd been here.

He needed to know his world could cave in around him at any moment. The only way he could save it was to stop pursuing her. Or else she would be forced to hurt the one thing precious to him.

A sigh escaped her lips, and she quickly sucked in. It was his neck or Janus's. Too much hung in the balance. She couldn't afford a mistake. With a glance at her watch, she slipped from the house the same way she'd entered. A plane awaited and money stood to be made.

Climbing in her car parked two blocks away, she glanced at the picture again, ignoring the flutter of her heart as her eyes brushed over Nick's face. She hadn't experienced control over a person like this since her Cold War days, and she wouldn't abdicate that power now for any emotion, even if the part of herself she had buried long ago stirred with his nearness. The engine roared to life, and she gripped the wheel, her knuckles whitening.

No. Never again.

Chapter 1

THE SKY EXPLODED in an array of fiery colors and Kaylan jumped, remembering the distant crash of buildings and buckling earth in the Haiti earthquake only nine months before.

"It's okay, babe. It's just fireworks." Nick pulled her close on the beach, his arms reminding her of her new life in California, away from the humid, tropical landscape of Haiti, and away from her family in Alabama.

Vibrant reds, blues, and oranges danced in the sky, leaving smoky silhouettes in their wake. Nick's team of Navy SEALs and their loved ones surrounded her—her new community. Logan and Colt lit fireworks on the beach and then darted away before they ignited, children squealing in delight as they burst. A campfire crackled in front of them on firewood piled in the sand, and the clear night sky grew hazy under the continual pops and smoke from children's sparklers. Kaylan couldn't imagine a better way to begin Labor Day weekend. She wished she could freeze the memory and frame it. Laughter mixed with the lap of waves and boom of fireworks. Children played tag, darting in and out of the waves licking the beach. Titus, Jay, and Micah stood near the fire with other guys from SEAL Team 5 and Support Activity 1,

1

roasting hot dogs and marshmallows. The women chatted or chased down kids.

Kaylan smiled to herself. It was picture perfect. The scene seemed so normal, hiding the fact that these men were conditioned for war. She squeezed Nick's arm a little tighter, knowing the time would come. He would have to leave.

His strong fingers ruffled her hair, gently sweeping strands from her forehead. Despite the warm evening, goose bumps danced down her arms, and she closed her eyes.

"What's going on in that head of yours, gorgeous?"

She turned her head to meet Nick's gaze, loving the fire found in the smoky blue. "Just making a memory."

His lips brushed her forehead. In one quick move he stood from their sandy blanket, pulling her with him. "Let's take a walk." He settled his arm around her shoulders, and once again she treasured the contact, knowing these moments would carry her through the long days to come.

A football whizzed through the air and smacked Nick on his back. "Yo, Hawk, get a room, man," Jay called, whistling at Kaylan.

Before Nick could react, Kaylan's brother Micah tackled Jay around the waist, and they both hit the sand. "I think you forgot you are talking about my sister." With one quick move Micah wrapped his arms around Jay in a headlock, his legs pinning the rest of Jay's body. Jay fought and kicked but Micah held firm, his arm still allowing Jay to breathe. Barely.

The rest of the team gathered around, dollar bills exchanging hands as quickly as their cheers and chanting filled the air. Kids joined in the frenzy, excitement glowing in their young eyes.

"Micah totally has this."

"No way. Jay wrestled in high school. Micah is toast."

Jay squirmed. His face turned red, whether from embarrassment or lack of air, Kaylan couldn't tell.

Nick chuckled. "Looks like Micah has it under control." He

turned Kaylan away from the crowd and moved up the beach as darkness settled around them.

The moon hung low in the sky, reflecting eerily on the waves capping and lapping the beach. Nick walked them toward the surf, the cool Pacific stretching to kiss their feet. Kaylan could barely see the water line, but the soft roar of each new wave soothed her.

She closed her eyes, turning her face to the gentle breeze and enjoying Nick's strong, tough hand in hers. Her feet left the ground and her eyes flew open as Nick swung her in his arms and jogged to the water.

"Put me down, jerk!" she shrieked, awaiting the plunge in the dark, cold ocean. Her panic built. She saw only blackness. "Nick Carmichael, don't you dare."

His boyish laugh tugged at her heart. "It's just water, Kayles." And in they went, Kaylan's jean shorts getting soaked, her T-shirt hanging on her frame.

Her breath caught in her chest with the chilly water. She could barely make out Nick's grin in the darkness as she swiped wet hair from her eyes. "Nick Carmichael!" With one good swing she sent a wave into his face. His eyes registered surprise before his smile quirked. Trouble.

"Oh, no, you don't. You already got me wet. Nick, don't you dare." Before she could back away, he grabbed her around the waist and they both went under an incoming wave. The salty taste permeated her mouth.

"All right, all right." She came up, sputtering and gasping for air in the icy water. She shoved at his chest as he steadied them both. His heart pounded beneath her palm, and his warm laugh melted her heart. She joined his laughter. Just like with her best friend, Sarah Beth, Nick's moods and reactions became more and more familiar to her. This laugh spelled pure joy. Contentment.

"Moonlight looks pretty good on you, even though you're wet."

She wrapped her arms around his neck as he pulled her close.

"You aren't too bad yourself, Mr. SEAL."

"I mean it, Kayles. Beautiful, kind, genuine, gentle. I couldn't be more blessed."

She was thankful for the darkness as her face heated. She could barely discern his smoky blue eyes, but she knew that look. The one he reserved only for her. He expressed himself better than she did, and occasionally it left her feeling behind the emotional curve.

He rested his forehead on hers, the waves lapping gently around their legs. Despite the chill, she felt warm with this Frogman in his natural habitat. Nothing could touch her.

The breeze ruffled her dripping hair, and on its wings came whispered words, "I love you, Kayles." The admission sent her heart pounding. She pulled away from him, unsure. She'd longed to hear those words but dreaded the possibilities that came with loving and losing. Sarah Beth's death in Haiti had taught her all too well the pain of losing someone she loved with everything she had.

"Nick…"

"Don't panic on me." He pulled her close, and she fought the urge to put space between them, the desire to run before she got hurt, before she lost another person she loved, before she fell so hard that the darkness enveloped her again. She could almost taste the Haitian dust clinging to the air, smothering the light and her ability to breathe.

"I can't. Nick..let's talk about something else." Sarah Beth's cry echoed faintly with the crash of buildings in her mind. Again Kaylan tried to pull away, memories of Haiti causing Coronado, California, to fade from her view.

His calloused hand cupped her chin. "Kayles, look at me. It doesn't matter that you can't say it right now. I just need you to know. I need you to trust me." His blue eyes reflected the glowing moon and never wavered from their hold on her face, on her heart.

"I love you." He drew each word out, making sure they reached every insecurity. "I'm not going anywhere."

She allowed the words to penetrate her fear, hoping against hope they would take root and blossom. Healing came slowly, but every day she grew stronger. Nick was key to the process. But there were some memories that could not be erased, some nightmares that bled into her daylight hours, stealing her most precious moments.

One day she would say it. One day she would feel it. But not yet, just not yet.

"Smile, gorgeous." He smoothed the lines on her forehead. His mouth tipped at the corner in the moonlight, and her body tensed.

"Don't you…" She squealed as his fingers found her rib cage. She twisted and fought, laughing so hard the harsh memories from moments before receded with the tide into the darkness.

"Nick Carmichael, let go!"

"You asked for it." He released her, and she began to tip backward into the waves, his laugh echoing in her ears.

"I don't think so." She snatched his T-shirt and pulled him in the water with her, her head dipping below the cold waves once again.

Their laughter filled the air as they rose to the surface. "How can you be so nice one second and so mean the next?"

"Mean? I make you laugh because I love you. Don't be so gloomy." His chuckle warmed her to her toes, and she threw her arms around his neck.

"I like you too."

His arms slipped around her waist and his face dipped toward hers. He could see all the way to her soul in the moonlight, and it was enough to stop her heart.

"I think it's a little more than that. But I'll wait to hear the words." His lips settled on hers, making the lingering fireworks pale in comparison.

"Ugh, break it up, you two."

Her brother's voice made her jerk, but Nick held her close, turning to face Micah on the beach.

"Bad timing, Bulldog. What's up?"

Kaylan tensed as Micah held up a phone. His silence spoke volumes. Her hands clenched in Nick's wet shirt.

"We gotta go, Hawk." His voice carried a warning over the crash of the waves.

"Is it..."

"Yeah. It's time."

Nick's hands slipped from her waist, and he waded to shore. Kaylan immediately felt cold. She followed him out of the surf. Up the beach several other SEALs that were part of Support Activity 1 kissed their wives or girlfriends good-bye before running for their cars.

"Babe, we gotta go. I'll call you later." Nick's eyes grew as distant as the skyline, his mind already miles away.

Kaylan refused to show her fear. "Be safe."

With a nod, they both ran to Micah's car. Moments later they peeled out behind their teammates.

Kaylan wandered back up the beach to the other SEAL families. She'd known when they left Haiti in July and when she'd moved to California to begin her dietetics internship the first of August that the time would come when Nick and Micah would leave. She'd come to hate every ring of his phone. But here they were, and she had the choice to panic or stand firm. She was the girlfriend and the sister of two SEALs. If they could race fearlessly into danger, then she could remain their anchor at home. She only hoped they wouldn't see the small cracks in her armor as she fought to hold herself together.

"Kaylan, Kaylan, Kaylan." Four-year-old Molly came bounding up, her blonde curls bouncing around her slim shoulders. Kaylan lifted her into her arms.

"What's up, Munchkin?"

"Where did my daddy go?"

Kaylan glanced at Molly's mom, Kim, who was busy wrestling sparklers away from her two boys. Kaylan smothered a laugh. They were as strong as their dad, Logan, the lead corpsman and one of the older men. Molly had his curly blond hair and pale green eyes.

"Daddy and the boys needed to work. You'll see him later."

"Are they going to take care of bad guys?"

"Yes, sweet girl." Molly was innocence in a beautiful, sweet package. The little girl wrapped her arms around Kaylan's neck as she walked them closer to the fire. Molly's blonde hair glowed, and her little hands felt sticky on Kaylan's neck. Water from Kaylan's clothes dampened Molly's shorts and T-shirt, but Molly didn't seem to care.

"Kaylan, know what?" She pulled Kaylan's head close, whispering in her ear. "My daddy's a hero just like Superman. Only he's better. He doesn't need a cape."

Kaylan's heart warmed and she kissed Molly's sticky cheek, tasting marshmallows from the s'mores. "Your dad is definitely a hero."

"Molly?"

The little girl squirmed to the ground when Kim called but turned back quickly to Kaylan. "Don't worry about Mr. Nick. My daddy says he is the best of the good guys."

The best, the bravest, the most sacrificial. The latter frightened Kaylan the most. Her hero without a cape, unafraid to face the barrel of a gun—even if it meant his life.

Chapter 2

NICK AND MICAH filed into the room they affectionately deemed The War Zone. Other members of Support Activity 1 entered behind them, excitement from the Labor Day festivities fading in light of a looming mission. The summer moon and pop of fireworks seemed distant now as Nick's mind honed in on unfinished business. His fiery kiss with Kaylan in the Pacific felt like a dream, smothered in the light of reality.

"This better be about Janus," he mumbled to Micah as they took their seats and waited for Senior Chief to speak. Her trail had gone cold as soon as he returned from Haiti two months before, and Nick itched to catch this terrorist, woman or not.

Senior Chief Collin "X" Williams paced the front of the room. He was so named for Professor X from his favorite comic, X-Men. He had the innate ability to read his men, assess their strengths and weaknesses, and send them into combat prepared. Nick knew he had measured every angle of the mission before briefing the team.

"Sorry to pull you away from the party, but duty calls. At zero three hundred hours we picked up satellite feed of a terrorist cell moving weapons over the border into Iran. We believe the weapons originated in Ukraine and Russia from our one and only."

Micah glanced at Nick, his brown eyes expectant. Payback would be sweet.

"Janus slipped her shadow. Her last known location is Yalta, Ukraine, and we believe she is still there. Not sure where her boss is, but we believe he resides somewhere in Russia. If we can catch this slippery fish, we may be able to catch the shark behind her." X rubbed his hands in anticipation. Unlike his comic book character, X boasted a full head of fiery red hair and a freckled face, browned by years in the sun. A toothpick hung from his mouth, forcing him to talk through gritted teeth. Nick often wondered how many toothpicks he'd swallowed.

"I want this chick bad. Her shipments are wreaking havoc on our boys in the sandbox, and I've had about all I want to take of being the loser in this scenario. It's our turn. She believes she's safe. This time we have the upper hand. I'm sending a team of six. You leave in forty hours. I need a working plan in twelve. This is a capture, no-kill mission. But do whatever you need to do to bring her in. Let's get busy." He tossed the toothpick in the general direction of the trash can as he exited the room.

The War Zone broke into a flurry of activity as the men jumped from their seats and pulled out maps of the terrain, ocean, and city. Nick paused to assess the action, studying each team member. He'd worked with all of these men before, trusted them, would give his life for them. As much as Nick could take care of himself, the SEALs innately operated in team mentality, an ideal that was beaten into every man throughout BUD/S. Each man used his strengths and abilities to play a role in planning and execution. All in. All hands. All the time.

Colt stood at the white board at the front of the room studying the mission details. Short and stocky, he had sandy hair mixed with faint traces of gray, giving him a distinguished look amidst his boyish charm.

The son of true California hippies, he had rejected his parents' lifestyle after the tragedy of the twin towers. While pictures of his childhood showed him sporting long locks, his short-cropped hair and brown eyes held a serious tone in adulthood. The terrorist attacks had bred a new generation of patriots, a bright spot in the carnage. A couple years younger than Nick, Colt owned the title of "team daredevil," always eager to prove himself, and was quite the poker player. Nick winced. He definitely wouldn't play him again anytime soon.

In the corner of the room, Logan, a veteran on the team, wrestled supplies and made a list of items to take with them. His little girl, Molly, held a special place in Nick's heart. Logan's wife, Kim, was pregnant with their fourth, and Nick marveled at the strength of their marriage. Too many SEALs tasted the bitter cup of divorce due to job demands. Nick wasn't willing to risk that with Kaylan, and he believed he could live up to his calling and marry the most amazing woman he'd ever met.

Besides Nick and Micah, Logan was the only other Christ-follower on the team. Nick firmly believed Logan's walk with the Lord remained the secret to his marital success. The man radiated calm and strength. "Redeemed" stretched across his bare back in gothic ink letters and drew many questions from their teammates. Logan never hesitated to share his faith. It oozed from every pore of his body in the confident way he led the team and the gentle way he handled his family. No one questioned his leadership or character. No one needed to. As far as Nick could tell, Logan's only weaknesses were his obsessive love for steak dripping with A-1 sauce and his babbling about the ranches in Montana. Nick left the room every time Logan started in on the topic.

Jay and Titus huddled close together talking logistics with Micah. As evident on the beach, Jay claimed the title of "team prankster." Built like a quarterback, he never backed down from a fight and usually could be found at the center of the problem. Jay rarely wore anything other than a cocky smile, but behind his deep blue eyes lay a pain and rage none of them dared touch. He was the comms guy of the team, handling communication with head-quarters and carrying the big radio. It took him no time to assess a situation and communicate it clearly. Little rattled him under fire.

The team knew Titus as Jay's better, blacker half. Rarely could they find one without the other. A native Texan, Titus claimed his dreams of becoming a SEAL saved him from the heartache of the gangs. A brilliant mind and talented linguist, Titus blended well in Muslim territory as he spoke Arabic, Farsi, and pieces of local tribal dialects. If he heard it once, he could repeat it. His dark skin bought him friends his white teammates might otherwise deter.

Merging from two different teams, these men accepted the call of Support Activity 1 and ran into danger whenever the situation deemed necessary. They truly defined SEALs, and Nick felt ener-gized and strong in their presence. They would enter together and leave together. No questions. No option. Justice was imperative. Janus continued to claim American lives. Even one was too many.

Kaylan opened her front door floating on a cloud. He loved her. Nick loved her. She leaned against her door and touched her lips. She'd known it all along, just didn't want to believe it. But she'd felt it in every kiss, every smile, and every encouraging word over the past nine months.

But she knew what loving led to—pain and heartache. Tomorrow didn't come with guarantees. Regardless of her hesita-tion, her heart galloped like her mare back at home when given free rein.

A head popped up over the top of the couch, and Kaylan squealed, throwing a hand over her mouth to stifle the sound. "Oh, my gosh. Megan! Geez, next time tell me you're there."

Kaylan's roommate rolled her brown eyes beneath thick, long

lashes. "Please. I can read your mind from over here. Stop blushing and thinking about soldier boy, or I'm going to puke."

"Yeah, yeah." Kaylan rolled with her roommate's attitude. She found an odd comfort in Megan's strength of will, even if it tended to repel others. At least they were building somewhat of a friendship in the month they had lived together. Kaylan met Megan through a college friend who'd moved out to California. Megan was three years older than Kaylan's twenty-three years and in need of a roommate. While emotionally distant and the textbook definition of sarcastic, Megan had a hidden charm that Kaylan felt determined to bring forth.

Megan had inherited a house from a rich grandmother. Situated on the outskirts of San Diego, near Coronado, it was the perfect distance from the SEALs and the beach. It wasn't extravagant by any means, but with the prices of California real estate, Kaylan was perfectly content with the small space in a good neighborhood. Kaylan paid rent to cover the taxes and utilities, but other than that, the house was paid for.

"You're so tough." She ruffled Megan's nearly black hair as she plopped down on the couch. "Just wait. Someday a nerdy activist will come along and sweep you off your feet. Then you'll get all mushy and emotional and, heaven forbid, have to talk about feelings. And I'll be here. Waiting to tell you 'I told you so' and full of all these great dating tips I've picked up in all my extensive experience." Kaylan sighed and placed her hand on her heart.

Megan snorted. "You live such a charmed life. My guy won't want to talk about feelings. They make you weak."

Her words stung. While Megan knew about Kaylan's home and family and relationship with Nick, she didn't know about Sarah Beth or the earthquake. *Charmed* fell far from Kaylan's radar. *Haunted* might be more appropriate.

"So did you actually watch the fireworks, or did you make them?" Megan broke into her silent reverie.

"Megan."

"C'mon, Kayles. You gotta let loose every once in a while. Just go with what feels good. You're such a prude. You're gonna get married anyway. Why does it matter?"

Kaylan shook her head and laughed softly, used to Megan's criticism of her morals. She struggled with her negativity but knew it covered a deeper issue. Maybe one of these days Megan would trust Kaylan with that secret.

"You know why, Megan. These guys you bring home sometimes...do you ever feel good when they leave in the morning?"

She shrugged and her grin turned wicked. A challenge. "Sure. Stress gone, happy, content. No strings attached."

Kaylan nodded. "What about a few days later?"

Megan's grin drooped a bit, but she didn't back down. "What about it?"

"I've watched you check your phone, waiting for a call. I've heard you cry at night when you think I'm asleep." Kaylan leaned forward and touched Megan's knee. "Megan, from the beginning this kind of a relationship was designed for marriage. One man, one woman for life. Nick and I want to wait and experience that after we make a permanent commitment before God and our families." Maybe Nick could talk to her. He had a past much like Megan's.

Megan's eyes frosted in the warm air. "You want to get real, Kaylan? Why do you scream in your sleep? Why do you shout people's names?" She leaned into Kaylan's face, her walls blocking any entry, guns loaded and aimed. "I think your faith is your shield and you're just scared." In one quick movement she rose from the couch, walked down the hall, and slammed her bedroom door.

Kaylan sighed. "Epic fail, Kaylan," she mumbled to herself. She couldn't talk about her nightmares with Megan. It meant talking about the earthquake and her memories. Maybe Megan was right. Maybe she was scared.

She hugged the turquoise throw pillow as her eyes wandered

the dark room taking in pictures of Haiti, her and Nick, her family, and a couple photos of Megan and the dolphins at the wildlife conservatory where she worked. Books lined a shelf in the corner of the room in perfect proximity to the overstuffed khaki couches in the middle of the living room. Pink roses sat on the bar, the gateway to the kitchen in their open-floor plan. The smell of the sea hung in the air, reminding Kaylan of the waves kissing her legs as she and Nick stood in the surf.

He loved her, but he was leaving. The reality stung even as her heart raced. She didn't know how to feel. Megan had one thing right: Kaylan was scared. No doubt about it.

"Lord, give me time with him before he leaves, please. Even a little will help. And please help me figure this out." She tossed the pillow on the chair and rose to get ready for bed, her overflowing heart battling her scattered mind.

Chapter 3

NICK'S FEET POUNDED the wet sand in the dark, wee hours of Sunday morning. He'd slept for two hours after helping his team prep to leave within the next thirty-six hours. He could sleep on the plane, but he couldn't sacrifice time with Kaylan. He wouldn't. Not now. Not when he might need to reassure her. Not when every fiber of his being wanted to be by her side.

She'd softened again over the course of the summer, her healing compounded after visiting Haiti again. She'd gained her weight back and then a little more, but he loved her gentle curves and the fullness of her face when she smiled. He loved every freckle on her nose and the crinkles in the corner of her eyes when her musical laugh graced the air around them. He loved that she loved with her whole heart, and he loved that she respected herself enough to be sure before she shared her heart with him. She may not understand her feelings, but her eyes lit up in his presence, as if he alone made her world spin. He couldn't believe how much he loved her. He would lay down his life in an instant to make her happy.

Kaylan's internship in San Diego kept her busy, but they still managed to see each other a couple times a week. Every certified dietetic internship required participants to complete rotations for clinical, community, and management nutrition. Over the coming months she would rotate between hospitals and a couple of non-profits, but she was gunning for a position that aided disaster relief because of her experience in Haiti. Despite her busy schedule, she still struggled to find a balance between living and grieving. Unfortunately the two were synonymous, but she'd learn how to cope and build new memories. She didn't talk about Sarah Beth much, but he'd catch her with tears in her beautiful green eyes every now and then.

They planned to go back to Alabama as often as possible. Pap remained strong, despite his previous mini strokes. Kaylan talked to him every Sunday afternoon, and Nick loved the old man's wisdom. Her other brothers, Seth and David, remained in Alabama, David advancing in his career as an accountant and dating Melody, and Seth playing football for the University of Alabama. Nick knew Micah and Kaylan missed their family. He wished he could shorten the distance for them. But it was the price they paid for being in the military.

He checked his watch. Zero five hundred. He'd have to hustle to watch the sunrise with Kaylan before she went to work. He sprinted the last quarter mile to his Jeep, pulled the key off the tire, and turned the nose toward her house about fifteen minutes away. He knew he'd find her on her front porch in the rocking chair, writing in her journal and reading her Bible, her hair wet from a shower.

Tedashii's "Make War" song blared over the speakers as Nick drummed his fingers on the steering wheel. The lyrics reminded him of how much he'd distanced himself from his past—a college playboy and party jock, the guy who knew how to have a good time and didn't care who he hurt along the way. But man, Jesus was good. The day it finally clicked had been Nick's sunrise moment, and he refused to go backward.

The wind cooled the sweat on his brow as he drove. He ran a

hand over his face, feeling the stubble and knowing it would be a while before he picked up a razor. Kaylan liked a little scruff, and he enjoyed not worrying about shaving when on a mission. He guessed it was the California hippie in him.

He exited the highway and turned onto her street. There she sat, third door on the left, her porch screened in, but open to sight. The stone and stucco house was a far cry from the rustic lake house her parents owned in Alabama, but she and Megan made it home.

Her auburn hair had grown longer, and he loved the loose waves. He chuckled at her awful posture as she bent over her Bible, her leg tucked under her on the chair.

"Hey, hey, beautiful."

Her smile melted his heart. Man, he loved this woman. She opened the door and flew into his arms. "You smell sweaty." Her laughter joined his as she leaned back to look into his eyes.

He swooped in for a kiss as the sky turned a deep turquoise in the blooming light. When he pulled back, they were both breathless.

"You sure know how to start a girl's day."

"Only yours, Kayles."

"You mean you don't have a date to watch the sunset with some chick tonight?" Her mischievous smile lit her emerald green eyes. "That sure is good to know. I don't share well."

"Brat." He poked her ribs, and she jerked away, giggling.

"Don't be mean, or you can't have your coffee."

He stalked her and backed her into the railing, his fingers striking all the right places on her ribs.

She squealed. "I give. You win!" She jerked away from him and opened the door to the house. "I'll get your coffee."

"Oh, no, you won't. You'll spit in it or something."

"Me?" She threw a hand to heart, but he knew better than to trust that innocent look. Her brothers had trained her well. She did not back down from a challenge, and she knew how to give payback.

"I'll get my own coffee, thank you very much." He kissed the freckles on her nose as he squeezed past her in the doorway, careful not to wake Megan as he grabbed a mug and poured his coffee.

Nick took a sip, enjoying the steaming, black brew. Pure adrenaline would keep him going until he left. Time with Kaylan was too short and too precious. He glanced at the waterproof watch on his wrist as he slipped back onto the porch. He would need to leave within the hour. A lot of plans still had to be made.

Kaylan patted the spot next to her on the loveseat, and Nick sank down next to her, immediately tugging her tight to his chest. Light spilled over the houses across the street to the east. The sunsets definitely trumped sunrises in California, but Kaylan insisted on her morning routine.

"When do you leave?" The mood immediately changed in the warming air.

He kissed her forehead, smoothing her damp hair from her face. "Tomorrow."

She turned her face to meet his, and he sensed the growing unease as her bright green eyes darkened a shade. "And when will you be back?"

"Kaylan, you know I don't know that."

She nodded, turning away from his gaze, but not before he saw tears. He shifted on the seat. "Babe, look at me."

Her eyes met his again, and she blinked away the moisture, swallowing hard. He silently willed her through it. *Attagirl.*

"I'll miss you," she whispered.

He ran his fingers through her hair, down her cheek, over her lips. His eyes never left hers, memorizing every feature. He knew this would never get easier, but he knew he would feel more confident knowing that he didn't have to leave her side when he came home. He was ready to share a home and a life with this woman.

He tilted her chin up and met her lips with his, hungry to hang on to this moment.

Every nerve came alive as his hand drifted to her neck, pulling her face closer to his, deepening his kiss. He didn't want to stop, wanted to stay like this forever. He tasted the vanilla coffee creamer on her lips, and his senses swam with the smell of her flowery shampoo. His grip tightened just as Kaylan pulled away.

"Slow down there, surfer boy." She tucked a strand of hair behind her ear, not quite meeting his gaze.

He ran a hand over his face, a nervous laugh matching her own. "Sorry. Not sure where that came from." His breathing came heavy, and his heart sank as he realized old patterns died hard. He grabbed her hand and pulled her from the seat. "Let's walk to the park."

"Nick, it's Sunday."

"Kayles, it's not even six yet. We'll be back in plenty of time. Besides, I can't stay long anyway."

The walk took several minutes, and Nick's desire cooled in the morning air. They walked hand in hand, and he enjoyed the simple pleasure of her fingers threaded through his. She trusted him. After his past abandonment, her struggle to let go of Sarah Beth, the renewal of their relationship, and her move to California, she trusted him fully. He treasured that confidence.

"Want to know a secret?" Her smile made the morning light shine brighter.

"I'm always up for a juicy secret."

"As a little girl, I always had this picture in my head of finding my guy and just fitting like lock and key. Maybe that's dumb. I'm not into the idea that there is only one person in the whole world for me. But I liked the idea that I would know because we would just fit together."

He smiled to himself. He loved when she broke down the remaining walls with him to share the romantic, vulnerable pieces

19

of her heart. That still came as a challenge to her. He squeezed her fingers.

"I think it's a perfect fit." Truthfully, her hand fit his like it was made for him. He kissed her fingers. "You know, if my team ever sees how sappy I am with you, they might lock me in an institution somewhere."

She paused as they stepped onto the playground. Plastic jungle gyms and a swing set surrounded them. She sidled up to his side and placed a kiss on his cheek, her breath caressing his face. "I won't tell," she whispered. She laughed and pulled back. "But don't go getting all macho around me just to save face. You're soft as a gummy bear when you finally let that thick armor down."

He winced. "A gummy bear?"

"Would you prefer teddy bear? Those are soft and cuddly and..."

"Nope. I think gummy bear is slightly more masculine than the other option. But we still need to come up with something else."

She used his arm for balance as she slipped her shoes off and wiggled her toes in the sand. He led her to the swing and sat down in the one next to her. Quiet fell as they propelled themselves into the air.

She broke the silence. "You know Sarah Beth and I loved to swing when we were little. We used to see how high we could go, and we sang this song about a rainbow as we flew back and forth." She went quiet a moment, and for the first time he noticed the faint dark circles under her eyes and the almost wild sadness that she seemed to hold at bay. "It's crazy how quickly it ended, how one day she was there, and the next day gone. There aren't any guarantees." She dragged her feet in the sand, bringing her swing to a stop. "I mean, what happens if you don't come back, Nick?"

A hint of the old bitterness crept into her voice. He jumped from his swing in midair, landed, and turned to stand in front of her. "You knew that was the risk you took dating me. I've never lied about it, Kayles." He ran his fingers down her cheek. "I love you. I want to build a life with you. Wake up every day together, have a family, grow old and fat and gray." He shrugged. "Okay, maybe not fat." Her gentle smile encouraged him. He loved that she still blushed.

"But you will have to decide if you can handle this. Kaylan, I believe with all my heart this is what God's called me to do. I want to protect those I love, this place that I love." Passion filled his heart as he thought about his team, and he felt proud to be a SEAL to serve his country, his state. To serve her.

He linked their fingers. "I want to protect you. But that involves sacrifice on my part and on yours if you choose to embrace our journey. It means partnering in something bigger than ourselves." He bent down in front of her. "Are you willing to do that?"

The blue sky hung like a canopy over them as he kept his gaze locked on hers. She leaned forward and rested her forehead on his. "I would do anything for you," she whispered and cradled his face. His breath caught at her gentle touch. "You are more than worth it. Just be patient with me. It's hard.' She leaned back to meet his eyes. Determination colored her tone. and her gentle hold on his face firmed. "But I can do this."

He pulled her out of the swing and into his arms, kissing her again until they needed to draw back for breath. Reality rushed back in with his ringing phone.

"What's up, Bulldog?"

"Time's up. Need you back, ASAP. We may be able to see Kaylan one more time before we fly out."

"I'll be there in half an hour." If traffic wasn't bad and he sped the whole way.

"I've gotta go." He and Kaylan hurried back to his Jeep, the air now stuffy and the neighbors waking for church or yard work. He pulled his keys out and leaned in to kiss her cheek. "Come by tonight? It may be late. I've gotta throw some things in a bag before we head out."

"I'll let myself in and wait."

He climbed in the car and started the engine. Kaylan leaned into the window. "Hey." Her green eyes pulled him out of work mode for a moment. "Go save the world."

He grinned and backed out of the driveway, his nose toward his next mission.

Chapter 4

AYLAN CHANGED INTO a sea green top and flowing
beige skirt for church, snatching clothes off her floor as
she went. She wished Megan would go with her. After
such a short time in California, Kaylan still hadn't made many
friends. Truth be told, she struggled with the idea. She knew to
love meant risking her heart, exposing vulnerable places she only
allowed the Lord and her family to touch. Despite everything, she
wanted a life in California, especially if she and Nick moved forward in their relationship as she hoped.

Still, no one could ever replace Sarah Beth. Kaylan still
remembered her bubbly laugh and all the late-night movies and
study nights in college. She remembered ballet recitals and their
first *NSYNC concert in seventh grade where they'd screamed
and cheered until the final note. A small smile tugged at her lips
accompanied by the sting of tears.

"No." She shook her head and blinked back the tears. "No more."
She tossed a pile of laundry in the hamper and then turned to her
dresser, intent on finding the necklace Nick had given her. The
story behind the lily medallion set her heart racing. His words
from the dance studio still reverberated in her mind: "The lily
symbolizes everything beautiful and pure. It embodies you."

"Where is it?" She sighed in frustration and ran her fingers through her hair, turning in a slow circle. She wasn't exactly neat, but she wasn't a slob either, and she took care of her things. She fumbled through the jewelry on her dresser again, matching earrings as she went. No sign of the lily.

Her eyes darted to the clock, and she groaned. Even if she left now, she would be five minutes late. She snatched her purse from the floor, bumping into the dresser in her haste. A frame fell and landed with a soft thud face down on the floor.

"You can wait," Kaylan huffed as she hurried from the room and out to her car, making plans to search for the necklace as soon as she got home. She wouldn't tolerate losing one of her most precious possessions because of messiness.

After a couple hours searching off and on, Kaylan finally admitted defeat. Her necklace had disappeared, but she would find it after Nick left. Instead of going crazy searching, she went over to Nick and Micah's house and began to clean. She vacuumed and dusted, washed their laundry, and emptied the refrigerator of perishables. She even watched a movie before turning out the lights.

Now, Kaylan lay curled on the brown leather couch in Micah and Nick's living room, the night hours stirring nostalgia and dreams. The digital clock on the end table read a little after two in the morning. As she burrowed further into the couch, she thought back to their time on the beach only two nights before. She still couldn't believe that Nick had whispered those three little words beneath the California moon. Goose bumps trickled down her arms as she remembered his gentle touch and the love in his blue eyes. His laughter as he dunked her in the ocean still set butterflies to flight in her stomach.

He loved her. That knowledge drew her toward him more than

she thought possible. In that moment on the beach it was as if a thousand invisible threads stretched between them, binding them. No matter the distance, she could feel their tug and knew it would take an act of God to slice through them. But she couldn't say it back, and she wasn't sure why. Something restrained her, and until she identified that thing, she would remain silent.

She curled tighter beneath the blanket and wondered when they would be home. She'd given up on the idea of packing for them. Since she had no idea where they were headed, she wasn't sure what clothes to pack or how many. Maybe watching the clothes selected would at least tell her the climate. She planned to spend time watching the news for anything weird while they were away, guessing and wondering where they might be.

The key scratched in the lock and Kaylan bolted upright. She squinted toward the door, her sleep-laden eyes adjusting to the light.

"Hurry, Hawk. We've got to be back in an hour. Time to roll."

"Just got to toss some things in my bag. I'm ready to catch this..."

Kaylan cleared her throat, and Nick and Micah whirled, fists clenched.

"Whoa. It's me." She chuckled and turned on the lamp. "Y'all are not instilling confidence in me. If I can catch you off guard that easily, what about the bad guys? There's only one solution."

Nick leaned over the couch, his smile adding to the light. "And what's that, gorgeous?"

Kaylan sighed and shook her head, the butterflies in her stomach taking flight again. "Take me with you. Clearly I'm the only professional here. How will you survive?"

A storm rolled over his blue eyes, and she sensed a thousand thoughts jockeyed for prominence in the stretching silence. Behind Nick, Micah crossed his arms with a smirk. It spoke volumes that he accepted their relationship as he watched their battle of wills play out. Nick beckoned her closer as he leaned toward her, his warm breath tickling her ear and sending shivers down her spine. "Not a chance," he whispered with a quick peck on her cheek. "Come sit with me while I pack. You can drop us off."

Kaylan forced her body to rise from the couch, her early morning catching up with her. Her rotation with her dietetic internship had the potential to be brutal the next couple of days as she caught up on sleep. But she wouldn't trade this time as she saw her heroes off.

She stifled a yawn as she entered Nick's room and plopped down on the edge of his bed, her back finding the wall.

"First things first," Nick said as he tossed his bag on the bed. He leaned down and tipped Kaylan's chin up, his lips meeting her own with a passion and determination that both scared and thrilled Kaylan. She wondered if deployments might possibly keep things fresh in their relationship. She would always miss him, but his homecomings would be even sweeter.

He pulled back slowly and rested his forehead on hers. Living in the same state, let alone within close driving distance, was new to their relationship, every moment precious.

"I hate this," he groaned.

She brought her hands up to rest on his face, feeling the blond stubble already growing on his cheeks and chin. He slowly raised his eyes to meet her own. Her breath caught at their intensity, and she realized for the first time how much he was trying to hold himself together for her, for both of them. Her racing heart settled and something deep within her grew still. She wouldn't make this more difficult for him. She was the girlfriend of a SEAL. She wouldn't break. She would send him off with her head held high and be waiting for him when he got home. The miles wouldn't sever the bond. Just as he fought for their country, she would fight for him, his sanity, his strength, his heart. She would let him go.

A knot formed in her stomach, testing her resolve. She slowly brought her lips to his again. "Go get 'em, babe," she whispered as she pulled back. She forced herself to bounce up from the bed, hoping her energy and focus on helping him pack would let him know she would be okay.

Micah rounded the corner as Kaylan grabbed Nick's few toiletries from the bathroom. "Seriously, dude?"

"I'm hurrying, Bulldog. Chill out."

Micah turned to Kaylan and rolled his eyes. "If you aren't going to help, then leave. And why haven't you been helping me, your ever-loving, favorite, second-to-oldest brother?"

"That's quite a title." Kaylan walked past Micah, tossing something in Nick's bag before she came back to slug her brother's arm. "We all know you are an expert packer because of your years living with me. Nick hasn't had the benefit of my expertise."

Micah eyed Nick's nearly empty bag and shook his head. "I'm thinking y'all were doing something other than packing." He approached her, his finger aimed at her face. "And as your favorite older brother, I should warn you that I can and will leave him on this mission if he isn't behaving himself with you. Tell me now, Kayles."

Her laughter spilled over as Nick's brows raised and he came to a standstill. "Leave me behind? Watch it, Bulldog. That's blasphemy. Never leave a man behind." He smirked. "And kicking my tail is highly questionable. We both know who always wins that fight."

Micah threw his chest out and approached Nick, reminding Kaylan of little boys arguing over who built the bigger mud pie. Kaylan stepped in between them, her laughter drawing smiles to their pseudo-tough faces.

"All right, hotshots. You made your point. Save it for the bad guys."

"You." She turned to Nick and stood on her tiptoes to kiss his cheek, sending him the smile she saved just for him. "Finish packing."

"And you." She turned to Micah, her heart dancing as she felt the familiar tug of home and family and Alabama. "Don't ever let Dave catch you calling yourself my favorite older brother. He really might bury you in a box and throw you in the lake."

Micah's grin bloomed, reminding her of his mischievous escapades as a child when he would hide her dolls or her dance shoes just so he could chase her around the house while she looked for them. "Dave doesn't have a violent bone in his body. Competitive, sure. Violent, absolutely not."

She shook her head. "I don't know. Challenge Melody, or me, or mom, or Gran, and you might have a fight on your hands."

Micah tapped a finger on his chin and pretended to ponder for a moment. Kaylan tried to sucker punch him in the stomach, but he moved quickly. Pinning her arms, he began poking her rib cage, sending her squealing.

"I give. I give. I give." Kaylan drew a deep breath as Micah let her go, sending her tumbling into Nick. Her ribs ached from his jabs and her constant laughter. She would remember this moment until they came home. Thankfully it wasn't a true deployment with their full team. They would travel with Support Activity 1, take care of their assignment, and then come home to prep for their next deployment a little over a year away. Kaylan knew they would travel and train all over the country as needed between now and then, but at least then she knew they wouldn't face enemy fire.

The knot in her stomach re-formed with a tug, and she took a deep breath, steadying herself again. Nick grabbed his bag from the bed and slung it over his shoulder.

"Drop us off, babe?"

She smiled up at him, now wishing the time hadn't slipped by so quickly. "Wouldn't miss it."

She looped her arm around his waist and followed her brother to the car.

Chapter 5

KAYLAN CUT THE engine as she pulled up in front of the team building. In the sudden silence she realized her brother and boyfriend were about to board a C-17 to another corner of the world. She knew a cause burned in their hearts. Their easy banter less than an hour before had faded, replaced by quiet resolve mirrored in their confident stance and determined expressions.

Micah had always been her protector. She remembered her fourth grade year when John Mark Turner wanted her to sign his cast. He'd had a crush on her since second grade, but Kaylan was a kid. She played with the boys the same way she played with her brothers. Anything other than that was the last thing on her mind. John Mark and his friend Andy cornered her after school. The whole class had signed his cast, but Kaylan didn't want to encourage him. His constant attention made her uncomfortable.

Andy told her to sign John Mark's cast or she couldn't go home. Kaylan remembered lifting her chin and trying to hurry past, but Andy caught her and pushed her into the potted bush growing right next to the front door. Micah had materialized at her side, his brown eyes burning with anger. He pulled her up, checked to make sure she was okay, and then in one swift move turned around and gave Andy a black eye.

Even as a middle schooler Micah deemed it "defending the defenseless" and his "constitutional right" despite the principal's counsel otherwise. He hadn't changed much. She studied him in the rearview mirror as he opened the door and grabbed his bag. He'd exchanged his childhood superhero capes for the uniform of America's elite, and he wore it proudly. Much like his superheroes, he didn't boast about his position. SEALs rarely did. Their confidence came from their knowledge of their training and their trust in one another. They were ready.

Now Kaylan was here to see Micah off. It seemed a bit more real this time. In Alabama she knew when Micah deployed, prayed for him while he was away, and talked with him when he called. But now she was here to say good-bye. A lump formed in her throat as he closed his car door. Nick sat next to her in the front, watching, waiting.

Her door opened and Micah reached for her hand. "Time to say good-bye, sis." Tears pooled in her eyes, but she blinked them back as she unbuckled and stepped from the car. Nick mirrored her movements on her other side, readying his bag.

"Be safe." Her voice cracked, but she cleared her throat quickly. "Take care of each other."

As he pulled her into a hug, she realized that the two people she loved in California would no longer be a phone call away. Panic built, but Micah's arms around her held her together, the way they always did when he defended her. Pride in him fought the panic.

"Hey." Micah held her away from him, leaning in close to see her eyes in the early morning darkness. "We'll see you soon. Don't let David or Seth steal my place or anything while I'm gone. We both know I'll always be your favorite."

She couldn't help but smile. "We'll have to agree to disagree."

"Hasn't anyone ever told you that you should agree with

everything a man says when you send him off to war? You don't
want me distracted or worried now, do you?" He crossed his arms
over his chest, and she fought a smirk.

"That's good to know. But I'm pretty sure you also taught me
not to lie, so..."

Micah held a hand to his heart. "You're killing me." He smiled
and his eyes wandered behind him. It was time to go. He pulled
her into a quick hug again and kissed the top of her head. "Take
care of the home front. We'll catch ya on the flipside." With a brief
nod to Nick, he jogged off to meet the rest of the guys.

Kaylan took a deep breath, realizing that this good-bye would
be much more difficult. She stood still, refusing to look at him as
the car door slammed, and she heard his boots scuff the pavement
as he approached. She leaned back against her car door, her heart
in her throat, wondering when Nick had become more important
to her than family. As important as, sure. But more important
than the ones who were her heart and soul? Not even Sarah Beth
had ever claimed this degree of affection.

Was she in love with him after all?

He stood in front of her ready to leave, a clear testament to the
dangers he would soon face, but he never wavered in his resolve.
She realized then that he had never wavered in his pursuit of her
heart, either. He was there, waiting for the fullness of her heart,
the depth of her commitment. He waited confidently and quietly,
never pushing, always reassuring.

Her breath caught, and she blinked as a tear rolled off her lashes.
A dim light from the building illuminated their parking spot, but
Kaylan felt as if they were the only two people in the world.

His hands, calloused from hard work and countless drills with
his team, cupped her face, slowly raising her eyes to meet his. He
stepped closer, his body a breath away, but she could feel the pull,
the chemistry of being near someone she loved. Loved? Was it
possible?

Another tear tracked down her cheek, and she tried to pull away, desperate to hide her weakness from him. But, as always, he wouldn't let her run. His thumb wiped away the tear, and his eyes held her captive.

"Don't hide from me, babe." His husky voice betrayed his frazzled emotions, and Kaylan realized he was fighting back tears as well.

She wrapped her arms around his waist. "This is hard, Nick. I've never had to say good-bye here, like this."

He ran his thumb over her bottom lip, his eyes traveling the course of her face. "God willing, we'll have many more times like this, but equally as many 'hellos.'"

Her heart galloped. Her mind flashed back to Rhonda's broken house in Haiti and to her last moments with Sarah Beth. It took sixty seconds to change the course of both of their lives. Sixty seconds to write a death sentence, and sixty seconds to create a lifetime of absence and agony. Would she never be free from the memories?

Only minutes before the quake hit, they had laughed and talked. They had witnessed the miracle of life in the slums. Even now Rhonda sent her pictures of that sweet baby. He was pulling himself up and would be walking soon. But Sarah Beth would never see.

Kaylan's breath came in shorter spurts. What if this was her last good-bye with Nick? What if this mission took him from her? She couldn't, wouldn't be able to bear another quake of that magnitude in her life.

"No. I can't do this. I can't do this. You can't go!" She clenched his shirt in her fists, her fingers aching from her tight grip.

The pressure on her face intensified. "Kaylan, look at me."

She couldn't. She remembered Sarah Beth's blue eyes as they gazed into the distance right before she breathed her last. This wouldn't be the last time she held Nick's gaze. It wouldn't.

"Kaylan Lee Richards." He gripped her shoulders. "Look at me." The intensity and passion in his voice shook her mind from the rubble. Unchecked tears streamed down her face.

"Oh, baby." He wiped them away and pulled her close, his hold fierce.

"I am not Sarah Beth," he whispered in her ear. "We are not in Haiti. Let it go."

"But what if…"

"No 'what-ifs.' Do you hear me? None of that." He pulled back to look in her eyes, his arms around her still cocooning her in a temporary bubble of safety.

"Hey, Hawk." Micah stuck his head out of the door. "We gotta go."

Nick's gaze never left her face. "Be right there." His voice sliced through the darkness, rooting her in the present. Time was running out.

His voice lowered and intensified, his words spilling from his lips, matching his urgency to make her understand before he boarded a plane to God knew where. "Listen to me. I am highly trained. I have a team of men who are confident and more than capable. We are ready. And we are SEALs, Kayles. We do our job because we love our country. But I do my job for more than that now. I do it for you." His fingers caressed her lower back, paralyzing her in his arms. "You are my reason to come home, Kaylan. The reason I fight for more than my country. I love you. I get that you can't say it yet. But you need to know. I love you. I will do whatever necessary to protect you, and right now that means taking out…" He stopped short, his eyes showing a split second of fear. "Right now that means leaving."

She couldn't move, couldn't speak. His hand came up to her face, tracing the tear marks before drifting to the back of her neck causing her face to heat. His lips hovered inches from hers. She could see the blue of his eyes, reaching all the way to her heart and strengthening the cords that bound them the first time he said

33

those three little words only days before. "I love you, Kaylan Lee Richards. Do you trust me?"

She nodded, fearing the tears would come again if she responded.

"Do you trust the Lord has a better plan for us than either you or I could write?"

Peace stole through the air as she remembered Jeremiah 29:11. Why did she always panic before she remembered Scripture? "Plans for a hope and a future," she whispered.

He nodded.

"Come back to me. Be safe." She wrapped her arms around his neck, desperate to capture the memory of his arms around her.

"Hawk!" Kaylan sensed Micah's impatience. Time was up.

Nick's lips stole hers, gentle at first then passionate, bordering on desperate as his hands gripped her neck and waist, holding her close to him. She sensed his love, his fear, his desire to make her understand.

Then with a whispered "bye," he was gone. And her tears fell like rain, yet her heart stood firm. She would see him soon. She had to.

Chapter 6

FOR THE FIRST time since joining the SEALs, Nick had left something behind. It wasn't something he could fit in a bag or carry in his uniform pocket. He left behind his heart with an auburn-haired, green-eyed beauty. And he didn't want it back. As far as he was concerned, she could keep it until he died. Which would not happen on this mission if he had anything to say about it. He shot up a prayer for Kaylan's peace and the decisions the team would need to make in the hours to come.

The roar of the C-17 permeated his thoughts as Kaylan slipped into the recesses of his mind. He locked away the memory, knew he couldn't allow thoughts of her to dominate his consciousness while they tracked Janus. It was time to catch a killer.

Nick's blood boiled at the thought of young men and women who had sacrificed their lives for their country at the hands of weapons Janus and her mysterious boss had provided to bloodthirsty tribal leaders. Would there never be an end to people's greed and lust for power and possessions? He thought of the verses in the Bible that prophesied that war would continue until the end of time. Great job security for him. But he fought to provide justice and an end to the bloodshed. He ached for a time of peace.

Would his children always know the cruelties of war? If he

stayed in the SEALs as he planned, his kids would gain an early understanding of duty, justice, and sacrifice. SEAL teams would die. Men, SEALs, they would know as family. He couldn't control it. Death respected no person or situation. It came. Nick thanked God for the promise of eternity for those who believe. It left a small measure of hope, brought purpose to the pointless skirmishes over land and religion.

Micah elbowed him, raising his voice over the drone of the plane, "You good, man?"

He gave a thumbs-up. "Just thinking about what's ahead."

"I want this chick so bad I can taste it. I hope our intel's solid. She hasn't stayed in one place long. Maybe we finally found her home base. Yalta, Ukraine, is a pretty busy port, though."

Nick shrugged. "May be perfect for anonymity." Nick remembered the first time they laid eyes on Janus in the jungle of Nicaragua. He'd injured his back in an explosion that night. He remembered his shock as the scarf slipped from their target's head and they discovered Janus was actually a woman. He wished he could put a real name with her face, a motive for her methods. But he was still in the dark.

Micah's voice broke his reverie. "Think she'll actually give up the big fish if we catch her? She was one of the coldest targets I've ever come across when we saw her in that bungalow in the jungle. I'd never seen someone so icy." He studied Nick. "Although..." His cheeky grin was back in place. "You come pretty close when something ticks you off. I usually know when to steer clear."

"Did you just compare my anger issues to a known terrorist?"

"If the shoe fits."

"Harsh, Bulldog. Harsh."

"Now, see, that's the look I'm talking about. Like you want to kill me."

Nick smirked. "Don't tempt me."

Micah pulled a black-capped pen out of his pocket. "How many ways could you kill me with this?"

Colt tipped his Angels baseball cap up from his eyes across from them where he'd been dozing. "Twenty-three," he answered. "Want me to demonstrate?" His eyes held that crazy streak he got right before he did something stupid. Nick blamed his hippie upbringing. He didn't doubt this kid could deliver.

Micah tossed Colt the pen and the rest of the team came alert, eager to see what the team daredevil would do next.

"The easiest and most obvious way would be to shove it through someone's jugular, making sure to hit the major artery in the process." Colt uncapped the pen. "Like so.' In one quick move, he aimed the pen at Logan's throat and with incredible speed moved in for his faux kill.

Matching his speed, Logan's hand came up and grabbed Colt's wrist, turning the pen and pinning Colt's arm in a position where the point now faced Colt's neck.

The team roared with laughter as Logan offered Colt a cheeky grin. "Never try to trick a dad while he's sleeping. I'm used to nightly attacks from arms much shorter than yours." He patted Colt on the cheek before letting him go. Colt's tan skin deepened to a brownish shade of red.

"Smooth move, dude. You'll have to teach me that sometime."

Logan settled back against his seat crossing his arms over his chest and closing his eyes again. "I can't give away all my secrets. Time to get some shut-eye, men. Who knows how much sleep we'll get on this mission."

Nick watched as one by one his teammates fell asleep. Exhaustion tugged at his eyelids, and his mind wandered back to the beginning of his SEAL career in BUD/S, where he first learned the life skill of sleeping wherever he could, whenever he could. He gave in to the urge and closed his eyes while his mind wandered. The drone of the plane lulled him to nostalgia, and he remembered the way he felt the first time he met Kaylan.

Sarah Beth and Kaylan were out on the lake in Tuscaloosa, Alabama, riding the family jet skis. Kaylan pulled a quick figure eight in the water, spraying Sarah Beth with white foam, her musical laugh echoing over the engine. Kaylan's hair hung limp in a ponytail and a few strands draped over her eyes. Her freckles stood in stark contrast and her cheeks tinged a faint pink from her day in the sun. Her joy washed over him, brightening the summer day. Sarah Beth and Kaylan anchored the jet skis and approached him and Micah on the deck, their laughter echoing on the lake.

Micah had run forward and picked Kaylan up, spinning her around in a hug. Her joyful spirit lightened the air around them. He felt a magnetic pull and knew without a doubt that Kaylan was someone special. She radiated life.

"Micah, put me down!" As he set her on the deck and turned to hug Sarah Beth, she approached Nick.

"You must be Nick. I'm Kaylan."

He stuck out his hand. "It's nice to finally meet you."

She looked at his hand and grinned. "That won't work in this house." She stepped forward and put her arm around his waist, rubbing her hand on his back with sisterly affection. "We hug. Don't even try to shake Mom's hand." She turned toward the house, unfastening her life jacket as she went, revealing a black swimsuit. She stopped when she realized he wasn't following. "Welcome to the family, Nick. We're glad you're here." She nodded toward the house with a smile and kept walking as Micah and Sarah Beth followed her.

The plane hit an air pocket, and Nick's mind flew back to the present. He still felt the same way about Kaylan now, breathless, hopeful of what could be, what would be if he had anything to say about it. For a time he thought marrying her was an impossible dream, something he cooked up in the heat of a summer morning.

Now he knew his gut instinct was correct. He was ready to marry this girl.

Life had changed her. Haiti had changed her. While his first memory was of a girl becoming a woman, Haiti had solidified the transition to womanhood. A hint of sadness colored the innocence and childhood laughter that once defined her. She used to say that Sarah Beth defined full life, but Nick knew better. Kaylan defined that all on her own. She just needed to discover the beauty that came after a person experienced brokenness. She was finding her way back, learning to laugh again, learning it was okay to love with all her heart. That joyful girl of summers past lay somewhere deep inside, ready to burst past the hurt and death of innocence. He had determined to help her find her way back to that girl, to remember the sweetness of a time when life was beautiful just for a moment and remind her that they would make more of those moments in the days and years to come.

With thoughts of summer days, sunrises, and an auburn-haired beauty, Nick drifted to sleep, Micah's snores providing just the hint of home he needed to relax and let go.

Chapter 7

NICK'S TEAM LANDED at the Naval Support Activity base in Souda Bay, Crete, at zero five hundred on Tuesday after about fifteen hours of travel time. Nick felt grungy and exhausted as he grabbed his bag and followed his team into the hangar where they set up a small briefing area in a corner. He shook his head, hoping to dispel the fog.

The sun shone brightly on this hot September day, and Nick took a deep breath, inhaling ocean air. What he wouldn't give to take scuba gear and explore the waters around the island. When he was a kid, his mom swore he was a fish out of water. "You should have been born with gills and flippers, son," she always told him.

Nick helped his team spread out maps and photos on small fold-out tables. Guys from the base rolled in a white board, dyed red in places from color that refused to be erased. "They're just kids." Micah nodded as they exited the hangar. "Do you remember when we were just kids?"

Nick shook his head. "It's been a while. But we definitely lost that boyish glow during BUD/S. They scrub that right out of you."

Titus approached Nick and Micah with cups of steaming coffee. "Anyone for Turkish coffee?"

"Turkish?" Nick accepted the cup, bringing it close to his nose to inhale. The strong scent cleared the lingering fog. He took a tentative sip. "Aren't we in Greece?"

Titus grinned, his white teeth in stark contrast to his dark skin. "I'm not always big on being politically correct. They call it Greek coffee now, but the recipe never changed. It's just political stupidity from the 1970s when Turkey invaded Cyprus."

"Well, aren't you just the walking encyclopedia?" Jay walked up and slapped Titus on the back. "Where's the café au lait, amigo?"

Titus rolled his eyes. "Well, to get a cup requires that you mind your manners. One of the guys here is a coffee connoisseur. He makes a mean cup of joe, and he's definitely identified some of the island delicacies. If you can act like a normal human being for five seconds, he might let you have a cup."

Jay chuckled. "Nah. That's what I have you for."

"T-Brown, rustle all of us up some of that coffee, and let's get down to business," Logan called as he checked some gear.

"On it." Titus disappeared through the hangar door, and Jay clapped his hands in anticipation. "It isn't alcohol, but I'll take what I can get. That smell is making my mouth water."

Micah crossed his arms. "The last thing we need is you caffeinated. You're like the energizer bunny without caffeine or alcohol in your system."

"Well then, that must mean you're ready for a rematch."

Nick smirked, "Meaning you're ready for another beating?"

"C'mon, Hawk. You let your boy do the dirty work for you last time. Let's see if you can hang." Nick couldn't ignore the playful challenge in Jay's eye. In one quick move he put Jay in a headlock as he dragged him toward the tables.

Logan chuckled and shook his head. "It's like working with a bunch of teenagers."

Jay landed a well-placed punch to Nick's gut, which doubled him over. "Little punk." Nick lined up to retaliate as Titus returned with the coffee.

"Seriously, you two? I wasn't gone for that long, and you can't keep Jay out of trouble for more than five seconds."

Micah grabbed some of the cups from Titus. "That's what we have you for. Aren't you his baby-sitter?"

"Man, please. I just keep him from breaking his neck."

Nick grunted. "Well, maybe you could teach him how to fight too. He's a little rusty."

"You white boys are lost causes. I could teach you moves that would terrify you. Street-gang style. Gotta learn to fight dirty."

Jay shook loose of Nick and crossed his arms in mock frustration. "T-Brown, you been holding out on me?"

"All right, all right. That's enough." Logan took a sip of the hot liquid and grimaced. "Down to business."

Colt, Micah, Nick, Titus, and Jay gathered around the tables where Logan had spread out a city map of Yalta, Crimea, in Ukraine. The white board behind Logan now looked like a rainbow had exploded, leaving all its colors behind. Diagrams, notes, and to-do lists cluttered the space. Charts, notes, maps, and supplies littered their corner of the hangar. Nick loved the controlled chaos.

Logan walked them through the plan, his eyes studying each man on the team, making sure they were fully engaged. "We think this weapons operation is fronted by a cruise line that sails the Black Sea and makes port in Eastern European countries. We'll take two Zodiacs from a ship anchored in the Black Sea to Yalta. Four will swim into harbor while two stay with the Zodiacs and watch our backs. Slip in, gather intel, and see if we can snatch Janus. We'll radio HQ once we have her.

"Our friend in the Agency fed us intel that Janus has pretty expensive taste. He confirmed that she lives on a small yacht anchored in the harbor. Since tourist season died down toward the end of August, we will have less interference. This is our target." Logan slid a photo in front of them.

Jay moved in to look at the boat. "That's a Ferretti 800

Superyacht. It would comfortably fit a couple of people but offer untold ease for one." His responding whistle stretched long and low. "Maybe I need to find a different day job." Nick popped him on the back of the head. "Kidding. Kidding"

Titus sat down and rocked back in his chair. "*The Jupiter*. How much y'all want to bet our chick has a thing for Roman mythology?"

The guys around the table grew still and Logan studied Titus. "Now how do you figure that?"

"She goes by Janus. But if you study Roman mythology, Janus was an obscure god known as the god of transitions. Some even considered him duplicitous, the god of choices. This ship is named *The Jupiter*, another name for Zeus, the most powerful god of Roman mythology. If I'm right, there may be a pattern or identifying mark that we can track."

Micah smirked. "Smarty."

Titus rocked back in his chair like he didn't have a care in the world. "Some of us like to read."

"So far intel has tracked four people who got on that boat today. Two left, which means as of right now they still have eyes on two, one being Janus. They will keep us updated as time draws closer."

Colt walked over to a laptop, pulled up the ship model, and walked his team through the interior. Anticipation charged the air as they set about finalizing plans. Nick would be part of the team to board the boat. Thanks to a childhood love of Russia instilled by his history teacher mother, Nick had gone on to take enough classes in college to achieve fluency in Russian. The language came naturally, rolling off his tongue as if he'd always spoken its strange cadence. Micah, Logan, and Colt would team up with him. Jay and Titus would run the two Zodiacs, ready for pickup and any other issues that might arise.

"We move out at zero one thirty, drop into the Black Sea at roughly zero three thirty. We're back here before zero seven hundred. Clean up, check your gear, get some shut-eye. Let's catch this witch."

Guys from the base directed the team to some bunks for sleep. Nick struggled with the time change every deployment. His brain said dive into the water and soak up the sun; his body screamed for sleep. The team settled into bunks, curtains shielding the light streaming in as the sun rose.

Micah yawned. "What day is it? My body is jacked up right now."

"September seventh." Jay's always playful tone fell flat.

For a moment no one spoke. Nick related to Jay like few could on the team. They'd both lost their dads. However, Nick had been able to tell his dad good-bye. Jay's dad had gone down in the 9/11 attacks. His death date drew near. Nick finally broke the silence. "How you doing with that, man?"

No one moved and Nick wondered if Jay would answer. When he finally spoke, Nick detected his pent-up emotion. "He's the reason I joined the teams, you know. When his plane went down, I thought my life had ended too. Then I got angry, so angry I don't remember much of my teen years. In one moment I became the man of the house. By the time I graduated from high school, I wanted to do something about those guys. I wanted revenge. But in BUD/S, I realized anger and revenge wouldn't get me through. Those emotions aren't powerful enough."

A heavy pause hung in the air, and Nick prayed Jay would keep talking. He'd never heard the details. Jay cleared his throat and then continued. "My dad loved this country. We flew the American flag loud and proud in front of our home in Jersey. He taught me to put my hand over my heart, to thank those who served, and to thank God for our freedom. I thought of my mom and brother, how I wanted to protect them from anyone who would ever do that to my country again. Vengeance turned to passion, and here I am."

For a moment the only thing permeating the stillness was the sound of base life happening outside their bunks. Colt's rusty, deep voice broke the silence. "I remember where I was on nine eleven. My parents were on this kick to find all the major surf spots in California and Baja after spending a year in Hawaii. We were traveling the coastline, my mom kinda homeschooling me when she felt like it. I was eleven and felt more at home on a board than in a classroom. That day I was up at the crack of dawn owning some sick waves. When I came into our trailer, a couple of the guys we were traveling with were gathered around the small TV. I watched the second plane crash into the World Trade Center.

"My parents were anti-rules. Anti-government. Shoot, they are the definition of hippies. But something inside me snapped. They didn't just hit buildings; they killed people. People, brah. I couldn't let that alone. Every time we got close enough to a library, I would disappear for a few hours, find newspapers and websites, and read about what was happening. I started finding books about SEALs and hiding them in my bunk. As soon as I got my GED, I walked into a recruitment office, shaved my awesome hair off, and set my sights on BUD/S. Those men thought they would injure a country. What they did was raise a generation of warriors instead. You don't kill thousands of Americans without serious consequences."

"Where were you, Logan?" Micah asked.

"University of Montana. Nineteen years old. I was at the school gym when the bulletin came on. I watched one plane, then two. I dropped the weights and headed to Kim's dorm. Know what she said as soon as she opened the door?"

"You smell like a sewer?" Nick chuckled, thankful Jay's sense of humor remained firmly intact despite the seriousness of the conversation.

"She said, 'I'm going to be a military bride, aren't I?' We finished school, got married, and here I am. She never wavered. I guess I

45

married a soldier in her own right. That woman is a greater patriot than anyone I know."

"How does she handle your deployments?" Nick wondered out loud, thinking of Kaylan back home.

"She believes that this is bigger than either one of us. She fights for her country by letting me go and holding down the home front. I have no idea how she does it, and sometimes I feel guilty for leaving her. But she shoves me out the door and tells me to go do my job and not to come home until it's done."

Nick watched Logan raise his hands in front of his eyes. "Sometimes I hold my kids and wonder what they would think if they knew of the men I've killed. Know what my wife says?"

"You need to use more lotion?" The guys howled as Jay made another jab.

"You make it really hard to tell a story."

Jay leaned over the bunk to peer down at Logan. "I'm done. For now. Continue."

"C'mon, Pops," Titus cut through the laughter. "What does Kim say?"

The silence lingered for a moment. "She says they're the hands of a hero and that she wouldn't have it any other way. Know what I think? My wife's the hero. I couldn't do this without her."

"My wife's the same way," Titus chimed in. "Liza had a cousin living up in New York when the towers were hit. A fireman in the city. Really shook her family when they couldn't contact him for hours after the buildings collapsed. She hates the work hours, but her biggest complaint is missing Texas. Heck, I miss it too, so those complaints I can handle. Where were you, Bulldog?"

"Getting out of the car for school. I'd just started tenth grade. My mom loaded us back up and took us home. We watched the news the rest of the day. I thought the world was ending. I was a superhero fanatic as a kid, and I kept thinking that Superman just needed to fly in and save the day. If only, ya know? The guys responsible for nine eleven taught their kids to hate America. But in the process they taught American kids to love their country and fight for her. In a way they hurt themselves more. Hawk?"

Nick thought back to that morning. "Mom woke me up for school with pancakes and bacon. She never cooked during the work week. I immediately thought someone died. I didn't realize thousands had. That memory didn't impact me fully until college. I looked around and hated my life. Found the Lord and wanted to fight for something bigger than myself. I wanted to do something that meant something. And I wanted a team to do it with."

"You think God actually cares, Hawk? We're killers. If He created life, aren't we violating some intergalactic law by taking it away? I mean, that's pretty serious stuff." Colt's questions shook Nick. He'd wondered the same thing before.

"Man, God doesn't care. He took all those people. He took my dad. What's a few more if we're actually doing it for a good reason?" Jay's voice held a bitterness that Nick understood well. His own voice had once held that tone.

"Jay, I don't think the Lord ever likes the loss of life. But we're human. And people are evil. God didn't kill your dad, man. Evil people who chose not to follow a good God did that. They'll pay someday."

"Whatever, dude."

Nick glanced to his right and kept going at Micah's encouraging nod. "My mom used to read me stories about King David, whom God called a man after His own heart. David's hands were marred with the blood of thousands that the Lord commanded he battle. He promised David victory, and thousands of mighty men fought with him. The first time I fired my gun on my first deployment, I got sick. I watched a man go down. It didn't hit me until we got back to base. I couldn't help but think of those stories and that God still loved David."

"So how does that justify the massive amounts of death in war, Hawk?" Colt's curiosity bled through his question.

Nick took a deep breath, praying his words would count for something later. "This war...it's ugly. We're fighting to protect our own and fighting to defend countless others who don't have a government to fight for them. I hate it. But I've got to believe that though the Lord doesn't like war, He allows it, and I'm going to wage it for the people I love. I'll answer to Him for what I've done. I fight, and I'm going to keep fighting."

The silence stretched again, and Nick shut his eyes, praying his words would take root. Praying that these men would understand the goodness of God, that His justice and mercy existed in equal measure.

Jay's deep Jersey accent jarred him from his drifting. "You know if we catch this witch, we'll be cutting off the weapons supply to the very guys that killed my dad. Fewer American lives lost."

Logan's voice boomed in the silence. "Let's get some shut-eye."

Nick drifted to sleep, preparing to make war.

They were coming. Janus ended the call and took another sip of bourbon, the amber liquid burning her throat and stomach. She grimaced.

How had they found her so quickly? She stood and walked to the windows, the smell of salty air faint but familiar. She squeezed the crystal glass in her hand and wondered if Nick was with the team that would try to take her out. She hated losing the upper hand. But this game wasn't over. Far from it.

She would have to disappoint them. She glanced toward the bedroom and the packed bag on the bed. No, she wasn't ready to be caught yet.

"Sorry to disappoint, little SEAL. But you will not catch me tonight. You may even catch more than you bargained for."

She paced back to her chair and studied the man sitting opposite. He had proved to be a useful distraction at times.

Ivan raised his brows at her perusal. "Is it time?"

"*Da*," she answered. "You know what to do."

Chapter 8

INTEL HAD LOST their vantage point on Janus. The call came thirty minutes before the drop-off. They'd seen Janus and a man periodically come up on deck, but for hours now, nothing. But the team was launching anyway. Her boat. Last confirmed location. Everything was a go.

A knot built in Nick's gut, and no amount of prayer eased the uncertainty. But he shoved it aside. No room to think about possibilities. They had a job to do.

Nick's head breached the water, his eyes barely above the surface. *The Jupiter* bobbed two hundred feet away. Micah touched his shoulder then submerged again, approaching the sleeping vessel. With his teammates by his side, Nick sliced through the water, taking slow breaths through his face mask, feeling the cool currents of the Black Sea moving around his body. Somewhere nearby Titus and Jay lurked in black Zodiacs, monitoring the area around them.

Micah hit the boat first, pulling himself up on deck and immediately scanning the decks, corners, and recesses with his rifle. He waved them on, and within seconds Nick knelt next to him with Colt and Logan by his side, their wet suits leaving growing puddles on the deck.

Logan signaled that Nick and Micah should check the cabin while he and Colt took the deck. They moved in perfect sync, the only sound the gentle lap of waves on the hull of the boat. A cruise ship sat anchored farther in the harbor, and Nick hoped no one lingered topside.

Nick followed Micah below, his senses alert for any sound or movement. The ship lay in stillness. Too quiet.

"Cabin is clear." Micah said, radioing the rest of the team. The two of them lowered their guns and looked around.

Lush blue carpet blanketed the floor. A bed flanked one wall, adorned with cream and gold coverings and pillows. Gold-filigreed trinkets sat throughout the room, and leather armchairs made up a small sitting area. Plush and lavish. Nick had to agree with their intel. Janus enjoyed comfort and had expensive taste.

"Maybe we missed her." Micah broke the silence, still studying the room. He approached a small desk sitting below a circular window and glanced through a few papers, careful to leave them undisturbed. "Maybe she stayed in a cushy hotel tonight or is enjoying a late night in Yalta drinking Ukrainian booze."

Nick approached the desk and immediately stilled. Lying on top of the letters and papers was a note written on thick, cream-colored stationery. The precise Russian lettering told Nick more about their target than the room ever could. His face drained of color as he read.

"Hawk, what is it?" Micah looked harder at the papers.

Nick picked up the stationery and turned it toward Micah.

Micah stilled, his brown eyes scouring Nick's face.

"It says, 'Catch me if you can.' Someone ratted us out."

Glass broke as a bullet whizzed through the window, embedding in the cabin wall opposite them. Nick and Micah immediately hit the floor as their radio erupted with Colt's shouts. "Shooter! Man down, man down."

Logan. Nick's stomach sank. Kill the shooter, then get Logan home to his family. He issued instructions to the men on the Zodiacs. "Jay, T-Brown, see if you can get eyes on our shooter. One shot through the portside cabin window."

"Three shots on the bow," Colt shouted. "I think it's a sniper, but he's an awful shot."

Sniper. Nick's own trade. He pushed his body up enough to catch a small glimpse of the cruise ship anchored just inside shooting distance. He should have known. He pounded a fist on the carpet.

"T-Brown, get eyes on the top deck of that cruise ship. Take this jerk out so we can get off this boat. Jay, radio HQ. Tell them we need surgeons available as soon as we get back."

"Hawk." Logan's voice shook over the radio, but Nick's heart leapt knowing he was conscious.

"Hang in there, man. Let's get off this boat."

"Grab anything we can hand over. We need more intel on Janus..." Logan sucked in a breath. "We need more to catch her."

"On it." Micah began pulling the mail and paperwork from the desk, then opened the drawer.

"Hurry, Bulldog," Nick hissed as he crouched and moved toward the door. Another bullet whizzed through the window. This guy was clearly shooting blind. It made Nick's blood boil. He hated getting shot at. He wished he had his sniper rifle in his hands. Payback would be brutal.

"There might be fingerprints." Micah grabbed a few pens and papers, shoving them in a waterproof bag and then stuffing them next to his chest before refastening his wet suit. He beat a path to the door on Nick's heels.

"We've got company," Colt shouted over the radio. "Speedboat coming from the west. I got eyes on three, all fully armed." Shots echoed from above, and Nick and Micah clambered up the stairs, stopping to appraise the situation.

"On deck," Micah called over the radio.

"Jay, T, we need y'all. Forget the sniper. We gotta get out of here." Nick swallowed his anxiety as he scanned the darkness.

Another round of bullets sprayed the boat, right above where Nick and Micah crouched. Sitting ducks with one wounded and a trigger-happy, inexperienced sniper. Not ideal.

"All right. That's enough of this." Micah looked to Nick. With a nod, they rounded the deck, firing back at the speedboat now beginning to circle *The Jupiter*.

Nick shouted over the roar of the speedboat. "Colt, you and Logan get to the stern and let's get off this boat. We'll cover you."

"Hawk, take port, I'll get starboard." Micah and Nick split and began firing. As the speedboat circled closer, Nick identified one driver and two shooters. The driver's blond hair glinted in the moonlight, probably Eastern European. Nick couldn't make out his face. The shooters both had caps pulled low over their faces, and their dark clothes blended into the night. Nick took careful aim and sent one flying over the deck and into the sea spray.

"One down."

Colt appeared, Logan slung over his shoulders, his steps quick and measured on the thin trail between the cabin and the boat's edge. "Hawk, help."

"Cover us, Bulldog." Immediately Micah appeared at his side, firing shots. The second gunner went down.

Nick grabbed Colt, steadying him, and then helped him lower Logan to the floor. A nasty hole gaped in Logan's calf muscle, blood still oozing from the wound. Logan's face was pasty, his eyes unfocused. Nick noticed Colt had already tied a tourniquet above the wound.

Jay's voice sounded over the radio, almost shattering Nick's ear drum. "Get off the boat! Incoming."

Colt swore as the speedboat barreled toward *The Jupiter*. Micah fired as Colt and Nick dove off the side, pulling Logan with them. From underwater, Nick heard another splash as Micah joined them, then they dove as deep as they could. The water lit up around them, and debris began to fall past them. Even with the currents, the heat seared the back of Nick's neck as he and Colt pulled Logan farther away, Micah swimming next to them.

Within seconds of surfacing, the Zodiacs pulled up next to them. Micah climbed over the side and then reached for Logan. As Nick helped Logan from the water, he noticed another gash in Logan's leg where a piece of metal from the boat had embedded during the explosion. He slid over the side and immediately turned to examine Logan's wound.

Jay swore as he watched from the other Zodiac. Colt quickly pulled himself into Jay's raft and began scanning the area

"Stay with us, man." Logan coughed up water and Nick knew a moment of panic for the kids, Kim, and the baby on the way.

"T, get us back, now!"

They sped away, leaving the remains of a yacht and speedboat crackling in the Black Sea, a crew of law enforcers, Nick assumed, approaching from shore. Bile built in his mouth. She'd outwitted them. Again. It was time to get to the bottom of this. They would get home. And they would get answers.

Chapter 9

KAYLAN COULDN'T WAIT to get off her feet as she entered her house and tossed the keys on the bar. The guys had been gone for four days, and she'd just gone to check their house and get the mail. Everything was as she left it. "I guess ole Mrs. Buckner finally croaked," Megan said as she stirred pasta in a pan on the stove.

"Megan!"

"It is what it is, Kaylan."

"That's sad. We didn't get to say good-bye." She sank onto a bar stool, her feet sore from her rotation. This month they had her stationed in a hospital, creating meal plans for different patients. She loved the nutrition aspect, but she was ready to finish the internship, take the dreaded registered dietician exam, and become Kaylan Richards, RD.

"I went by at the beginning of the week and took Mrs. Buckner some soup. She didn't look so good. Real pale. Barely able to move on her walker." Megan glanced at Kaylan. "It's kind of sad her family didn't take care of her. They would have thrown her in a shabby nursing home and never thought twice. I'll miss going over there to watch *Wheel of Fortune* when I take her dinner."

Kaylan nodded, thankful for the small glimpses of compassion she saw in Megan. Her friend was tough out of necessity. Life had dealt her some rough blows. Megan had lived in the house for a year before Kaylan moved in and had visited her ailing grandmother for a year prior to inheriting the house. Mrs. Buckner had been friends with her grandmother, and Kaylan knew Megan had grown more attached to their elderly neighbor than she let on.

"Guess we will have a new neighbor soon." Megan smirked. "I'm guessing we'll take her cookies? I think your Southern hospitality is rubbing off on me."

Kaylan laughed and allowed the full brunt of her Southern accent to color her words. "Stick around, darlin'. There's more where that came from."

"Oh, wow. Shoot me if I start talking like that."

Kaylan hopped off her stool and began to pull ingredients from the cabinets. "Not a chance. I'll have you saying 'y'all' in no time." She held up two bags. "Since you are making pasta salad, I think I should take cookies to this dinner tonight. Should we make chocolate chip or M&M?"

"You're in the mood for chocolate."

Kaylan snuck a small handful of M&Ms. "Always. So what'll it be?"

"Chocolate chips." Megan turned off the burner and drained the water over the sink. She preheated the oven, and the two moved around the kitchen in perfect sync, sneaking handfuls of chocolate until the cookies were in the oven. Their next-door neighbor, Nina, had invited them over for one of her monthly "Pick-a-Little, Talk-a-Little" dinners and tea. She liked to get the ladies on the block together once a month to gossip and eat. She was on neighborhood watch and took her job very seriously. Megan had refused to go to dinner until Kaylan accepted for both of them. They had an hour before the festivities began.

Megan hopped onto the kitchen counter. "The dough is the best part. We should just take that."

"Oh, so true." Kaylan licked the spoon before placing it in the sink and running the water.

"Where's lover boy been lately? Haven't seen him in a few days."

Kaylan didn't take her eyes off the spoon. "Work got crazy. Both of our hours have been all over the place this week." She shrugged. "We'll figure it out." She knew she wasn't exactly lying, but she wasn't telling the whole truth either. For a moment a longing for Sarah Beth hit her, and she physically ached. She never would have had to lie to her, even about Nick being gone. She winced.

"Uh-oh. Trouble in paradise?"

Kaylan forced a smile. "Everything's fine. What about you? I haven't seen Lance lately."

"That ended last week."

"You haven't even been together for two weeks."

"Flings are easier, Kaylan. Nothing serious, no strings attached. Just fun and then done."

Kaylan shook her head. "That doesn't sound very fun to me."

"Yeah, I'm sure. From what I can tell, you have a perfect family, perfect boyfriend even if he is military, perfect friends, and a perfect life. You wouldn't know what it's like to move from place to place every year, your mom out of your life and off with some guy, your dad too consumed with his job in the military, promising face time then never showing up. You wouldn't understand..." She stopped short, her face filling with pain and anger. She quickly lowered her gaze, her dark hair falling to hide her eyes. With a sniff she lifted her head. "Forget it."

Kaylan watched Megan for a few moments, her heart racing. She knew what she had to do, but it was the last thing she wanted to share. *Lord, please. Anything but that. I can't talk about that.* She waited, hoping the urgency would pass. She'd rather face the barrel of a gun than talk about what happened to Sarah Beth. Not yet.

But Kaylan couldn't shake the stirring deep within her. Kaylan could tell Megan why Jesus loved her, or she could be honest, risk showing Megan the most vulnerable place of her heart and what God had done. She could acknowledge that she still didn't understand the why, but she knew where her hope came from and because of that she could live a life full of joy. She wasn't there yet, but one day she would be.

Kaylan hopped from the counter and grabbed Megan's hand. "Come with me." Megan pulled her hand free but followed Kaylan to the bookshelf in her room that held photos of her and Sarah Beth over the years. She handed one to Megan, taken in Haiti.

Megan glanced at the framed photo in her hand and then back at Kaylan. "Okay, I'll bite. Who's this?"

"That is my best friend in the world. And this is also a big reason my life isn't perfect." She grabbed another frame housing a photo of her and Sarah Beth trick-or-treating as third graders. Kaylan was dressed as a scarecrow and Sarah Beth as the Tin Man. It seemed appropriate. In the end Sarah Beth really did have the biggest heart of all. She'd encouraged Kaylan to live joyfully. Kaylan could never thank her enough for that.

Kaylan sank onto her bed and patted the spot next to her. "I know you think I've lived this charmed life, and in reality, I have. It's been incredibly sweet and incredibly blessed. Up until a year ago I lived in a safe bubble of family, friends, and college. Life was good."

"Yeah, I think you're only proving my point." Megan moved to stand up, but Kaylan put her hand on Megan's arm.

"Wait, please. You need to understand. You need to know that I really do understand some of your heartache."

"How could you possibly? This Sarah girl sounds pretty spectacular to me. Looks like you're set in the friend department."

Kaylan shook her head, her eyes welling with tears. More than ever she understood that despite outward appearances, one could never really know or understand the broken stories or the beauty that lay hidden in some people's hearts. *Lord, I don't want to.*

Again the urge to speak overwhelmed her, and she continued, praying for the right words. "In late December Sarah Beth and I went to Haiti. That's where everything changed."

"I don't get it. I've heard you talking to that Rhonda lady and Abraham on the phone. You have pictures of Haiti all over the house. How could that experience possibly be bad unless..." She grew still and her eyes searched Kaylan's face. "Kaylan, please tell me...no. You weren't...you weren't in the earthquake, were you?"

Kaylan swallowed the growing lump in her throat, unable to speak. She nodded, tears beginning to fall, but she remained calm. "Sarah Beth and I were in Rhonda's guest bedroom when the quake hit. I managed to roll under my bed right before part of the room caved in, but...Sarah Beth didn't quite make it to cover. Once I managed to climb over to her, she..."

Megan reached for Kaylan's hand and patted it awkwardly before squeezing, nearly causing Kaylan to wince at her strength. She thanked the Lord for the pressure. It kept her focused. "They didn't find us until the morning. By then, well, Sarah Beth went to be with Jesus. She..." Her voice cracked and Megan intensified her grip. Another tear slipped down her cheek, and Kaylan realized Megan was crying too. "She died in my arms. It wrecked my world. I spent the next few days trying to help as many people as I could. A little boy I had played with died. I know I shouldn't have favorites, but Reuben"—she smiled through her tears—"he was something special. So many gone. I still have nightmares."

"That explains a lot. Kayles, if I'd only known, I wouldn't have given you a hard time."

Kaylan covered Megan's hand with her free one. "I should have been honest from the beginning. It's just, it hasn't even been a year, and there are times I still struggle. I probably will for a while."

"So how do you get over something like that? How can you still say God is good? Doesn't seem like He cares much to me."

Kaylan shrugged. "I still struggle with that too. But I know

He's good because I saw what He did in the midst of the destruction. He is a master at bringing beauty from brokenness, Megan. You can trust Him with your hurt. You can trust me with whatever you aren't saying."

The kitchen timer went off, and Megan jumped from the bed as if electrocuted.

"I'll get that. Thanks for telling me about Sarah Beth." She placed the frame she'd been holding on the bed. "Maybe some other time." She turned and hurried from the room.

Kaylan replaced the photos and ran her finger down the glass protecting the shot of Sarah Beth and her in their Halloween best. "Miss you, Bubbles." Her mind raced back to her first meeting with Sarah Beth in kindergarten, blowing bubbles on the stairs, and the beginning of a beautiful, lifelong friendship. In truth, it had been lifelong, only ending in physical death. And they had an eternity together one day. That thought made the tears dry and a small smile break through the lingering sadness.

She started to leave the room and noticed the frame she'd knocked to the floor in her hurry to get to church on Sunday. She retrieved the frame and placed it on her dresser, then stopped. The smiling faces of a foreign couple stared back at her, the bar code from the store at the bottom of their portrait. She knew there'd been a photo of her and Nick at the beach in that frame just last week. She searched the floor and came up empty, then picked up the frame and studied the back. No loose edges. Maybe Nick took it with him for something.

She shook her head. She still couldn't find her necklace, and now this. Maybe she was losing her mind. She wandered toward the smell of cookies, making a mental note to talk to Nick about the photo when he returned.

Chapter 10

K AYLAN AND MEGAN rang the doorbell of Nina Ander-
son's home next door, balancing a plate of cookies and a
pasta salad. The woman loved her flower beds. Kaylan
spotted a few tools lying in the dirt, probably abandoned for
dinner preparations.

"Here we go." Megan rolled her eyes and Kaylan elbowed her,
careful not to jostle the pasta salad clutched to Megan's chest.

"They just want to get to know us. They are our neighbors, after
all."

"Kaylan, how many times do I have to tell you? We are not in
the S—"

The door opened to a woman Kaylan had never met. Wispy
blonde hair hung loose to her shoulders. Light blue eyes stared
back from a pale face with angular cheek bones dusted by makeup
that enhanced her facial features. She was dressed to impress.
Designer shoes, black skinny jeans, and a button-down, solid red
shirt. Kaylan was glad she'd taken time to throw on a dress.

"You must be Kaylan and Megan." The woman extended her
hand. "I'm Cathryn Brady. I moved in across the street a few weeks
ago." She stood back and motioned them inside. "Nina is finishing
up in the kitchen."

Megan spoke for the first time. "Welcome to the neighborhood. Where did you move from?"

"Chicago. Before that, I moved from here to there with work. Enough to appreciate meeting new faces."

"Wow. My family moved everywhere growing up, and all I got from it was a bad attitude." Megan chuckled at her own joke.

Kaylan inwardly winced and moved past Cathryn toward the kitchen. "I guess we can just put the food down in here?"

"Well, of course you can," Nina said as she swept into Kaylan's view, a potholder in one hand and spoon in the other. "Welcome, welcome to our little gathering. Looks like you have already met Cathryn. Over there we have Taylor, Jenna, and Beth." She pointed to three ladies circled around the rectangular wooden table. What looked to be salad dressing dripped from the spoon as she chattered away.

A woman with raven-black hair approached Kaylan and Megan. She looked to be about the age of Kaylan's mom. Her designer jeans paired with a tailored blazer spoke of a woman who knew how to make an impression and dress for her audience. "Kaylan, Megan, I'm Jenna. Nice to meet you." Her faint accent intrigued Kaylan.

Kaylan introduced herself and Megan as they laid the food they'd brought on the kitchen counter. "And where are you from?"

"My mother was British. My father American. I am a child of two countries. But I find I prefer California."

Megan whistled. "California is definitely a melting pot. Is anyone in the room actually from California?"

Taylor raised her hand, her smile shy as Nina bustled past her. "Just me and Taylor it seems. But the world is too large to be from any one place. Wouldn't you say, ladies?"

A murmur of confirmation greeted Kaylan's ears as small talk resumed throughout the room. Kaylan took a deep breath, delighting in the aroma of home-cooked food. Nina definitely knew how to make a room both cozy and eclectic. The walls radiated a rosy hue, catching the golden rays of the California sun. Mustard yellow, olive green, and dusty blue chairs encircled the wooden table, and teapots of all shapes, sizes, and patterns adorned the surfaces around the kitchen. It may not be home, but Kaylan would take it.

Nina turned from the stove and motioned to the ladies around the table. "Let's eat." As they began to talk and eat, Kaylan took in the assortment of women and their familiarity with one another. Nina with her short, spiked gray hair and spunky personality made quite the hostess. Beth lived at the end of the block with her husband and their three kids, two of whom were teenagers.

Taylor and her husband had been married for a few years and liked to take an exotic vacation every summer. This year they'd been to Tahiti and stayed in a hut on the water. Megan peppered her with questions.

Jenna was single and a CEO at a major corporation in San Diego. Work kept her busy and traveling, and when she wasn't working, she trained for marathons, 5Ks, and Iron Mans. She'd moved to the neighborhood four months earlier and enjoyed the monthly get-togethers with the ladies.

Cathryn, who was in sales, was a jet-setter, frequently away on business trips. She'd moved in not long after Jenna and was still unpacking. "I haven't had time to hire a housekeeper yet. One of these days I'll get around to it," she chuckled as she took a sip of tea.

As Nina stood up to serve dessert, Kaylan leaned closer to Cathryn. "I may have a solution to your housekeeping problem."

Cathryn raised delicately plucked eyebrows. "Oh?"

"Well, I have an internship right now, but I could use some hours at a job to help pay the bills."

"Perfect. It wouldn't be many hours. I've unpacked most of the house but haven't had time to tuck it all away yet. I could use the help."

"My pleasure." Kaylan smiled, thankful for a distraction and a way to make some money while Nick was away.

Nina waved a hand through the air as she placed Kaylan's cookies on the table with a tray of lemon bars and a teapot. "No more business talk over dinner."

"My apologies, Nina." Cathryn offered a small smile before leaning over to Kaylan and whispering under her breath. "Stop by in the next couple of days."

Kaylan nodded in response as the dessert was served. She'd missed her family around the kitchen table, but if she couldn't have that, maybe this group of women could help fill the loneliness she'd experienced since moving to California. And maybe it would be good for Megan too.

Chapter 11

NICK PACED BACK and forth in the hospital hallway, his stomach rumbling in anticipation of dinner. They'd been in Germany a little over three days, and if they got the green light, the team would fly out that night on a plane headed home. He ran a hand through his hair and for the fifth time that day wished for a shower and a razor. The hair on his face was starting to irritate him.

Grabbing another cup of coffee, he headed back to the waiting room where the rest of the team had taken up residence. How they had escaped with only one gunshot wound blew his mind. Micah had a cut over his eye from a piece of debris, and Colt had a few bruises, but it was nothing unfamiliar to them.

He rounded the corner and almost ran into the doctor, who was updating the rest of the team on Logan's progress. Nick stilled as the doctor's words registered in his sleep-deprived brain. "...infection. We gave him antibiotics, but it will take a few days to see if they work. We're going to bandage him up and send him home for doctors there to decide. We've done all we can do for now."

"And if the antibiotics don't work, sir?" Titus broke the silence.

The doctor shook his head and removed his glasses from the bridge of his nose. "He could lose his leg below the knee."

"Doc, why would he lose his leg? I thought we got here in time." Jay stood up, his nervous energy clear. He hated hospitals.

"The bullet severed his artery. He lost a lot of blood, and the debris lodged in his muscle, severely damaging his mobility. Because of pollution in the water, infection set in. We are working to contain and eliminate it right now with medication. But I think the best move is sending him home. He and his wife and the doctors will be able to make the best decision together. This is only my immediate recommendation."

"Thanks, Doc, for all your help." Micah stood and shook the doctor's hand.

The doctor pointed at the gash he had butterflied shut above Micah's right eye. "Take care of that. No fights, got it?"

"Yes, sir." Micah's Alabama accent intensified in his exhaustion, and right now he looked about dead on his feet. None of them had slept much since bringing Logan in.

Jay and Titus still blamed themselves for not getting the sniper, but Logan would hear none of it. "You two were exactly where we planned, covering our backs around the perimeter, so shut up or get out. This could have happened to any of us, and I wouldn't wish it on any of you."

The only thing that helped Logan was Tim McGraw and old John Wayne DVDs that they managed to rustle up. If Nick listened hard enough, he could hear the cheesy cadence of Western music and the muffled sound of old rifles filtering down the hall.

Nick wanted to shoot something. As soon as he got back, he would hit the shooting range and stay there until all his adrenaline faded. Then he'd run for another hour or so on the beach. He hated to lose, and he hated to fail on a mission.

"So now what?" Colt threw his arms in the air. "Logan's career may be over. And we didn't even catch this chick." He walked to the wall and slapped it.

Nick sank down in a chair and hung his head. "They've got

a baby coming soon. And the kids…they'll have a tough time understanding this."

Jay paced the room then stopped and made eye contact with every one of them. "They won't do this by themselves. Hear me? We will be there every step of the way. Even if that means we all pitch in and get Logan a prosthetic and then give him heck as he learns to walk. Got it?" He pointed. "No matter what."

Titus clapped him on the back. "That was never an option, Jay, man. I love those kids like my own, and Kim. Kim has just taken Liza under her wing. Helped her adjust to SEAL life. They will never want for anything, not if I have anything to say about it."

Jay resumed his pacing. Nick knew he would burn off the anger, the feelings of abandonment he faced in a crisis that reminded him of losing his dad.

"I'll call Kim. See how she's doing." Nick stood and held up his Styrofoam cup. "Anyone need a refill?" Colt and Micah handed him their cups as he exited the room.

He pulled out his military issue phone and slowly dialed Kim's number. At least Logan wouldn't come home in a flag-covered box. But the circumstances still wouldn't be easy.

"Hello?" Molly's sweet voice rang over the phone line, and Nick pictured her as she'd been at the Labor Day party on the beach. So happy, so full of life. His heart broke.

"Hey, ladybug. It's Uncle Nick."

"Uncle Nick! Where are you? Are you coming home soon? Can I talk to my daddy?"

"We'll be home before you know it." He ignored her other questions, squeezing his eyes shut to block out the stark, sterile white of the hallways around him. "Molly, can you put your mom on the phone?"

"She's right here. See you soon, Uncle Nick. Can you give Daddy a hug for me, and tell him I love him?"

"Sure will, ladybug. Now put your mom on." He gritted his

teeth and took a deep breath. They would figure something out. They would get through this.

He heard the static sound of shuffling on the other end of the phone before Kim's alto voice cut through. "Nick, what's wrong? Is Logan okay?"

"Kim, we're coming home soon. Doc just cleared him. He's doing okay, ordering us around like always. I'm sure he'll call you again shortly, but I just wanted to check on you myself."

"I wish I could be there." Kim's tough veneer cracked, and it was all he could do not to reach through the phone and hug her.

"Kim, he's alert and watching John Wayne movies, if that tells you anything. I'm about to call Kaylan and ask her to get the kids so you and Logan can have some alone time when we land. You will get through this like you always do, one step at a time together."

Silence greeted him, and he heard a small sniff.

"Bring him home, Nick."

"We are on the first plane back. Stay close to your phone and e-mail. We'll see you soon."

He hung up and checked his wristwatch. It would be about zero eight hundred in San Diego. Kaylan would be arriving at work soon, assuming her morning commute was smooth. The phone rang three times before he heard a breathless "Hello?"

"Kayles, it's me."

"Nick! It's so good to hear your voice. Is everything okay?"

He exhaled, her voice a balm to his exhaustion. "We're headed home pretty soon. I don't have long. Listen, can you do me a favor?"

"Name it." He heard the sound of a car alarm engaging and guessed she had just parked.

"Can you help Kim by taking the kids so she can come pick Logan up when we get there?"

Her hurried breathing stilled. "Nick..."

"Kaylan, I can't say much. Please. Can you check on her tonight and then take the kids when you get word we are about to land?"

"Absolutely." She hesitated. "Are you okay?"

"Missing you. But other than that, I'm fine."

"Miss you too. Come find me when you land? I'm sorry I won't be there."

"This is more important. We'll have lots of these, God willing."

"Come home fast, babe."

"As soon as I can. Love you."

He could almost hear her smile over the phone and see the blush creep over her cheeks. "Bye."

Nick ended the call and grabbed the cups off the desk to refill them. He wasn't sure how, but they would get through this with Logan. No matter what it took. A SEAL didn't leave a man behind, in death, in life, or in loss of limb. Their brotherhood ran deeper than blood, and Nick would give anything to make this better. Janus had better pray she died before he found her.

Chapter 12

I T'D BEEN A little over a week since the team left California. And it had taken only a moment to change one's life forever. The plane engine shut off, and Nick and the team grabbed their gear. Logan sat in a wheelchair. He'd refused to be too medicated to see Kim, but Nick noticed the faint strain on his forehead and the way he clenched his fists when he believed no one was looking. Watching him, Nick realized he'd never seen such courage. Molly hit the nail on the head. Her daddy was a hero in every sense of the word, and the world would never know it.

"You ready, man?" Nick grabbed the handles of Logan's wheelchair as the rest of the team gathered around. Every eye solemn, every heart carrying the weight of a wounded warrior.

Logan made eye contact with every man in the group. "Hold your heads up. This isn't your fault." He looked up at Nick, and Nick again saw a flash of pain cut across his face before Logan concealed it. "Take me to my wife."

Ground crew scurried around, checking the plane and putting it to bed. X waited with Kim, but Nick had eyes only for her. Again, he thought he'd never seen a stronger warrior. Logan married well. Kim stood head erect, eyes clear, with an American flag in one hand and her other resting over her stomach as if comforting their unborn child.

Nick realized the rest of the guys were still following right behind him, ushering Logan all the way home, to his family, his heart, and his purpose. They all stood a little straighter when they saw Old Glory in her hands, and Nick knew Logan didn't regret the events of the past week. He'd done what he set out to do—fight for the country he loved. Kim came forward and wrapped him in a hug.

Only Liza and Kim waited for them. Most of their families lived in other states, and Logan and Titus were the only two married, although Nick and Colt were close. On a full deployment this moment would be sweet and much more energetic, but Nick thanked the Lord for the low-key greeting. It gave Logan and Kim the chance to react however they saw fit.

Liza came forward and met Titus. Nick noticed Titus hug her a little tighter. It could have been any one of them. They could have come home in boxes. Nick sent up a silent prayer of thanks for safety and protection. Kim took Logan's wheelchair from Nick and began to push her husband toward the waiting car. He would go to the hospital for more testing and hopefully find an antibiotic that would treat the infection. The pain became more difficult to mask with each passing moment.

Nick looked to Micah, his jaw clenched tight. "Let's get answers, Bulldog."

"No need to tell me twice."

X approached both of them and shook their hands. "Welcome home. Glad you're safe." He nodded toward the buildings behind him. "Let's go debrief. I want to hear what happened. And I hear we might have more info on Janus." Titus, Jay, and Colt appeared behind Nick and Micah, and X greeted them.

"We'll see. Gotta hand it over to intel." Micah held the bag like it contained an infectious disease. With every piece they discovered about her, they came one step closer to justice, but this info had come at a price. A price they'd all signed up for but still hated to see in actuality.

"Miss Kaylan, why isn't my mommy home with my daddy yet?" Molly lifted her Barbies and placed them in the pink house sitting in the middle of her bedroom floor. For the past hour Kaylan and Molly had undressed and redressed each Barbie. Kaylan peeked through the door to find both the boys playing Mario Cart on the Nintendo.

"Well, your mommy went to meet your daddy so they could have some alone time before they see you." Kaylan tapped Molly's nose with a smile.

Molly rolled her eyes, her dramatic personality in full swing. "Oh, Miss Kaylan, I know all about alone time. Conner and Tanner leave me alone all the time." She put her hands on her hips. "They always want to play ball but never with my dolls." A pout furrowed her little brow. "I hope my mommy gives me a baby sister when her stomach explodes."

Kaylan smothered a laugh. Logan and Kim had decided to find out the gender of the baby when they delivered. Kim was due within six to eight weeks, and Kaylan secretly hoped they had a baby girl too. For Molly's sake.

Molly grew still as the ringing of Kaylan's phone sounded through the room. Her pale green eyes doubled in size as Kaylan answered.

"Kaylan, it's Kim. Can you bring the kids to the hospital? Logan is ready to see them."

"Sure thing, Kim. They've already had dinner, and they've been waiting for this phone call." Conner and Tanner came to stand in the doorway, Tanner the spitting image of his daddy.

"And Kaylan, can you maybe prepare them a little before they get here? Just tell them he's in the hospital. I'll tell them the rest before we go in to see Logan."

Kaylan inwardly groaned. "Sure. We'll be there in about thirty minutes."

The boys ran from the room to put on their shoes, and little Molly pulled her sandals on her feet.

Kaylan ended the call and stood from the floor, calling through the house, "Whoever makes it to the car in the next sixty seconds gets free ice cream!"

All three kids sat buckled in the car in thirty.

The automatic doors slid open, and Kaylan walked through the hospital door with all three kids in tow, each markedly more subdued than they'd been at home, despite their stop at Mickey D's for drive-through cones. Kim waited for them by a few armchairs.

"Looks like Miss Kaylan let you have ice cream. I guess we'll have to ask her to baby-sit more often." She hugged all three kids as Kaylan stood back and watched.

Molly's green eyes filled with tears. "Mommy, why are we at the hospital? Where's Daddy? I thought only sick people come here."

Kim crouched down in front of her daughter and played with her braid. "Daddy hurt his leg while he was working, and the doctors want to check some things. But he'd like to see you."

"Is it bad, Mom?" Seven-year-old Conner's eyes never wavered from his mother's.

"We'll see. Let's just go see Dad. He's missed you guys." She reached for his hand.

Kaylan followed Kim and the kids to another wing of the hospital. She marveled at how strong this young mother remained.

She didn't know the extent of Logan's injury, but Nick wouldn't have called her if it hadn't been important.

She wondered how she would handle a phone call like this when she had kids one day. She blushed, realizing she'd pictured Nick's blue eyes and rich voice in her daydream. Maybe her feelings ran stronger and deeper than she wanted to admit.

She pictured a little green-eyed daughter or towheaded son and almost ached for that kind of life. But she knew she needed to fully understand this community first. Kim practically lived as a single mom most of the year. Kaylan admired how Kim commanded her home with ease and a firm hand, handing the leadership role back over to Logan when he arrived home. The Carpenter kids appeared well-mannered and energetic with a strong faith in Jesus. Kaylan prayed they never lost that faith.

They approached a waiting room where Nick stood leaning in the doorway. She stopped, her eyes drinking in the sight of him, scanning him for injuries. He'd slipped back into board shorts, a gray V-neck, and flip-flops, his face smooth of scruff and his blue eyes stormy. She closed the remaining feet between them, and he lifted her into his arms, burying his face in her neck, his grip tight with pent-up emotion. Her heart thudded from more than his touch. Something had gone terribly wrong. Desperation and sadness poured from him, and she clung to his neck as he set her down, leaning back only to look in his eyes.

"Welcome home."

He ran his thumb over her chin and tipped her face to meet his eyes, his lips covering hers in a kiss filled with pain and passion. She knew him too well to miss the rage and hurt he tried so well to hide. She'd never seen him like this before. She pulled back and rested her head on his chest.

"Thanks for taking care of the kids."

She laughed. "Those have to be the easiest kids I've ever baby-sat in my life. Kim and Logan definitely should win some kind of award."

Someone cleared his throat behind them, and Kaylan pulled away to find her brother with his arms crossed.

"Excuse me, what am I? Chopped liver? I do believe it's my turn for a hug and welcome home. I was out there too."

Kaylan rolled her eyes with a smile and met her brother in a tight hug. "Are you sure you aren't my baby brother? That was an awful lot of whining." She pulled back and noticed the butterfly bandage over his eye for the first time. "Micah Richards, what did you do?"

"Well, it's a great story actually. I got in a fight with this huge tiger shark."

Nick rolled his eyes and grabbed Kaylan's waist, pulling her back against him as she listened to her brother.

"So I'm wrestling this shark the size of an elephant, and Hawk wouldn't even help. I finally beat him and got nothing but this little scratch."

"And let me guess…all you have to show for it is one lousy tooth?" Her voice dripped with sarcasm.

Micah threw his arms into the air as the rest of the team chuckled in the waiting room. "Exactly. Now it will just be a legend."

"Uh-huh. Did someone look at that?"

Micah's eyes squinted into slits. "You sure you're my baby sister and not my mom?"

"You'll wish I were Mom when she gets hold of you."

Micah's voice turned serious. "Kayles, we don't need to tell her. This will heal and be no big deal. You're going to have to get used to a lot of tall stories and vague answers. There's a lot you don't know, and there's a lot you never will."

Nick's arms tightened around her waist before he let her go.

She hugged Micah again, leaning into him under his arm. "Well, I'm glad you beat the shark. And I'm glad you're so tough."

A cry came from down the hall, and Conner walked out holding his sister's hand. Kaylan let go of Micah and walked to meet the little girl. Molly ran the rest of the way to Kaylan and leapt into her arms, her tears soaking Kaylan's t-shirt.

Nick came up and put his hand on Kaylan's back, leaning to peer into Molly's eyes. "Hey, ladybug."

"Uncle Nick." She reached for him, and Kaylan let her go as Nick took her weight. For the first time she got a small glimpse of what life would be like with Nick, with children. Her heart warmed at the thought.

"What's the matter, ladybug?" Nick smoothed away Molly's tears.

"My daddy got hurt. Why didn't you protect him, Uncle Nick?" Her tears nearly broke Kaylan's heart, and she saw pain flash across Nick's face. The guys behind him bowed their heads. Jay paced.

"Sometimes things happen that we can't control, Molly. We got him home as quickly as we could, and the doctors are going to take good care of him."

She nodded and leaned her head on Nick's shoulder as he rocked her. Kim came out of Logan's room with the boys.

"Kaylan, do you mind taking the kids home and putting them to bed? I'll be home in a little bit."

Kaylan looked to Nick, who answered for both of them. "We'll both take them home. Why don't we stay with them tonight? I'll take them to school in the morning since Kaylan has her internship. That way you can stay with Logan tonight."

Relief flooded Kim's face. "Are you sure?"

"Our pleasure." Nick nodded to the men who had gathered around them.

Jay stepped forward. "I'll follow you and bring an overnight bag for Kim and Logan."

"But…"

Kaylan intercepted Kim before she could protest. "I'll pack it. Don't worry." She hugged Kim. "We've got it under control."

The group followed Kaylan and Nick out to the cars. Nick took the keys from Kaylan and climbed in the driver's seat. The kids were silent. Kaylan watched him close his eyes for just a moment and realized he must be exhausted. He turned on the car and pointed it toward the Carpenter's home.

Kaylan wove her fingers through his free hand. The streets had emptied of most of the traffic at 10:00 p.m., most people at home getting ready for the workday to come. "Hey, why don't you go home and get some sleep tonight? I've got the kids. I can go in a little late in the morning."

The car stopped at a red light and Nick met her gaze, his voice low over the sound of the radio playing Shane and Shane. "We made a promise we would be there for Kim and Logan. I'm going to help tonight."

Kaylan nodded, knowing better than to argue with his decision. Once he made up his mind, only an act of God could undo it. She ran her fingers through the hair at the back of his neck, and he leaned into her touch like a cat responding to a good back scratch. Not for the first time did she realize that she had the love of a man she didn't deserve. A man who put others before himself, no matter the personal cost.

Chapter 13

I T TOOK ALMOST an hour for Molly to fall asleep. Kaylan curled up on the bed next to her, stroking her hair and listening to her whimper until she finally went limp. She looked so innocent with her arm wrapped around her teddy bear and her thumb in her mouth. Her hero lay injured in a hospital bed, and that rocked her world.

Kaylan remembered the feeling of seeing Pap right after his stroke. Usually strong and capable, he'd looked feeble and confused. It shook her to her core. She couldn't even imagine having that feeling as a four-year-old.

Kaylan exited Molly's room, pulling the door closed behind her. She tiptoed across the hall and put her ear to the door of Conner and Tanner's room. Deep breathing. The boys had remained subdued, taking in every bit of the situation. They'd stayed close to Nick when they got home as he helped them unwind and get ready for bed. Thankfully they crashed as soon as their heads hit the pillow.

She wandered down the hall to the family room where Nick sat on the couch, his elbows resting on his knees and his head in his hands. The TV played an episode of *I Love Lucy* in the background, and Kaylan smiled as Lucy tried to talk Ethel into one of her crazy schemes. It reminded her of Seth and Micah. They'd always been in one hair-brained scheme or another growing up, usually with Micah as the mastermind. But Seth had an ornery streak all his own.

Leaning on the couch behind Nick, Kaylan grabbed his shoulders and eased him back into the chocolate suede couch. The room felt like Montana—outdoor paintings, rustic furniture, and pictures of the family in white shirts, jeans, and cowboy boots adorned the space.

Kaylan wrapped her arms around Nick and kissed his cheek. "How ya doing?"

He turned his eyes to meet hers, and she saw the exhaustion and something else. She could almost see his mind running ninety miles an hour.

"I missed you." He placed a gentle kiss on her lips and then tugged on her arms. She walked around the couch and sank next to him, curling into his chest, reassured by the sound of his heartbeat. On nights like this she wondered how she'd lived life before him. It somehow felt fuller now, as if a missing piece had found its way into her life. They chuckled together as Ricky showed up and caught Lucy in trouble.

Nick's eyes remained cloudy despite his laughter. She ran her fingers down his face, drawing his eyes to hers. "You're here with me, but your mind is still in a different country. Are you okay?"

He sat up on the couch and she followed, turning to face him, the suede changing color with her movement. He reached for her hands. "Let's play a game. Twenty questions. Things we may not know about one another."

Kaylan smiled, amazed he could orchestrate a lighthearted conversation when his face held so much worry. But she had to remember that SEALs worked hard and played hard. If they wore their work all the time, they would be emotionless machines. "All right. You go first."

"What do you want to be for Halloween this year?"

"Alice in Wonderland and the Mad Hatter."

Nick threw his head back and laughed. "Oh, no."

"Oh, yes. You'll look cute in all that makeup."

"No guy should ever wear more makeup than his girlfriend."

Kaylan smirked, causing Nick to chuckle again.

"Change that. No guy should ever have makeup on period, but especially in this circumstance where I would need more just to play the part."

Kaylan leaned in close as if about to kiss him. "Please?"

"No, ma'am. Play fair."

Her lips hovered right over his. "Please, babe?"

Nick leaned away, arching his back over the armrest. He gently pushed her back, his smile amused. "I'll think about it."

She gave in, her back sinking into the couch. "Most dangerous thing you've ever done. Outside of the SEALs, of course."

"Street racing. Sophomore year of high school. Had the car at about 110 and climbing. Went into a turn, and the car went up on two wheels. Thought I was going to flip." He shook his head. "Seriously the dumbest thing I've ever done. Thankfully it corrected quickly, and I finished the race."

"Did you slow down any?"

The smile that warned of trouble bloomed. "Nope."

"Of course not. Your turn."

"Most embarrassing moment."

Kaylan groaned. "Most definitely falling on my face during a dance recital."

He winced.

"Yeah, not good. I was thirteen and it was our big Christmas performance." She thought for a moment, the television casting an eerie glow in the dark room. "What did you want to be as a kid?"

He didn't even hesitate. "A teenage mutant ninja turtle."

She burst out laughing.

He rubbed his hands together. "All right, my turn. Where do you see yourself in five years?"

The change in tone caught her off guard, and she fidgeted, unsure how to answer him. "Well, I guess that depends."

"On what?"

"You only get one question at a time."

"You didn't answer the original question, Kayles." He reached for her hands again, running his thumbs over the top. His touch still sent shivers racing down her spine. She forced her brain to concentrate. "Where do you see yourself in five years?" he repeated.

She took a deep breath, her heart racing . "I guess I see myself working for a natural disaster relief organization somewhere, helping them create emergency strategies and provide nutritional food in the midst of a disaster like I experienced."

"Is that it?"

She shook her head, cautious to finish. "I see myself married and starting a family. My turn. I'll turn that question back to you."

He shrugged. "That's easy. On a SEAL team, maybe Six." He met her eyes, and for the first time since their reunion at the hospital, they appeared crystal clear and deep. Her breath quickened. "Married to you. Starting a family. That's what I want, Kayles." He brushed a loose strand of hair behind her ear, his voice lowering to a whisper. "What do you think about that?"

Heat crept up her face hidden in the dim flicker from the television screen. "Are we still playing?"

"No. I need to know a few things. We need to talk about this. It's just me, Kayles." His fingers caressed her wrist where her pulse betrayed her racing heart. "What are you afraid of?"

What fears held her captive? Abandonment, loss. The fear of letting someone in that deeply again. She knew she cared for Nick in a different way than Sarah Beth, but if they kept moving this direction, she would have to let him into all the ugly insecurities, the bad attitudes, the bitterness, all the broken parts of her heart. She would be fully known, and that thought frightened her. Would he still love her the same way if he really saw how weak she could be? He needed someone strong.

"Kayles…"

She had to trust him with something, had to help him understand why she moved so slowly.

"Baby. Can you answer me?" His face filled with hesitation for a moment, and he cleared his throat. "Do you…do you not want this?"

She gripped his hands as if he would slip from her grasp. It hit her then, the weight of her desire. She realized she wanted him more than her job, more than moving closer to her family, more than she wanted someone who worked nine-to-five.

"Nick, I want this more than anything. Okay? It just terrifies me."

Relief filled his face. "Why does it terrify you?"

"If you only knew what's inside me, the pain, the bitterness from this year. Trust me, you wouldn't like what you see. But I would have to show you all of that."

He cupped her face in his hands and focused all his intensity on her, his eyes piercing to her heart, shining a light on all the hidden places. "I want to know every part of you, even the dark places. Kaylan, that's what forever is all about. I'm not expecting you to be perfect or put together."

"But you are. All the time."

"Hmm. I think you need to talk to Micah. Kaylan, I stay calm because I have to. But inside I'm dying. Sometimes that manifests as anger, sometimes withdrawal, sometimes pride and cockiness." He smirked. "You should have seen me in college. Much worse. But I am far from put together. And you've got to let me see those things too, babe. I want to know. I want to understand you. And I want to know how we can fight that stuff, be better together."

He grinned. "How many kids do you want?"

"Five."

His eyes glowed like giant orbs. "Are you kidding? How about three."

"Hey, you asked a question, and I gave you an honest answer. Don't discourage me."

He smirked. "That is not a weapon for you to use."

She grinned. "Consider it a one-time thing. How about three and we can adopt two from Haiti?"

"That's still five kids, Kaylan."

She rolled her eyes. "Fine. I'll consider a negotiation. Maybe."

His grin hit the danger zone again as he leaned in for a kiss. "We can negotiate while we're practicing," he whispered against her lips.

Every fiber of her body responded to his touch, but she knew trouble when it knocked. She giggled and pulled away from him, jumping off the couch. "Okay, and with that, it's bedtime."

She padded down the hall and returned with sheets and a pillow for the couch. She handed them to him, and he tossed them on the cushions. He stalked her as she backed away, trying not to encourage him. "Don't I get a good-night kiss?"

"What did you just call that?" She pointed to the couch and then bumped into a wall, a picture frame rocking next to her head.

He pinned her with his arms, his eyes drifting to her lips.

"Nick Carmichael, you are trouble tonight."

He leaned in close, his lips a breath away, making her heart leap into her throat as she wrapped her arms around his waist. "No. Just in love with you." The words made her head spin as his kiss stole her breath away.

After a moment he pulled back, his hands now cradling her face. "Just so you know, I love you no matter what. It's not a conditional thing."

"My head gets that. My heart doesn't trust it."

He thought for a moment. "Kaylan, how are you sure of the Lord's love for you?"

Unexpected tears came to her eyes, but she blinked them away. "I guess I didn't think about that until the earthquake. But now I understand it better. He didn't leave me when I raged at Him, never abandoned me when my heart grew bitter. He sent me sunrise after sunrise to remind me of the beauty that comes after the darkest night." She wrapped her arms around his neck. "And He sent me you to walk through it."

"God knows your heart, every beautiful, messy bit of it." He tucked a strand of hair behind her ear. "How do you know what love is? How do you measure it?"

"I guess you can't."

He nodded. "Sure you can. Love comes from God, Kayles. It's deeper than we can ever understand, purer than we'll ever know, and unconditional no matter what we do, how far we run from Him, or how much we push Him away. We know it, because He is the embodiment of love itself." Nick brought her fingers up to his lips and kissed them. "Kayles, I'm not perfect. I never will be. I can't promise to never leave in the physical sense. I'm a soldier. But I can promise to never stop loving you and never base it on circumstance.

"Kayles, if He can love a prideful, playboy, college athlete who wanted nothing to do with Him, then I can love others no matter what. I'm not scared of the dark places, baby. Trust me. But more than that, trust Him with those dark spots. I promise, my love for you is unchanging. It's purer than I've ever known."

Peace settled her racing heart, and she leaned into Nick's arms, feeling a security and depth there she had yet to discover. *Lord, teach me to let him in, to let people in again. I don't know how.*

A lesson she learned in Haiti came flooding back. She would tackle this relationship one step at a time. She would open her heart, and she would remember what it looked like to love with all she possessed. Then she would understand how to love Nick as he truly deserved. And she wouldn't stop trying until that became a reality.

Chapter 14

NICK POUNDED THE sand, running in and out of the surf three days after returning home. Lecrae blared in his ears, and water danced around his ankles. It felt good to be home. He had a date with a gorgeous girl that night, one whose heart rivaled her good looks—pure gold.

There was still no word on Logan's leg. The whole team rotated in and out of the house, helping Kim take care of the kids. Kaylan, Nick, and Micah planned to take them to the beach the next day—get them out of the house and hospital, away from talk of their dad losing his leg.

The phone rang, breaking through his music. He slowed to a stop and put his hands on his knees trying to catch his breath before answering.

"Yeah, Bulldog."

"Dude, you need to hit the gym more if you are breathing that hard after a little run."

"Did you call for a purpose while you lounge around the house before work?"

"Yep. Have you been through the mail since we've been home?"

"Um, don't think so. I've been kinda busy. Why?"

"Nikolai Sebastian...that name mean anything to you?"

Nick nearly stopped breathing.

"Hawk. Did you hear me? Do you know who that is, or...or is this you?"

Nick cleared his throat, his heart still racing. No one knew that name. "It was on my birth certificate and my service records, but that's it. I never use it. No one knows. My mom always called me Nick Anthony after my dad. Is there a return address?"

"Nah, man. Whoever it was didn't even put your last name on the envelope. Want me to open it?"

"No! No. I'll be home in a few."

Nick practically sprinted the last half mile to his Jeep, curiosity pushing past his burning muscles and aching chest.

He threw the keys in the ignition, slammed the car into gear, and peeled out of the parking lot, his wheels threatening to fishtail on the thin layer of sand covering the concrete. Within minutes he made it to the house he shared with Micah, close to the base and close to the beach.

Throwing the door open, he immediately went for the table where a nondescript white envelope lay waiting for him. Micah walked in from the living room as Nick examined the writing. The style and formation of the letter seemed familiar, like he'd seen it before but didn't know it well enough to identify immediately. He flipped the envelope in his hand, the back as blank as a chalkboard on the first day of school.

He tore into the envelope and pulled a thin sheet of paper from inside. No. He froze, his heart settling like a stone.

Micah picked up the envelope and shook out a picture. Lifting it off the table, he turned it toward Nick.

Nick wanted to swear but bit his tongue, immediately tasting blood.

"Hawk, why is a picture of you and my sister in this envelope?" Micah snatched the note sheet out of Nick's hands. Nick reached for the picture, a shot of him and Kaylan at the beach, covered in sand from a game of volleyball. Kaylan had this picture up somewhere in her house.

His heart sank all the way to his toes. Kaylan.

"Hawk, what does this say?"

Nick licked his lips, his voice shaky as he responded. "It's Russian. It says, 'It's me or her. Take your pick.'" He met Micah's eyes, his fear full blown. "It's the same handwriting as the note we found on *The Jupiter*."

"Janus," Micah spat. "How did she get this picture, Hawk?" Micah met him nose to nose. "How the heck did she get this picture of you and my sister?"

"I don't know. But here's another question: How does she know my full name? And why didn't she use my last name? No one has ever called me Nikolai. And no one spells it like that. Who is this woman?"

Micah tossed the paper on the table. "I'm calling Kaylan. Get that stuff in a Ziploc bag and let's take it to base now. First Logan and now a picture of Kaylan. This chick just messed with the wrong Frogmen. Time to call in my buddy in the FBI."

Janus's gaze drifted to the calendar. Nick would have her letter right now. She'd sent it to Victor, then had him send it from Moscow. No way the envelope could be traced back to her exactly. No fingerprints. No DNA. Nothing. She'd even selected the paper from the stash she'd purchased in a Ukrainian market. Let him wonder how much she knew and where she stalked him.

He would not ruin her life. Not again.

She poured vodka in a tumbler and gazed around her new home. She'd furnished the rooms exactly as she liked them. She'd purchased new furniture, a new coverlet, and pillows for the bed. Money was no object.

Men always wanted weapons, and her boss knew where to find them. She offered her clients an endless supply, terrorists or politicians. Sometimes the line blurred. If she pocketed some of the profit now and then, the big man remained oblivious. His bank accounts overflowed.

She'd alerted her boss. The team had returned. From what she'd gathered, one appeared injured and might possibly lose a leg. She had a man on it, a rather handsome one at that. It amazed her how talkative nurses could be over coffee with a handsome stranger after a long night on shift.

She took a swig of the vodka, thankful for the taste of home. She really did prefer the bourbon, though. Or maybe a nice glass of wine charged to the boss's account.

Her chest tightened. They were too close, and he breathed down her neck like a dragon, one step away from writing her death sentence. How to take care of both problems?

She wouldn't live the rest of her life behind bars, and the SEAL team knew too much, would chase her to the ends of the earth until they ended their mission. Maybe it was time to look into real estate on a remote beach somewhere.

But if she couldn't run, one option remained. She could run right to the thing the team wanted most. Her boss.

Her hands began to shake. If only she were as noble as Andrei, as kind, as self-sacrificing.

A car jerked to a stop down the street, startling her. The glass slipped from her hands, shattering into prismatic shards. Her heart raced and she gripped her chest.

Enough.

Nothing could change the past. And nothing could save her now. But she'd vowed long ago that no man would ever control or manipulate her again. If she couldn't scare Nick away, then she would do whatever necessary to ruin his life and her boss's in the process.

It was the only way.

Chapter 15

KAYLAN FINISHED UP her meeting with Mr. Armitage. With his invasive surgery looming, she would need to take care and plan his diet accordingly. The hospital dietician continually taught her how to keep track of each patient's medical chart and diet. It could be an overwhelming task at times, but Kaylan decided to adopt the SEAL mentality of never giving up. She would learn this and be better for it.

Kelly, one of the nurses, stuck her head in the room as Kaylan rose to leave. "Kaylan, two guys are out in the hall making a fuss looking for you. Can you please make them shut up so the patients can get some peace and quiet?"

"That's weird. Yeah, I'm coming." She waved at Mr. Armitage and hurried from the room, following the loud voices coming from near the nurse's station.

"If you won't tell us where she is, we'll find her ourselves."

"Sir, if you don't calm down I'm calling security."

"Ma'am, this is an emergency."

Kaylan began to jog, recognizing her brother's voice. Micah never showed up at work. And he never yelled unless something had happened, usually something bad. She entered the open area around the desk and immediately spotted Micah and Nick. Kaylan rushed forward.

"Micah, calm down. I'm right here. What is going on?"

Micah immediately grabbed her arm and pulled her down the hallway out of earshot of the nurses.

"Micah, that kinda hurts. Let go."

"Bulldog, you need to calm down."

Micah released Kaylan's arm and took a deep breath. "Kayles, I'm sorry. We just couldn't find you, and it was like Haiti all over again and I panicked."

"Oh, Micah." She stepped into her brother's arms, kicking herself for never realizing the toll their trip to Haiti must have cost him as well. She wasn't the only one who'd been hurt. He'd tried to find her for days, only to locate the ghost of the girl she used to be.

She pulled away from her brother. "Okay, now what is the big deal? Is the family okay? Pap, he didn't have another stroke." She fought fear and panic in equal measure as she battled to stay calm.

"No, it's not the family, Kayles."

Kaylan couldn't think of what else could possibly warrant a work invasion. She glanced at the clock. She could go home in two hours. What was so urgent?

Nick held up his smart phone, a grainy photo displayed on his screen. "Do you recognize this?"

She took the phone from him, squinting at the pixelated shot. "Yeah. It's that picture of us after playing beach volleyball the first week I moved here." She smiled. "It's one of my favorites. That's funny, though. I meant to ask you about that."

"Ask me about what?" His guarded tone sent her heart fluttering.

"Well, it was in a frame sitting on my dresser, but I can't find it. I assumed you took it on your trip with you and would give it back when you got home."

His eyes widened.

"I'm guessing that's not what happened?" She looked from one to the other, annoyance building like a geyser. "Look, you two. Enough of the SEAL code of secrecy. Why are you here, and what's the big deal with this photo?"

Nick leaned in closer. "Kaylan, this picture showed up in a letter mailed to me this morning. A letter that has the name written on my birth certificate that no one knows or uses. The letter contained a threat with the photo. Babe, I need you to ask to leave early and come home. We've got to figure this out, but we can't talk here."

A thousand thoughts raced through her head. Who sent the letter? How in the world did they get the picture? Did that mean…"Does that mean someone's been in my house?"

Nick and Micah looked at one another, and she knew. "No way. Someone's been in my house. Someone you're trying to catch? I've got to tell Megan. We've got to get Megan." She fumbled for her phone in the pocket of her scrubs.

Nick stilled her hands. "We called the FBI and looped in our superiors. The FBI will send agents who will keep a low profile. We'll take care of Megan. We don't know for sure they've been in your house."

"How else would they get that picture, Nick? They didn't bother to hide the empty frame. Obviously they wanted me to notice. I just thought I was losing things."

"Things? Things plural, Kayles? What else have you lost?" Micah's voice rose again.

Her eyes darted to Nick. "Please don't be mad. I'm sure it's in my room somewhere."

"Kaylan."

"I can't find the necklace you gave me. I know I took it off in my room. But I haven't been able to find it since. But don't worry. I got sidetracked, but I'll tear my room apart this weekend and find it."

The blood drained from Nick's face and Micah's eyes grew wide. They looked at one another. "Please don't tell me…"

"We don't know that yet, Bulldog."

"Wait, you don't think whoever took the picture took my necklace, too?"

Nick placed his hands on her shoulders. "Kaylan, please go tell them there is an emergency and you need to leave."

She shook free and took a step back towards the station. "No. I have less than two hours left, and I want to finish."

"Kaylan Richards, do not make me swing you over my shoulder. Get your tail in the car."

"No, Micah." She gritted her teeth. "I am going to finish. Whoever this person is, they are not going to walk into my home and violate that space, then steal my opportunity here too. No way."

"Kaylan, please."

"No, Nick." Her voice shook, but she refused to waver. After a few moments of a silent standoff, resignation and a hint of pride flashed across his face. "I would never ask you to play it safe or to give up something, mostly because you wouldn't want me to. It goes against your very nature to give up. Please. Let me finish."

He slowly nodded and pulled her into a quick hug. "We aren't leaving until you are in your car and on the way to the house."

"Fine. But go somewhere and be quiet, will you? I want my coworkers to like me, and you aren't helping." With a small smile their way, she left them looking a little lost as she set her sights on finishing the day strong, no matter how much her hands shook.

Chapter 16

EVERY INSTINCT IN Nick told him to grab Kaylan and run as far away as possible. They could be happy somewhere else, anywhere that Janus couldn't find them. A shack in Haiti. The beach in Australia. A cottage in England. He didn't care. Any other option seemed better than reality...one of the most-wanted arms dealers in the world knew his girlfriend's address.

Nick had to concentrate not to step on Kaylan's heels as he and Micah flanked her all the way to her front door. "Kayles." Nick placed his hand on her waist and nodded to Micah.

Without a word his friend took the keys from Kaylan's hand and unlocked the door, then went on ahead to check inside. Nick pulled her close to him and kissed her cheek before glancing around the neighborhood.

"Is this necessary if you called in the FBI?" Kaylan's soft voice reinforced his protective instincts. "I don't see why you can't just take care of this."

"It's necessary because this is way out of our hands. We asked them to keep a low profile, and we already told them all we could, but this isn't optional, Kaylan." He motioned for Kaylan to follow him into the house.

Micah met them at the door. "No one's home."

"Anything look out of place, babe?"

She walked through the house, her eyes darting back and forth. They followed her down the hall to the guest bathroom and Megan's room then into her room. She shook her head. "It just looks lived in. Neither of us has been home much the last couple of weeks. I really wouldn't know."

Nick looked at her nightstand then to her bookshelf in the corner. "Think significant items. Things you might not notice right away but that would carry a lot of sentimental value for you, or us, or your family."

Her eyes darted around the room, then she shook her head, tossing her hands in the air. "Nothing. I can't think of anything. If whoever this is wanted to freak me out or take things I can't replace, they already took my necklace. They took a photo. I'm officially freaked out."

Micah nodded to her nightstand. "Anything in your drawers or under your bed?"

A faint pink tinged her cheeks and Micah chuckled. "Besides clean laundry, sis."

Nick did a double take. "You keep clean laundry under the bed? No way."

She turned on him, her pink face now red. "Hey, you said be vulnerable; this is vulnerable. I didn't have time to fold it yet, all right?"

A grin spread on his face. "You aren't as neat as you're trying to pretend."

She threw her hand over her heart. "My fatal flaw. Now can we get back to this?" She got down on her hands and knees and reached under the bed skirt, retrieving the wood box Nick had given her right before she left for Haiti.

Opening the lid, she rifled through a few papers. Then her hands stilled and her face went white. Nick immediately knelt at her side. Under a few letters lay a picture of her and Sarah Beth, both with red x's over their faces. Kaylan's face boasted a question mark over the x.

Micah punched the wall before turning to face her. "You are not staying here tonight. We are moving you now!"

Nick picked up the photo and turned it over, trying to touch it as little as possible. In the same Russian script he read, *Continue to chase me, and she will end up like her friend.*

"Nick, what does it say?" Kaylan's voice shook as she leaned in to him.

He looked at Micah, and a silent understanding passed between them. Panic built in Nick's gut and threatened to spill over. Never had he been so scared in all his life, not even when he couldn't locate Kaylan after the earthquake. And he couldn't control or fix any of it. He knew how to fight the enemy on foreign soil. He knew how to operate within the cloak of night and anonymity. He knew how to use the water as a shield and his body as a weapon. He knew how to use his mind to outwit and outlast any opponent. But he did not know how to protect his girlfriend in her own home on American soil, and the thought paralyzed him.

The front door banged open, and a high-pitched yelp sounded from the living room. He and Micah shot to their feet, every nerve in Nick's body ready for a fight.

"Hello? Anyone home?"

Kaylan moved past the two of them to greet her roommate. Nick followed her down the hall.

"Well, I see soldier boy's here." Megan smiled as she dumped grocery bags on the kitchen floor.

"Soldier boy?" Micah glanced at Nick and grinned.

"Looks like he brought his sidekick with him."

Nick choked down a laugh and put his arm around Kaylan, watching Micah process Megan's comment.

"Sidekick? How do you know he's not *my* sidekick?"

Megan looked at him and smirked. "It's okay, Micah. Everyone either has one or is one. Just accept your role in life."

"Do you have any other flavor besides sarcastic?" Micah's voice held a teasing bite.

Nick could see this getting out of control. "All right, all right." He glanced at Micah. "Hey, Megan, can you do us a favor?"

She hopped up on the counter. "I guess that depends."

Nick looked at Kaylan, wondering if this would come better from her, praying she had the discretion to keep it vague.

She nodded at him, then turned to her roommate. "Megan, would you mind checking your room to see if anything's missing?"

Megan's eyes grew wary as she looked from Kaylan to Nick to Micah. "Why?"

"There's a couple things from my room that are missing, and I need to know if it's just me."

"Do you think someone has been in the house?"

"We're not sure, Meg. But we need to find out."

"Think valuable or sentimental things," Nick encouraged.

"Well, that's a short list." Megan hopped off the counter. "Perks of a rocky childhood. Give me a few and I'll check." She disappeared around the corner.

Kaylan turned to face them when Megan left the room. "It isn't safe for her either. If y'all don't want to tell us what's going on, then fine. I understand. Kind of. But you need to tell her enough to convince her to leave for a few days. I won't have her hurt by whatever psycho has a problem with you or me."

"We understand, sis. I promise we'll take care of it." Micah plopped down on the couch and grabbed the remote.

Nick couldn't stand still. He had to do something. He reached for Kaylan's hand. "Let's go talk to a couple of the neighbors. Follow my lead, okay?"

She trailed him out the door and onto the porch. "You don't really think the neighbors had anything to do with this, do you?"

"No. But we're going to find out if they saw anything." He locked eyes with her. "Subtly. This person is good. The last thing we need is to cause people to ask questions or let this character know we're asking around."

"Let's start with Nina." Kaylan motioned to the middle-aged woman watering her flowers next door. "She's the neighborhood busybody. All three of her girls are in college, and I think she just misses the ability to mother. Did I ever tell you her husband designs video games?"

Nick grinned. "Remind me to never mention I'm in the military around him. I don't want to be part of the next generation of couch warriors."

Nina saw them coming and waved as Kaylan and Nick crossed into her yard. "Kaylan, so good to see you again. Isn't it nice that the weather allows for flowers as we move into fall?" She gestured to the yard around them, waving the hose in the process and grazing their feet with water. Kaylan jumped back, giggling in spite of the reason for their visit.

"Oops, so sorry. Can't help it. I talk with my hands all the time. My girls tell me I will never lose a beat if I go deaf someday." She chuckled and cast a glance skyward. "Fingers crossed that never happens."

Nick smiled, but his heart wasn't in it. He felt exposed out and about in the neighborhood. They didn't know where Janus lurked. They only had a grainy shot from a bungalow in South America. His eyes wandered the neighborhood. A black car sat toward the end of the block, and he had a feeling Micah's FBI buddy resided inside. He squeezed Kaylan's hand, hoping she would direct the conversation. She replied with gentle pressure. Nick refrained from smiling. They were becoming an old married couple already if they could read each other's body language.

"Nina, have you seen someone around our house the last couple of weeks dropping something off or anything like that?"

Nina's eyes lit, and Nick knew they would have to be careful with their questions. If they could just ask the right one, maybe she would talk and let something slip that she wasn't even aware was important.

"Uh-oh. Did you miss a package delivery? You and Megan know you can always have things sent to our house since I work from home and all."

"We really appreciate that, ma'am."

Nina groaned. "Ma'am. You Southern people make me feel so old." She studied Kaylan and Nick. "Come to think of it, I haven't seen anyone around your house, but I've seen some action over at Mildred's old house." She motioned to the house across the street.

"Like what?" Nick asked as he glanced in that direction.

Nina leaned in close, her short pixie cut curling around her ears, the gray giving her a distinguished look. "I guess her absentee kids finally decided to show up and clean out her house." She shook her head, her light brown eyes sad. "She was an amazing woman. Too bad they didn't spend more time with her."

Nick squeezed Kaylan's hand again.

She responded in stride. "Anything else, Nina?"

She sprayed another arc of water towards the flowerbed. "I did see someone wandering around the neighborhood at night around three a.m. a couple weeks ago. You know these teenagers, never up to any good. Thank goodness my girls made it through that stage and are in college now."

Kaylan smothered a smile. "Well, I guess it was nothing then."

"Oh, nothing is ever nothing, dear. I know what I saw." She bit her lip and blushed. "Of course, I can't be completely certain since it was dark and across the street. But I'm sixty-eight percent sure."

Nick scanned the houses around the block again and moved his arm around Kaylan's shoulders. "Anyone new to the neighborhood?"

Nina shrugged. "No. Not for a few months anyway since Jenna and Cathryn moved in. Both of them travel quite a bit. I suggested they should just move in together. We should all look out for one another, you know." She leaned in close again, and Nick struggled not to laugh at his mental image of middle-school girls gossiping over the latest new kid in class. He could barely hear Nina over the water rushing from the hose. "If you ask me, though, I think Jenna has a man coming to see her."

"I haven't seen anyone over there," Kaylan chimed in.

Nina rolled her eyes. "That's because he doesn't want to be seen. But I saw someone slip out just the other night when I was out for a late-night stroll with our dog, Roxy. She went crazy barking at a man who climbed into a black car."

"Do you know what kind of car it was?"

Nina waved the hand holding the hose again, sending a stream splattering against the stucco walls of her home. "That's my husband's area of expertise." Nick could tell she grew bored with the conversation. She walked over to turn the water off.

"You sure it just wasn't another teenager?" Nick grunted as Kaylan elbowed him in the ribs, but Nina appeared not to have heard.

"I've got to get supper on, but I hope you find your package, dear. Please let me know if I can be of any help." She waved to them both and disappeared inside.

Kaylan turned to Nick as they moved out of Nina's yard. "I don't know whether to laugh or be terrified that Nina sees ghosts wandering our neighborhood while I sleep."

Nick tugged on her hand as he looked up and down the street. "Well, I know where we are going next." He only hoped Jenna and Cathryn would be as talkative as Nina had been. Kaylan had said her new neighbors were reserved but kind, and she was usually a good judge of character. But right now Nick didn't trust anyone, even the sweet gossip now cooking supper next door.

Chapter 17

AFTER KNOCKING ON Jenna's door and finding no one home, Nick advanced on the next house on their stop. Kaylan said Cathryn traveled a lot and that much was clear from her front yard—no personal touches, no unique floral decorations, only plants that thrived on their own. Kaylan rang the doorbell.

"Too bad we missed Jenna. She's amazing. She lived in England growing up and runs in marathons and relays all over the world. But you'll like Cathryn too. She tells great stories. She's lived all over the place. Can you imagine what an adventure that would be?"

Despite the gravity of the situation, Nick smiled at his girlfriend, loving the way her eyes lit up despite her nerves. Always looking for the best in people, that was his girl. As much as he admired the trait, he couldn't reciprocate. He'd seen too much. He trusted few, and those few had earned it.

The door swung open and a short, blonde, middle-aged woman stood before him. Surprise swept across her face before she schooled her expression in a smile. "Kaylan, so nice to see you again."

"Sorry to just drop by like this, Cathryn. This is my boyfriend, Nick."

"Nice to meet you." Nick extended his hand. Her grip was firm and quick. Maybe they did the kissing thing where she was from. He shoved his hands in his pockets. "Kaylan told me some of your stories from dinner the other night."

Cathryn smiled. "When you've lived all over the place, there is a lot to tell."

"How long have you lived in the neighborhood, Cathryn?"

"I moved in a few months ago, but I travel a lot for my job. Sales keep me very busy. And please forgive me. I would invite you in, but I still have boxes sitting out. Kaylan has kindly volunteered to help me."

Nick kept his eyes on Cathryn, but squeezed Kaylan's hand tighter.

"Yes, just let me know when you want to start."

"I leave for another business trip in a few days. Come over any time in the evening, and I will show you what needs to be done."

"Sure. Happy to help."

Nick squeezed her hand again.

"Oh, I almost forgot, have you seen anyone hanging around our house lately?"

Cathryn's smile drooped a bit. "Not that I have noticed. But I am gone a lot. Is everything all right?"

"Oh, yes. Megan and I just weren't sure if we missed a package."

Cathryn gripped the door. "Sorry I couldn't help. I hope it turns up."

"We appreciate it." Nick began to pull Kaylan off the porch, sensing the neighbor would grow suspicious if they asked anything else. "Nice to meet you."

"And you as well," she said before closing the door.

"Well, now that we have officially ruled out my neighbors, can we please figure out what to do with me and Megan?"

Nick wrapped his arm around Kaylan as he scanned the street, every nerve tingling on high alert. "We didn't rule out all your neighbors. That Jenna lady wasn't home, and I didn't even start working the block."

"Babe, Jenna is fine too. You heard Cathryn. Just busy ladies who make enough money to live by themselves."

They reached Kaylan's porch. Nick stopped and turned Kaylan to meet him. "You know what I love about you?" He searched her eyes, seeing the fear she held at bay.

"Oh, so many things, I hope."

He chuckled. "Definitely your humility." He kissed her forehead, then cradled her face in his hands, his thumbs stroking soft skin. "I love your heart. I love that you see the best in people. You did that with Eliezer in Haiti. And you do it with me. But that also scares me, Kayles. People aren't all good."

Her eyes softened a fraction, some of the fear fleeing under his gaze. "Sometimes people behave better when someone gives them the opportunity."

"I don't have that luxury, Kayles. I need to protect you."

She wrapped her arms around his waist. "Sometimes people just need someone to believe in them, invest in them, point them to Jesus."

"Oh, babe, I don't doubt that. My life is proof. But I don't trust anyone right now. And I need you to trust me, and be more aware of those around you. Can you do that?"

Her eyes searched his. "What's going on, Nick? What aren't you telling me?"

"You know I can't tell you."

"Why?" Frustration colored her tone. "Some part of your job is threatening my safety and my roommate's. Why can't I know?"

Nick fought for patience, his combat-ready, no-nonsense Navy SEAL mode slipping to the surface. "Kaylan, please drop it."

"No, I want you to answer me."

Micah stuck his head out the front door. "Thought I heard voices. Megan said she didn't find anything missing. Everything okay out here?" He stepped outside as his gaze shifted back and forth between Kaylan and Nick, clearly unsure who to side with.

"I was just asking Nick why I can't know what's going on since it affects Megan and me."

"Oh." Micah met his best friend's gaze. "You know we can't answer that, sis."

"Maybe you should make an exception."

Nick chose his words carefully. "Kaylan, I hope this is the last time you and I have this conversation." She flinched but didn't waver. "I can't talk about what we do on most missions, especially this one right now. I most likely won't ever be able to, and if you can't accept that, you and I are in for a very rocky relationship. Believe me, I will always tell you as much as I can. I will always invite you to be part of the process, and you can trust that when I leave, I am always out there doing what I am doing for you. This time some crazy person decided to make it personal. So we had to involve the FBI. We will inform them when we discover anything that they need to know. I realize this is asking a lot, but it is the price you pay for dating a SEAL, and you do have a choice in that. So decide what you want before we make this more permanent."

Kaylan looked back and forth between Nick and Micah, her face beet red. She tossed her hands in the air and rolled her eyes, clearly biting back an angry retort. "Fine. So now what?"

"I'd like you and Megan to stay with us the next few days, at least until we figure out a game plan."

Before Kaylan could respond, Megan appeared behind Micah with a duffel bag slung over her shoulder. "Micah filled me in. I'm going to my boyfriend's house for a couple days. Call me when it's safe to come back home." She glared at Nick as she passed him and headed out to her car.

Kaylan groaned, clearly torn on whether to chase Megan or leave it alone. With a cry of frustration she threw open the door and stalked into the house. Nick and Micah followed her inside,

Nick wound as tight as a ticking time bomb. Silence descended in the room as Kaylan plopped down on the couch. Micah stood sentry at the door while Nick perched on the couch armrest facing Kaylan, fighting to stay calm.

Not only was he frustrated that he didn't know how to protect her, but he was also frustrated that they would never have the kind of relationship where he could tell her everything. He could live with it until she questioned it. Then the walls came up and the claws came out to defend his position. He knew she was still learning his community, but terror fought his need for her to understand quickly.

"Kayles, look…"

She threw up her hands. "No, don't, Nick. I get it. And I'm sorry I asked. Just promise you will tell me what you can. It's hard for me to know what or who to be afraid of when I don't know what I'm looking for. And everything and everyone in California is strange or a stranger right now. Am I supposed to live suspicious of everything?"

Micah crossed his arms and leaned against the wall. "Kaylan, this will be over soon, we hope. This is just a precaution. We just need you to trust us. You can trust the SEALs we've introduced you to and their families."

"I just want to protect you, Kayles." Nick leaned forward and brushed a stray strand behind her ear, thankful when her eyes softened and she didn't pull away.

She nodded, chewing on her lip. He could almost hear her racing thoughts. With a sigh she stood. "I'll go pack a bag."

Nick watched her go and then met Micah's eyes.

"She'll get it, Hawk. She's just scared and reacting."

Nick began to pace, adrenaline coursing through him as he calculated ways to catch Janus. "I'm scared too, man. But we've got to find a way to stop her before she hurts someone else we love."

Kaylan fought tears as she unpacked at Nick and Micah's place. Dealing with the threat to herself was bad enough, but to have her roommate involved without any choice in the matter made her restless and angry. Kaylan's heart broke for her friend. She hated to send Megan into the arms of another jerk. She knew this guy would dump Megan within the month, knew that Megan used physical intimacy to medicate her pain. Kaylan knew as soon as this ended, Megan would be more surly and sarcastic than ever. And Kaylan hated it. She hated that these men took advantage of Megan, hated that Megan believed she couldn't do better. Hated that Megan allowed it and encouraged it. But most of all Kaylan hated that she didn't know what to say or do to change it. Kaylan knew there was a Father who desired to heal Megan, if only she would let Him.

Nick knocked on the open door to Micah's room, and Kaylan quickly wiped away a tear. Not fast enough, though. Nick immediately came to her side.

"Babe, I'm so sorry. This is just temporary. We'll figure this out."

Her eyes filled, but she blinked the tears away and focused on unpacking her clothes on Micah's bed. "It's not that, Nick. Well, maybe a little. It's Megan." She met his eyes, her heart racing at letting him see this side of her. "I hate involving her in this. I hate that she went to her latest boyfriend's place. I hate that he will use her and then dump her. And I hate that she doesn't think more of herself."

Nick nodded and sat on the edge of the bed as she continued to unpack. "What's her background, Kayles? She said she had a rocky past."

"She won't tell me much. But from what I gather, her mom left when she was a kid. She was the only child of an Army soldier who knew how to drink but not how to raise a kid. They moved around a lot, and she got pushed off onto whatever family would take her when he deployed."

Nick studied her. "So now she's anti-government, anti-military, and anti-people. That explains why she went for sea animals and marine biology."

Kaylan offered a small smile. "She takes care of them, and they love her." She met Nick's eyes. "I think that's why she has a hard time with you and Micah and with me dating you. Deep down I think she sees a situation like her parents. And I think she seeks affirmation in these guys she dates, but she doesn't expect them to stay long, because she never experienced depth or longevity in relationships growing up."

She sank down on the bed next to him. "It just breaks my heart because I want so much better for her. And I want her to know what it feels like to be treasured by a guy, not for what she does but who she is." Her face heated. She reluctantly met those piercing blue eyes she loved so much. "Like how you treat me."

Nick smiled—the one he reserved just for her—and the warmth wrapped around her heart. "You make it easy, Kayles. Most of the time." He kissed her forehead.

"Nick, I'm serious. Did Micah ever tell you about Caleb?"

His jaw twitched and she knew. "Micah wasn't too impressed with that guy."

"Neither was the rest of my family." Her mind drifted back to her junior year of college when she'd met Caleb. She'd been like Megan once upon a time. Not in the extreme sense, but she'd once settled for a guy that controlled rather than treasured her. An engineer and student body president, Caleb could charm his way into any and every setting. Brilliant and handsome, he'd pursued Kaylan with an interest she couldn't ignore.

They'd dated for a few months before she began to notice his manipulation and his passive-aggressive tendencies. Because of his accolades and stellar reputation, she blew off the indications, thinking her radar had malfunctioned. Inside she was suffocating. He got angry when she spent time with Sarah Beth and refused to call or text her back the next day. Any time she had a family event, he insisted on being present. After six months of dating and his insistence that it was time to talk to her dad, Kaylan finally got the guts to call it off.

"I get a small piece of how she's feeling, Nick. But I wish she could see that she is worth far more than how these guys treat her. I wish she knew that she is made in the image of the God of the universe."

"She's got to figure that out for herself, Kayles. Pray and keep pointing her to Jesus. He loves her more than you do."

Nick pulled her into a hug, and she thanked God for the safety and blessing of a man who loved her enough to let her be exactly who God had made her. Maybe one day she would have enough courage to be fully herself. Slowly but surely she crept closer to that reality.

Chapter 18

NICK LOVED HAVING Kaylan in California. Despite the threat of Janus, the weekend stretched before them, and Nick planned to enjoy it with one beautiful woman. With Micah's help he'd thrown together an impromptu team night at the beach. Jay arrived with Logan's kids. Still no word on his leg, but it didn't look good. Yet one more loss he would add to Janus's tab. She continued to rack up quite a list.

"Uncle Nick!" Molly skipped up and flew into his arms. She was the child of a SEAL, all right, fearless and trusting of their community. She knew he would never let her fall. He gave her a hug as he watched her brothers run down the beach to play a game of catch with Jay and Titus.

"Hey, ladybug. What's going on?"

"I brought my board and my wet suit. Will you get in the water with me?"

Nick studied the sky. They still had a couple hours of daylight left before the sun dipped below the Pacific Ocean and ushered in the night watch. Nick looked to Kaylan.

"I haven't learned either." She shrugged. "I think it's about time I did."

Molly rolled her eyes. "Miss Kaylan, I am not on the baby level anymore. I can teach you how, no problem." She squirmed from Nick's arms, her attitude in full effect. "Race ya!"

She took off to Jay's car to slip her wet suit on over her swim suit. Nick nodded at Kaylan to do the same. "We can't let her beat us." He took off like a shot to his Jeep, his competitive nature refusing to back down even to the four-year-old that had captured his heart.

Within twenty minutes they stood in the surf, Molly walking out as far as her little legs would take her then fighting the waves as she climbed on her board. What would happen if Logan lost his leg? He might never be able to teach Molly to surf. A muscle in his jaw twitched. Heat flooded his face.

What if something happened to him someday? What if he could never stand and hold Kaylan again? What if some teenager with something to prove set a roadside bomb, and Nick returned less than whole or in a flag-covered box?

He shook his head. He couldn't play the "what-if" game. The reality remained that he would rush into a situation to fight with his brothers and for his country any day of the week. But he couldn't control the consequences—win or lose.

He held the board while Molly practiced paddling, the waves cooling him as the sun slowly arched closer to the horizon, the sky turning shades of gold and orange. Kaylan sat on the beach talking to Liza, Titus's wife, sidetracked on the way to change into her suit. Nick looked at the little girl in front of him as she giggled, blissfully unaware that her daddy's life may have changed forever.

At times he wondered why God didn't stop the evil in the world. He'd wrestled with his inability to fix Kaylan's hurt after the earthquake. She'd wrestled with the goodness of God. The more time that passed, the more stories from Haiti filtered to both of them about people coming to Christ despite and because of the awful circumstances, of people finding more strength than they knew existed to help each other. They heard stories of changed lives. It helped him better understand the goodness of a sovereign God who saw the big picture when Nick didn't. But evil men who killed others? Nick wondered why the Lord didn't just wipe them out.

Where did justice fit into all this? And how did Nick reconcile the fact that he killed people for a living? How was it possible for God to be just and merciful in equal measure, and if that was God's character, what would that look like in Nick's career? In all honesty, there were moments in combat when he didn't think twice about pulling the trigger. Training and the intense urge to protect his home, his family, and his team overrode any sense of hesitation under gunfire. He didn't want to take a life, prayed he wouldn't have to. But he refused to back down when the situation called for it.

It was a weight he would always carry, always wonder about. What made him different from these men he wanted God to take care of? They fought a war of belief and philosophy, not one of compromise. It was as the Bible said; he didn't make war against flesh and blood but against mentalities and influences much deeper than anything human.

"Uncle Nick, let me try. Let me go." Water splashed his face as Molly kicked, snapping him out of his reverie.

"I don't know, ladybug. Maybe next time."

She stopped paddling and gazed up at him with her pale green eyes. In that moment he knew he would have trouble if he and Kaylan ever had a little girl. Molly knew how to shoot an arrow straight to his heart.

"Uncle Nick, please?"

He groaned and gazed out at the waves rolling in. These were baby waves, ones that she could just ride into the beach if she even managed to stand up like they'd been practicing. He took a deep breath.

"All right, ladybug. You can give it a try."

"Woohoo!" Molly took off paddling. He knew she wouldn't go

out far. He slowly moved her direction, prepared to bail her out if necessary. He heard Kaylan cheer her on from the beach.

He breathed in the sea air and immediately felt his body relax. No stronger drug existed for Nick that could rival the tug of the sea. His mom used to say that he was born with fins and gills and that's why they couldn't find his birth parents. They lived under the ocean. For a while that answer satisfied him. He felt more at home in the surf than with his feet firmly planted on land. Now, he wanted to know who his birth parents were, even more so since that letter arrived with his birth name on the envelope.

Molly turned back toward him and started paddling with her little arms. She pushed up from her board and slowly managed to stand on wobbly sea legs before tumbling into the water. With quick strokes, he swam in her direction, ready to let her cling to him when her head crested the waves. She came up sputtering, her little eyes blinking furiously to dispel the water. He tugged her board to her, and she clung to it as she wiped water from her face.

"Uncle Nick, did you see me? I stood up! That was one mean wave." Her jaw rattled from the cold but her grin melted the chill away.

Nick chuckled, leaning on the other side of the board, his toes barely scraping the sandy ground beneath their floating bodies.

"Check you out. You'll be a pro in no time."

"Yeah. I'm going to learn to surf to pay for things." She shook her head, and her smile drooped. "I don't want to do what Daddy does. I want to wrestle waves, not people."

Nick bobbed with her board. "I think your mommy and daddy will love whoever you decide to be."

"Even if I don't fight bad guys?" Her big eyes nearly broke his heart.

"Molly, why do you think you need to fight bad guys?"

"Because my daddy does. Because he's a hero and takes care of people." Her bottom lip protruded in a pout, and he wished he could ease her confusion and hurt.

Nick reached across the small board and stroked her arm. "Molly, your daddy and I decided we wanted to fight bad guys to protect you and people we love. But that doesn't mean everyone has to do that. If everyone fought bad guys, who would win surfing competitions or stay home and take care of things?" He tapped her nose and smiled.

"Zactly. Plus, I don't want to get hurt."

There it was, Molly's fear lurking right below the surface. Nick squeezed her hand. "Baby girl, you might get hurt surfing one of these days, or riding your bike, or playing with your brothers."

"Or my new baby sister."

Nick smiled, praying Molly got her wish. "Or your baby sister. But Molly, we can't live afraid to get hurt."

"Oh, I know that, Uncle Nick. I live with two boys. They hurt me sometimes when we play."

Nick nodded in agreement. "I bet they do. But know what? You'll be tougher for it. Things happen in life that hurt, Molly."

"Like what happened to my daddy?"

"Yes. But those bad things often help us become better people. You understand?"

She tapped his nose like he did to her all the time and giggled. "Sorta. One more time?" She breezed past the serious moment, ready to play. He wished he could refocus that quickly. Oh, to be a kid again without a care in the world. He prayed she never lost her innocence.

Nick helped Molly climb back on her board and then treaded water as she fell into the waves one more time. How did you explain the idea of pain to a four-year-old? Kids understood the physical ache but couldn't always identify the sentiment that ran much deeper. He wished he could wrap Molly in a bubble and keep her far from a broken heart or the decision that might be coming for Logan.

But all he could do was coach her through the waves and pray her through the ache. One day she would see that pain only polished a person, as the waves polished the sand on the beach, washing away the messy bits to reveal the treasures hidden beneath.

Shadows lurked just outside the fire line as the group sat roasting marshmallows on the beach. Nick cringed when his phone buzzed in his short's pocket. Lately every time it rang there seemed to be bad news. Kim's name illuminated the screen. He closed his eyes and answered the call.

"Nick." Her voice broke. Nick stepped away from the laughter of kids and smoke of the camp fire to see the starry night.

"Kim, just tell me."

"The antibiotics didn't work and the muscle has too much damage from the shrapnel. They...we decided. He's going to lose his leg. We will work to get a prosthetic so that he can function and have a normal life. But..." She sniffed back tears. "I don't know what to tell the kids. Can you bring them to the hospital?"

Nick ran a hand over his face and kicked the sand. He tamped down the rage causing his hands to shake. "Yeah, Kim. We'll load up and bring them."

He could hear her breathing on the other end. "Hawk, it's not your fault. You all need to know that." Her voice shot straight through the phone to all the questions and anger boiling in his heart and mind. "You know he would have rushed into all of that again. You know he would rather it be him in this bed than one of you." Anger colored her voice. "Don't you dare for one second dishonor his sacrifice by blaming yourself. You know this is a commitment you all made. And those of us who love you, commit to make it with you."

"Kim…"

"Just bring my kids, and we'll talk more when you get here." She sobbed just as the call disconnected.

He stared out at the waves and at the moon illuminating the horizon line. The vastness of the ocean terrified him at times. Its strength couldn't be compared, measured, or replicated. It often reminded him of the Lord—able to soothe one minute and destroy the next. He had a healthy fear, but the cadence of the water still called to his soul. Saltwater blood. He smiled at the memory of his parents, feeling the ache of missing them magnified more than usual.

Logan hadn't died over there. He could at least be thankful for that. His kids wouldn't grow up without their dad. The bullet hadn't affected his brain. They would still learn from the amazing man he remained. And they would go their whole lives knowing their daddy was a hero.

Nick groaned. How did he do this?

Gentle hands wrapped around his waist, and he smelled the faint scent of lavender mixed with sea spray as Kaylan stood behind him. For once he leaned into her strength.

"Is it Logan?" Her voice barely carried over the waves.

He could only nod. "Kim needs us to take the kids to the hospital."

"You know the guys won't stay behind."

He nodded again. "Where one goes, we all go. When one grieves, we all grieve." He counted on their presence. "We promised they wouldn't go through this alone." He turned to put his arm around her. "This is my family, Kaylan, and they're hurting. And I can't fix it." His eyes stung from the pull of tears. He had to stay strong.

She placed a gentle kiss on his cheek. "Then let's go take care of them." She pulled back to look in his eyes. "Together."

His lips found hers, slow and steady, finding comfort in the familiarity. Every day he wondered how he could possibly love this woman more, but every day his love for her grew. If this moment portrayed a lifetime with her, then he couldn't wait.

Nick turned to face the group and met Jay's eyes. He shook his head. Jay swallowed, his jaw locking and hands clenching. Nick could feel his anger burn hotter than the fire. Janus would pay, one way or another.

"Hey, kids, let's go see your dad." Nick tousled Conner's hair and reached down to pick up the blanket spread out on the sand.

The boys jumped up, racing to the car. Molly came to Kaylan, reaching for her hand, her eyes drooping. Without a word everyone else cleaned up the beach and kicked out the fire, following Nick and Kaylan to the cars.

Whatever came next, they would weather together. Even in loss of limb, Nick wouldn't leave a man behind.

Chapter 19

FOR ONCE THE white dominating the hospital ward didn't feel clean and crisp. It felt too sterile, too cold. He dreaded the conversation to come. Like in days past, the team gathered in the waiting room. Jay and Titus pulled out the notepad they had stashed under a couch and resumed their last game of tic-tac-toe. Nick wasn't sure who dominated the score chart at the moment.

Micah settled into a chair and flipped through the same sports car magazine Nick had seen him peruse at least ten times. His eyes kept drifting to the USC football game blaring from the TV in the corner. Colt pulled a rubber ball from his pocket and set it in motion, bouncing it from the linoleum floor to his hand. In the same way Nick chewed gum to create a repetitive mindless motion, Colt played with that red rubber ball. He claimed it channeled his nervous energy into something he could control. Nick shook his head. Whatever worked to maintain Colt's sanity was fine by him.

Kaylan slipped her hand in his in the doorway. "Kim and Logan are telling the kids now." She leaned into his arm. "I can't imagine what that would feel like."

He studied her face. "What would you do, Kaylan? If I got shot and lost a limb like Logan, how would you handle that?"

He watched fear flash across her face before resolve settled in. "We won't play the 'what-if' game, Nick. If it happens, we'll handle it."

A sob and scream echoed down the hall, and Nick bolted to Logan's door. Molly lay curled on Logan's chest, sobbing. Nick noticed the strain in Logan's face as he masked the pain from his little girl. Tears filled all their eyes.

Nick couldn't handle it. He broke through the guys who had gathered behind him and charged back down the hallway, stopping short when it ended with a window. His anger blinded his vision. Nick framed the window with his hands, his knuckles turning white on the wall. He jerked at the gentle contact of a hand on his back.

"Don't touch me right now, Kayles."

"Nick..." She reached out again.

"I'm serious, Kaylan." He stared out the window but could only see his reflection staring back, his eyes blazing and jaw set. He smacked the wall with his hand, his palm stinging as he channeled all of his anger into the motion. And once he started, he couldn't stop.

"Nick Carmichael." Kaylan's voice cut through the red. He gripped the window ledge to still his hands. His eyes stung with tears.

"It should have been me. God, why wasn't it me?" Kaylan's face reflected in the window, and he saw fear and concern. She'd never seen him lose it like this before. Normally he maintained control.

"Where's God's justice in this? Where's His mercy? This isn't fair." He rested his forehead on the window. "I wish it'd been me."

A tentative hand came to rest on his shoulder, and he fought to control his anger.

"Babe, please don't say that again." Her gentle tone cracked through, and he hung his head. Unfortunately he knew this feeling

117

all too well. He'd felt it when his buddies died in the desert, when his parents died. But it had never stung so bad as it did with Logan.

"Hawk." The voice echoed down the hallway, and Nick spun his head so hard his neck popped. Logan stood just outside his door, leaning on Kim, his face white but determined. "In here. Now." The kids filed down the hall as the guys entered Logan's room.

Kim helped him settle back onto the bed as he winced. A shock-wave of pain shot through Nick at his buddy's pain. Rage filled him once again toward Janus and those selfish enough for power and money that they would hurt others who stood in their way.

The room fell silent as a tomb, and a sickening feeling filled Nick's gut. This conversation shouldn't be necessary.

Logan made eye contact with every one of them. "You all need to cut it out. No pity for me, you got it? I wouldn't want any of you in this bed or in this situation." He gripped Kim's hand. "I need you all to do me a favor."

"Name it," Colt spoke up.

"I need you to help Kim and the kids, especially with the baby on the way. Until I figure out how to get a prosthetic so I can get on my feet again, I need to know that we won't be flying solo."

"Logan, is that even a question in your mind?" Micah chimed in. "We swore at that hospital in Germany that no matter what happens, you and your family will not go through this alone." He shook his head. "You don't even need to ask that."

Nick glanced around at the guys in the room—jaws set, arms crossed, determination and loyalty written in every facial expression, every movement. The Carpenters wouldn't be alone at all. He imagined they would have to ask the team to back off at some point.

"We're here, Logan, every step of this," Nick reassured. The guys moved to file out of the room but halted at Kim's voice.

"One more thing." Kim let go of Logan's hand and approached them, making eye contact with every Frogman. She squared her shoulders despite the tears, and Nick knew why Logan had trusted this woman to walk by his side in the SEALs. She was a SEAL in her own right.

"I don't know what happened out there, but I know you are chasing someone big." Anger filled her voice. "I don't care what you have to do. Just finish it. Get 'em."

Nick allowed a grin to slip through the rage he held at bay. "Count on it."

They would catch Janus. It was only a matter of time.

Assuming the role of "the steady one" in the relationship felt unfamiliar to Kaylan, but over the weekend she and Nick had subtly switched roles. As she processed their relationship and a future with him, she realized there would be times when she would need to be strong for him. Now seemed to be one of those times. Even the threat from a stranger paled in comparison to her concern for Nick.

To keep her mind off her mysterious stalker and Logan's condition, she'd channeled all her energy into caring for the kids and Nick and Micah, just as she had found a project to keep her sane in the weeks following the earthquake. Now Nick had grudgingly consented to let her fulfill her promise to Cathryn to clean and unpack her house.

No sooner did she ring the doorbell than Cathryn pulled the door open. Kaylan entered the house, her eyes catching a glimpse of a car parked down the street, the same one that had parked there when she had gone to stay with Nick and Micah. The FBI. At least Nick could rest easy. She couldn't be alone even if she wanted to be.

"Kaylan, thank you for coming over. I hope you are hungry. I made dinner."

"Thanks, that sounds great." Kaylan stepped through the doorway into a homey and elegant world. Original floral paintings hung from the walls. Soft, pastel pillows graced an ivory suede couch. White walls and sheer curtains created a bright atmosphere that drew Kaylan in.

She followed Cathryn through to the kitchen. Two plates filled with salad sat on the table. Cathryn gestured to a seat, and Kaylan sank into a cushioned chair. "I know you are from the South, so I made some tea. Would you like some?"

"That sounds perfect, thank you." In truth, Kaylan rarely loved anyone else's tea as much as her gran's. No one else made it quite right. She took a sip and forced herself to swallow. Not enough sugar. Not enough lemon. But it was the thought that counted. She picked up her fork.

"I hope you like salad."

"This looks delicious. My mom makes salad all the time back home, but every time I buy produce for one it goes bad. Nick usually wants something more substantial than salad, and I gave up trying to bribe Micah to eat it ages ago."

"Micah..."

"Micah's one of my older brothers."

"Two brothers. You must have been lonely."

"Three actually. David, Micah, and a younger brother, Seth. And I was anything but lonely. I loved having brothers, and my best friend was around all the time."

"And where is she now?"

Kaylan set her fork down and took a sip of her tea, immediately regretting the decision. She worked to temper the sinking feeling in her chest at the thought of Sarah Beth. "She's not around anymore. Do you have any kids?" Kaylan glanced around, looking for any family photos.

Cathryn's laugh sounded more like a bark. "I never married. My job is my baby."

"Any other family?"

Cathryn's mouth flattened. "No. My parents have been gone for quite some time."

"I'm sorry."

"Don't be. I meet interesting people all the time. And I like being on my own. It is nice to have neighbors, though."

They ate the rest of their meal making small talk. Afterward Kaylan placed her napkin on the table and stood, grabbing both of their plates and taking them to the sink. "Well, what would you like me to do?"

Cathryn stood. "Leave those in the sink and follow me. I will show you."

Kaylan slipped the plates in the sink and turned to follow, almost hitting her head on an open cabinet above the sink. She reached to push it closed and stopped. Lines of pills and vitamin bottles lined the shelf with several natural remedies packed in the tight space. Cathryn was either a health nut, fighting off a really bad cold, or sick. Either way, Kaylan didn't feel like she could ask, not yet anyway.

Kaylan wound her way back to the one spare bedroom. The house was small, like most on the block, small but high in price. Kaylan hated that about California. A double bed stood in one corner and a desk rested against another wall. Four boxes sat in the center of the floor waiting to be unpacked.

"I need to unpack these and a few boxes in the kitchen. I will ask that you avoid reading through any files you come across. Some of my clients prefer absolute privacy. Just stack any paperwork in the drawers, and I will go through it."

"No problem." Kaylan glanced at her watch, anxious to get back to the guys. "I'll unpack these tonight and just organize, and come back another time to finish it up."

Cathryn smiled. "Thank you. That will help. Maybe come by

and clean once a week? I will give you a key in case I am not at home."

"I can manage that. Thank you for helping me out with this job."

"It isn't much, but I appreciate a clean house, so this works for both of us. Let me know if you have questions." She turned and left the room, leaving Kaylan to dive in.

Kaylan unpacked the boxes, arranging office supplies, paper work, and décor in piles. She quickly made the bed with sheets and a quilt she found. The quilt appeared to be old, in fact the only thing in the house not in pristine condition. Kaylan guessed it was probably a family heirloom.

Within an hour she was waving good-bye to Cathryn. She paused at her car and glanced at Jenna's home a few doors down. She might as well suggest her help cleaning while she was out of town too.

Jenna opened the door in running clothes, her phone and ear buds in her hand. "Kaylan, what a surprise. Is everything all right?"

"Oh, yes. Sorry to bother you. Actually..." she turned and looked back the way she had come. "I'm helping Cathryn unpack some of her stuff and clean about once a week and wondered if you could use the same since you are out of town so much."

"How thoughtful. Actually I could use a hand. Maybe Saturday or Sunday afternoons. It wouldn't take you long. My housekeeper just got married and moved out of town. You have perfect timing."

"Great!"

"Come in and I'll get you a key."

Kaylan walked into the living room and noticed a series of tribal masks hanging on the wall. Jenna waved her hand around. "My brother is a photographer and travels all over the world. He likes to spoil me with interesting finds. Makes it feel exotic in here, don't you agree?"

"I love it," Kaylan replied, approaching the wall and studying the pictures hanging with the masks. "If you both travel, do you see one another often?"

"Not as much as I would like. You have brothers, correct?" she called from the kitchen.

"Yes, three. I'm actually thinking about going home to see two of them this weekend."

Jenna reentered the room, carrying a key. "Oh, how lovely. Where do they live?"

"Alabama. That's where my family's from."

"Does your boyfriend go with you when you go home? Nick, isn't it?"

Kaylan took the key from Jenna. "When he can. He works with one of my brothers. My family kind of adopted him a few years back."

"How wonderful. That must make it easier on your relationship."

Kaylan smiled. "It does." She took another look around, noting the clean and modern look mixed in with the exotic. "Do you want to show me around or just let me figure it out when I come?"

Jenna's black pony tail swished as she talked. "Just make yourself at home when you come. Cleaning supplies are under the sink in the bathrooms. Vacuum and mops in the hall closet. I'll be gone the next two weekends, so just do what works best for you. You are a lifesaver. I'm so glad you thought of it."

"No, thank you. Every little bit helps since my internship takes most of my time." Kaylan opened the front door and stepped onto the porch.

"I'll write you a check and leave it on the bar."

Kaylan smiled and waved. "Enjoy the rest of your workout," she said as Jenna closed the door. Kaylan jogged to her car, thankful that a few things were panning out, and headed to the guy's small house in Imperial Beach. Anticipation built as she drove.

They all needed a break, a way to clear their heads, unwind, and laugh. She had only one solution. It was time to go home.

She'd looked up flights on her lunch break at work. They could hop a plane to Alabama on Thursday after work and spend a long weekend. Now to convince the guys. Since they wouldn't let her return to her house yet, they were stuck with her presence at their place.

She entered the house and found both guys in the living room watching Sports Center and Monday night football. Settling into an armchair, she enjoyed the sound of their jeering and laughter until halftime.

"I have a suggestion." She muted the TV. "I think we should all go back to Alabama this weekend. What if we flew in Thursday night, spend time with the family, get out on the lake, and go to Seth's game on Saturday? They're playing the Florida Gators." Kaylan couldn't help the smile that spread across her face at the thought of home and Bama football. "Please?"

"Sis, I'm not sure if we can get the time off."

"You won't know until you ask, Micah. Please, I think it would be good for both of you. Logan's surgery is scheduled for Monday morning. We'll be back in time. Mom said she already has tickets for the game. Some of their friends who were going canceled. Please?" She batted her eyelashes, drawing a laugh from the guys.

"I'll ask, babe." Nick stood and reached for his phone.

"Whipped." Micah coughed and Nick dropped his arm around Micah's neck in a headlock.

"She's right, Bulldog. It will be good for us both to clear our heads and have some fun out of town this weekend."

Kaylan silently cheered. She'd make sure they both relaxed and enjoyed the weekend. She remembered their effort to make her smile after Haiti. They hadn't lost a brother to death, but they had lost a teammate they trusted in combat. She would help them unwind so they would be better prepared for the next steps in their assignment.

Fear and anger battled for dominance in her heart as she

thought of this enemy the team chased. Her new home had been violated, her new family wounded, and the man she cared for felt trapped. She felt the bond between her and the SEAL family strengthen as her heart fused with their cause.

Nick reentered the room from making phone calls. "Looks like we are good to take Friday off. But we both fly out for training on Tuesday, so we need to make sure we get back Sunday night to give us a day to get ready."

She jumped from the chair and kissed him. "I'll purchase the tickets." She practically skipped to her room. Sweet home, Alabama called her name, and she was responding to its inevitable tug.

Janus smiled. She'd rattled them enough to move Kaylan. More surprises would follow. Perhaps if she rattled Nick enough, he would quit chasing her. She took a long drag on her cigarette. Probably not. She would have to strike out at everything he loved. Even then, that might not be enough. If the United States government had her in its sights, she might need to go into hiding.

From her vantage point Janus had watched Nick with Kaylan. Every time he left the house, he scanned the neighborhood casually, always alert for trouble or subtle nuances. Janus knew that look. Determined. Protective. Concealed rage that he kept tame in Kaylan's presence. He might be a formidable opponent after all. She knew the character of SEALs all too well. They were relentless and loyal to their own. They believed in what they fought for— their country, their families, and their brotherhood—whether or not they agreed with political decisions or direction.

The most dangerous kind of person was one who believed in something greater than himself. Their direction never wavered. Their very life philosophy made them nearly invincible, for no matter how terrible the circumstance, they could cling to one thing in the darkest night—hope. But then they died for it, just like Andrei, her brother who wanted to protect everything and everyone the USSR stood against.

She squeezed her eyes shut. She could still see him kneeling in the dirt, hands tied behind his back. Blood dripped from his mouth and one of his eyes was swollen shut. Something sticky matted the left side of his hair, but he looked up at her with one blue eye, confident of his actions even on his knees. The sound of gunfire in her memory made her eyes fly open. She could still see that blue eye. The same shade as Nick's. Maybe that's why Nick fascinated her.

She took another drag on the cigarette and stepped away from the window, licking her dry, cracked lips. Her heart raced. For the first time she tasted the bitter brine of fear. She refused to be caught. But she wouldn't let Nick die like Andrei either. If she had to hurt him to keep him away, make him stop, she would. Even if that meant sacrificing the one thing he loved most.

Janus squared her shoulders. Time to set the next plan in motion. Reaching into her pocket, she gripped a chain and pulled it out, studying it in the twilight. A dangling lily.

Nick should have left well enough alone.

Chapter 20

THEIR PLANE LANDED in Alabama around midnight on Thursday, and Kaylan could have kissed the ground she walked on. Home—Southern accents, home cooking, Alabama football, family, and the lake she'd grown up on. Even as she crawled into her bed that night, she couldn't believe the peace she felt. Already the fact that a killer shadowed her seemed like a movie instead of her life.

She woke early the next morning, despite the day off, eager to see a sunrise. She donned her bathing suit and cover-up, planning for a day on the lake. Warm sun, the wind on her face, and even the murky smell of lake water called her name. Anticipation tugged her feet down the stairs. Even the slight fall nip entering the air wouldn't stop her.

Fresh, black coffee brewed in the pot near the stove. She opted for hazelnut coffee from the Keurig with Irish cream flavored creamer. Her mother had repainted the breakfast nook again, this time a warm cranberry color. A pastel-tinted sky filled the bay windows facing the dock and lake.

"Hey, gorgeous." Kaylan jumped at Nick's deep voice and his arms wrapping around her waist. Coffee splashed her hand as she steadied her mug. "Oh, babe, I'm sorry."

She shook the liquid from her hand and turned in his arms, careful not to spill any more. Wrapping her free arm around his neck, she pulled his face down to hers. His lips tasted like coffee. As in the months after Haiti, once again she found safety in his arms. But while he had sought to comfort her then, it was her turn to be the comforter.

"Why didn't you sleep longer this morning?" she whispered against his lips.

"I couldn't miss an opportunity to spend the morning with you." He kissed her again, and she leaned into his embrace. And in the warmth of her family's kitchen, wrapped in Nick's arms, she knew. She loved this man with everything in her. No matter the danger, no matter where the government sent them, she would follow Nick Carmichael anywhere.

She would tell him today. Her heart fluttered with her realization.

It was time.

Compared to the Pacific, the lake water warmed her to her toes. She knew fall approached and the time to winterize the jet skis and boat drew near, but for now she enjoyed the sun on her face and wind whipping her hair as she raced Nick on the jet skis. Water drops collected on her sunglasses, and she waved to neighbors on the shore as they zipped past. Nick lifted his hand off the handle. "Is that all you got?" he mouthed before speeding off in front of her.

No way could she let him win. More than once she'd flown off a jet ski while riding with her brothers. She leaned in close to the bars and pushed the jet ski to fifty miles per hour. Her skin pulled taut in the wind whipping past her. Up ahead Nick stopped and jumped into the water to float, his life jacket collecting around his face, a Frogman in his natural habitat. She followed suit, the water cresting her head as she plunged into the deep.

The life jacket ballooned around her as she floated on her back in the water. With a quick tug her head jerked below the water line, causing her to panic. A wave lapped over her head as she came up sputtering to Nick's laughter.

"That was not nice, Nick Carmichael."

His chuckle reverberated on the water. "I can't be sweet all the time." He unbuckled his life jacket and slipped it on the seat of his jet ski.

"Nick, we aren't supposed to take those off."

He looked around the calm lake, absent of boats this time on a Friday morning, and shrugged. "I never swim with a life jacket. It'll be fine." He swam back to her, his eyes the only visible part of his face as he approached.

"Don't start that," she warned, then squealed as he grabbed her around the waist and unbuckled her life vest. "Nick..."

His hands stilled. "Do you trust me?"

"With all my heart."

He studied her for a moment, then slipped the life vest free from her arms, tossing it on the floating vessels. She wrapped her arms around his neck, their legs treading water in sync in the gentle, bobbing waves. As he leaned in to kiss her, she pulled back and shoved his head under water. Laughter spilled from her until he jerked her below again.

They both came up sputtering and laughing.

"Truce," she shouted, backing away from him.

He reached for her, and a nervous giggle spilled from her lips. "Nick..."

Keeping his hands to himself, he leaned forward to kiss her. "Deal. I promise."

She studied the rivulets of water that dripped from his hair down his face and the way his body maintained buoyancy with ease, truly a fish in this water. He found peace in the toughest waves.

"I've been thinking." Her heart galloped as she licked her lips, tasting lake water.

"That's a pretty dangerous pastime for you, isn't it?"

"Watch it, mister." She smiled. "Sarcasm is dangerous too."

His arms repelled the water around him. "All right, all right. What's been going through that gorgeous head of yours?"

"I've been thinking a lot about Sarah Beth and how much I loved her, how much it hurt when she died." She blinked back the prick of tears, wondering when the pain would lessen. "I've watched you and thought about that night on the beach. And I've watched Logan and Kim as they weather this crisis, Kim's strength, Logan's leadership.

"I've thought about what love is. That it's less about how I feel and more about a commitment. A choice. I've watched Kim choose what's best for Logan, stand by his side, and still parent their children. She honors and respects Logan's sacrifice. She chooses to love him no matter what shape he is in. Because she trusts him." Kaylan closed the distance between them, slipping into the hollow of his arms. He stilled in the water, his gaze curious.

"Kayles, what are you trying to tell me?" His eyes searched her face as he wrapped an arm around her waist, supporting them both as they bobbed in the waves.

"I'm saying that I've been scared to love you. Scared to lose you. But when I look at what God says love is, Nick, you love me as Christ calls people to love others. More than once you've been ready and willing to lay down your life for me, to do whatever is necessary to protect me. You've been patient in my fear, constantly pointing me to Jesus." Her eyes filled with tears, and she couldn't wait to share her heart, all of her heart with him.

"Nick Carmichael, I love you with all my heart. I think I have for a while, but it took me a while to identify or express it. I want to follow you as you follow Christ. I'll trust Him to take care of you as you once trusted Him with me after Haiti. But I will not live in fear any longer." She laughed, her heart feeling free with the words. She framed his face with her hands, staring into his gorgeous blue eyes. "I love you, Nick. And I want a future with you."

His lips covered hers, and for a few glorious moments she allowed everything she hadn't allowed herself to feel pour into her kiss. It felt appropriate that all good things in their relationship happened in and around water. It somehow made each experience more powerful, more meaningful.

They both pulled away breathless. Nick rested his forehead on hers, keeping them floating in the gentle waves. "Do you know how long I've waited for you to realize that?"

"Wait, you knew?" She pulled back to look at him.

"Kayles, you said it. Love is a choice, not a feeling. You've demonstrated love in your actions, your words, and your respect for me for months now. I think you were expecting it to feel like something different than it does."

She nodded. "I think I was expecting these giddy, over-the-top feelings. And there is a measure of that when I'm with you."

"I get that. But you and I have experienced the nitty-gritty of life together the last year. When we first met, I was over-the-moon infatuated with you, like a little kid with my emotions. But this last year? We've had to weather the absolute worst, and we've still managed to care for one another and move forward. That's love, Kayles. And I love you too, Kaylan Lee Richards."

He kissed her again, and she relished his words, the meaning taking root in a greater way than it had on the beach. Her heart finally found a home with the man she adored on the lake where they first met. Their future began today.

He tugged her back to the jet skis, and she climbed on the back, the seat scorching her legs.

"Kayles, can I talk to your dad while we're here? You know...about the future?"

She could read a subtle case of nerves he fought to hide, and her stomach knotted. The future. This was a big step. She took a deep breath and smiled. "Whatever you want to do, babe."

He slipped his life vest on and grinned the smile he reserved only for her, the kind that made her heart race and rooted her all at the same time. "Race you back."

Before she could even snap her vest, he took off like a shot. A smile spread across her face, and she thanked the Lord that life would never be boring with this Navy SEAL. She revved her engine and followed in his wake, her jet ski dancing back and forth across the waves he'd created on the way home.

Chapter 21

NICK LOVED WATCHING Kaylan in her element. Her family had her heart, and with her guard down, she loved with all she had. After their morning on the lake, he had noticed a subtle shift in her—less independent and more open with him, like all her walls from Haiti and his abandonment years before had finally crashed to the ground. Her eyes truly revealed her heart, and with her admission, he saw the joy, pain, and occasional fear that flared from time to time.

In true Richards' fashion the kitchen island held a healthy spread, compliments of Marian, who watched the interaction among her four adult children with pleasure. Scott and David were taking a long lunch break, and Seth had just returned from class. Scott bantered with his sons, his arm slung around his daughter. Pap and Gran watched from the kitchen breakfast nook. The old man motioned to Nick, patting the seat next to him on the bench seats framing the bay windows.

Pap nursed sweet tea, which Nick knew from experience tended to be more sugar and lemon than tea. Gran had the brew down to a science without a recipe. He'd watched her make the tea with practiced hands many times during his stay with this family. Nick sank into the cushion, accepting a glass of tea from Gran before she went to join her daughter around the island.

"How are you doing, young man?"

Nick grinned. "I'm doing well, sir."

Pap nodded to Kaylan. "It looks like you are keeping my grand-daughter happy. Thank you."

Nick loved the twinkle in Pap's eye. Despite his stroke, he remained as spunky as ever. "My pleasure. She makes me happy too."

"Am I hearing wedding bells anytime soon?"

"I guess you will need to talk to her about that." Nick chuckled, appreciating Pap's bluntness.

Pap shook his head. "No, sir. You're the one that has to do the asking. So I'm asking you."

"I've wanted to ask for a while. As of today, I think she's finally ready."

"Ah, I see." Pap turned to look out at the lake and then back at Nick with a cheeky grin on his face. "That lake has always been a magical place to her. I guess it's only appropriate she came to terms with her feelings out there, as well."

"She told you what we talked about?"

"No, son, but knowing my Sugar the way I do, it didn't take me long to figure things out. Now to business." Pap dropped a large manila-clasped envelope on the table. It made a dull thud as it landed, telling Nick Pap had stuffed it full.

"What's this?"

Pap folded his hands on the table and leaned closer to Nick. "I know how important it is for you to find your family. So I used some of my connections with the powers that be to find your birth parents. There aren't many hard facts but a lot of trails. I actually found your dad, but it seems your mom wanted to stay anonymous."

Nick opened the brackets and removed the bundle. He sorted through some of the sheets until he found what appeared to be a military record with a scanned photo paper clipped to the top. Air Force.

"That's your father. Airman First Class Thomas Murphy. He worked ground crew at a base in Germany in the 1980s before the fall of the Berlin Wall. He hailed from Kansas City, Kansas. His family owned some cornfields, but he didn't want to stay in Kansas his whole life. He enlisted at eighteen and accepted the position in Germany at twenty-two. I only discovered your relationship because I had some strings pulled. Perks of being a judge for so long. Friends in strategic places. It was buried in your file. I don't think your adoptive parents even knew."

Nick studied the photo, same strong jaw and angled nose, similar dusty blond hair. His blue eyes seemed determined to prove himself, a young kid set to conquer the world. The face staring back at him seemed as foreign as it was familiar. His dad. Biological dad.

"Do you know what happened to him?"

Pap flipped the file to another page and pointed to the bottom. Bullet wound on a day off in the city at the age of twenty-five. Robbery was expected since he was out of uniform. He was sent home to Kansas to be buried, a hero who died too young and unfairly. But death never fought fair.

Nick glanced back up at Pap, who watched him closely, and Nick allowed him a window to his quiet struggle. "I'm not sure what to think or how to feel about all this. Maybe I wasn't expecting him to be dead. Maybe I never actually thought I would find this. I mean, we share the same blood, but he's not my dad, you know?"

Pap nodded. "Blood binds us, but it's not definitive. Family is also a choice, as you well know from growing up with two people who loved you with everything and didn't share a drop of your DNA. I think it's okay to have mixed emotions. Pray through it. Sort through it. And put the search to rest."

"You said there was nothing on my mom? How could she be a

ghost? And if my dad was in Germany, how did they meet, and how did I end up here?"

"All good questions. I couldn't find all those answers. I did find this." Pap reached across the table to tug another page loose. A birth certificate and a note. Nikolai Sebastian caught his eye. The same name Janus had written on the envelope mailed to his house. The name no one ever used. "You were dropped off at US Mission Berlin, which operated as a sort of embassy in West Berlin during the Cold War. You were passed off to a member of the State Department with a note declaring your father was a member of the United States Air Force. A couple of soldiers volunteered to take you home once they were released. You wound up in the California system before your parents adopted you as a baby. This is a note from a member of the State Department responsible for your relocation."

He scanned the note.

This baby was left at our doors on May 25, 1984. The note left with the baby said only his name: Nikolai Sebastian, a squadron number, and the name Murphy, with Air Force written next to it. CPS was called, an investigation commenced, and the baby was placed with a couple within a month.

It was signed *Mary Statton*.

"That's where the trail ends as far as your mother is concerned."

Nick looked away. His eyes found Kaylan's across the room as laughter and jokes reached his ears. He had everything he ever wanted. Yet he still hoped for answers. Maybe some of the men who served with his dad could give him insight into this mystery woman. If his dad died at twenty-five, then Nick had been conceived at least before that. His dad's buddies would be late forties, early fifties. He could track them down.

He turned his focus back to Pap. "Thank you for taking the time to do this, sir. It means a lot."

"You're family now. As good as blood." Pap winked. "And even if you didn't make my granddaughter's face light up, I would still help you out. You aren't alone, son."

Nick shook his hand and rose from the table. Joining the family, he dropped his arm around Kaylan's shoulders, realizing he would officially belong to this family in a matter of time. No matter his own background, his kids would have parents, grandparents, great-grandparents, and uncles.

"Gran's sweet tea give you a stomachache, Hawk?" Micah punched his arm. "You're turning kinda green."

"That's from your company, Bulldog. I turn green in your presence," Nick joked.

"From jealousy. I knew you would admit it someday."

"Mark the date, bro," Seth said as he took a bite of chicken. "It'll never happen again."

"Wishful thinking, Mike," Dave said, pounding his brother on the back.

Micah threw his arm around Dave's neck. "You know you want to be me too. Get away from that desk job and play with guns and exploding things."

"The fact that they let you do that just means that they need their heads examined. And I work very well at a desk."

Micah and Seth both rolled their eyes. "I have no idea how you do that. I'm thankful God gave you the numbers brain and not me," Seth quipped. "Although football stats are right up my alley."

"Speaking of..." Kaylan cut through her brothers' banter. "Y'all gonna give us a good game tomorrow?"

Nick smothered a grin. Kaylan's accent deepened at home or when she got off the phone in California after talking with her family. He never got enough of that sound.

"Heck, yes. Roll Tide!" Seth held up his glass, and the rest of the family followed suit. He glared at Nick's silence.

Nick laughed. "I guess I better learn to be a Bama fan."

Chapter 22

NICK HADN'T CHEERED so loudly in all his life as he sat next to the Richards clan Saturday night at Bryant-Denny Stadium. They all sported Alabama colors, and with the exception of the SEAL teams, he'd never felt more at home. Seth had worked his way up after a year as a redshirt and made several good tackles during the course of the game. Alabama won 31–6 over the Florida Gators.

"Roll Tide!" Kaylan shouted as they stepped out of the car after hours at the stadium.

"Did you see Seth sack that guy? I may need to stop messing with him now. Our baby brother's all grown up and playing on national television." Micah threw his arm around Kaylan.

Kaylan patted his arm. "Maybe there's hope for you too." She and Micah reached the porch first with Nick and her parents trailing behind.

Nick spotted a brown box sitting on the welcome mat.

"Huh, that's funny. It doesn't look like there is postage on this. Maybe the neighbors dropped it off." Kaylan reached to pick it up. "Who's Nikolai Sebastian?"

Warning bells sounded in Nick's head, the ease of the last couple days fading. "Kaylan, don't touch it."

Micah jerked her out of the way just before she touched the brown wrapping as Nick leaned down to inspect the package.

"Nick, is everything all right? Why don't you just bring it into the house and you can open it there," Marian suggested, oblivious to the charged energy radiating off her son and Nick as she and Scott moved past him to unlock the front door.

"I think it would be best if I opened it out here. I'll meet you inside in just a minute."

Scott caught Micah's expression and reached for Marilyn's hand to lead her into the house. "Anyone interested in hot chocolate?"

"Sounds great, Dad. I'd like some in a minute." Kaylan looked between Micah and Nick, and Nick nodded that she could stay with them. "Be right in."

As soon as the door closed, Nick pulled out his military-issue pocketknife and sliced into the small box no bigger than a box of Chinese takeout. A note sat on top on the same paper and with the same Russian script as the other notes. *You owe me a yacht. Continue to chase me, and your debt will increase. I may just take something you love.*

Nick's heart stopped beating as he lifted the note. Kaylan's lily necklace rested at the bottom of the box on blood-red tissue paper.

"Hawk." Micah's voice dripped with caution and anger. "Fill us in, man."

Nick lifted the necklace from the box, and Kaylan caught her breath. "But how…"

Nick placed the trinket around her neck, thankful to have it back where it belonged. But what it now represented terrified him more than he cared to admit. "Babe, would you mind going inside while I talk to Micah? Go ahead and make us both mugs of hot chocolate."

"Extra marshmallows in mine, pretty please," Micah added, his attempt to lighten the mood falling flat to Nick.

Kaylan looked back and forth between them. He watched the

war to argue or agree battle within her. Finally she nodded. "You got it."

As soon as the door shut, Micah lost it. "No way. You have got to be kidding me. They know where my family lives. What's worse is it looks like that package was hand delivered, meaning Janus most likely knew we were here this weekend!"

Nick popped a piece of Juicy Fruit in his mouth and began to pace. "Let's talk through this. We've received two packages: one at our place with a photo of me and Kaylan, and one here at your family's house with Kaylan's necklace. We've also found or received four notes: one on the boat, one in the mail at our house, one on the back of a picture of Kaylan and Sarah Beth, and one here." He stopped pacing and hesitated to ask the next question. "What's the common denominator?"

Micah leaned against the porch railing, his fingers tapping with nervous energy. "Hawk, with the exception of the note on the boat, the common denominator is my sister. I would think the target is me since she's my sister and this is my family's place. But the packages and letters are all addressed to you. In Russian. Like whoever is writing knows you can read it." He stilled completely and locked eyes with Nick, revealing his combat-ready side that forever lurked just below his playful, carefree exterior. "Hawk, Janus or someone close to her is targeting you."

Nick's steps quickened as he resumed pacing. "Why would the right-hand woman of one of the most dangerous arms dealers in the world target me? Our whole team has been after her, but we only have the intel we've been given by the big wigs. CIA has had a target on her back long before we ever heard her name. Why start dropping clues, leaving threats? Why me and not someone else on the team? And why Kaylan?"

Micah shook his head. "That last question worries me the most. It implies someone has watched you enough to know she is your one weakness."

"How is that possible, though? She only moved to Cali in August. It's been a couple months. The rest of the time, it's been long distance between California and Alabama and Haiti. There's no way..."

"There's no way this person would truly understand Kaylan isn't just another girl unless they'd been watching the two of you for a long time," Micah finished.

Nick stopped pacing and faced Micah. He fought panic and rage that Janus had somehow reached into a safe and fun weekend to scare him and Kaylan. This wasn't how SEALs fought. But somehow she'd managed to make it personal. They needed to end this.

"I'll call X and the Feds, let them know what's up. Janus or one of her minions is on American soil. If they have any more leads, we need to know. Surely with the SEALs, the FBI, and the CIA all working different angles, we can catch Janus soon."

Nick lowered his voice. "I'm ready for this to be over. We better figure out a plan to have eyes on Kaylan while we are gone at training."

"I know just the duo for the job."

They entered the house and Nick went to the kitchen for his hot chocolate, the peace accumulated over the weekend now drained. For now, he could only pray and sit tight. If it came down to the wire, he wouldn't let Kaylan out of his sight.

Janus studied the lake house from her position in a tree house across from the driveway. Old books and action figures littered the corners, and Janus inhaled humidity, longing for her yacht and the comforts of home it once offered. Well, at least the closest thing she had to a home since childhood.

She watched as Nick and Micah finally entered the house, glancing around before firmly shutting the door. As if that could keep her out. They were so easy to rattle. Americans thought their teams were so elite, but break them down, hurt them by harming what they loved the most, and they wept like babies. They knew nothing of loss, nothing of terror. Nothing like what Janus saw as a child in Russia. She still remembered the door crashing open and Stasi pouring in, her brother hauled away and her father doing nothing while her mother wept. Life hadn't been worth living east of the Wall. No place for children.

She lifted an action figure. What would it have been like to raise a son? Like Andrei. Or a daughter, like herself. She bolted upright, the action figure cutting into her palm as something foreign and wet rolled down her cheek. No weakness. She'd made her choice, the choice she'd had to make her whole life—anything to survive. And she'd do it again. Even if it hurt someone else.

Coughing seized her lungs, and she attempted to smother the sound. She'd seen some of the best doctors in Eastern Europe. Too much vodka, too many cigarettes, too much running. She grew weary just thinking about it. She glanced at her watch in the moonlight. Business called.

A plane waited for her in the morning. She had a meeting with a client regarding weapons. Janus didn't care what they did with them. She asked few questions, her main objective to collect the money. Her boss wasn't a patient man, and he demanded cash up front.

She shuddered despite the warm night. If he ever knew she dipped into the payoff from time to time, he would kill her in the most gruesome way possible. But she hadn't survived this long by throwing caution to the wind. Except once when her emotions overrode her good sense with a handsome soldier that set her heart racing. But that had been a long time ago. Janus would never allow herself to experience that pain again. No matter what.

Chapter 23

ONDAY CAME TOO quickly for Kaylan as she began her rotation at a relief organization, learning the foods to plan in case of a natural disaster. Fortunately for the organization, and unfortunately for her, she was all too familiar with this dire scenario.

As she met with the manager and learned more about what the next month would look like, Kaylan struggled not to flash back to the days following the quake. People stood in line for days with buckets hoping for water or food. The deaf or impaired were thrown out of line so that the "normal" could survive. People trampled others in their pursuit of survival.

More than the proper food, Kaylan knew they needed proper planning to get food to people as quickly as possible, with people on both ends ensuring the supplies reached the final destination. As she formulated a proposal and plans, the hole in her life that Sarah Beth once filled seemed bigger than ever. And in those moments her fear Nick wouldn't come home magnified irrationally. Everything seemed out of control. "See you tomorrow, Bill," she waved as she left for the day. Already the weekend felt like it had never happened.

Megan's car was parked out front when she got to Nick and

Micah's. Kaylan hoped things had ended with the guy of the week. As much as she loved her brother and boyfriend, she would love a girl around, especially one who would make light of a situation that kept Kaylan up at night.

"Hey, babe," Nick met her in the kitchen and bestowed a quick peck on her lips. "Can you come in here for a second?" Twining his fingers through hers, he led her into the living area where Megan waited with Micah in what seemed like a silent standoff.

Kaylan almost laughed. "What's going on?"

"Sidekick over here called and said I needed to come over." Kaylan could tell her roommate was uncomfortable being anywhere near a military base. No wonder she hadn't wanted to stay with the guys.

Kaylan sank down on the edge of the couch and looked at her brother and boyfriend. "All right, spill it. What's going on?" She fought to keep the panic at bay but could tell nothing from their calm demeanors.

"Micah and I both have training out of town for about a month. And we need to talk about living arrangements."

"Okay, well, I'll just move out of Micah's room and back into my house."

"Kayles, I'm not sure about that."

"You aren't going to be at your place. Clearly whoever this is knows your address as well as mine. Megan and I will be better back at our place. The FBI can watch us there just as well as here. Just let me know which of the guys will be in town so we can call if we need to." She shot an apologetic glance in Megan's direction. "I'm so sorry about this, Megan."

Megan grimaced, then shrugged. "It was starting to get a little boring around our house anyway with you being Miss Perfect and all." A glimmer of a smile graced her mouth, and Kaylan silently cheered for Megan's grudging support.

"Kaylan."

Kaylan's eyes shot back to Nick. "Nick, you can't control your training schedule. I can't live in fear, and I really can't do anything if you won't tell me what or who I'm watching out for."

"You know I can't tell you."

"Babe, I need to move on with life right now unless you have another idea."

"We figured you would pull the tough act on us. So we do in fact have another idea." The front door opened, and Colt and Jay filed into the room.

"How's it going, ladies? We're your new body guards." Jay grinned, winking at Megan, who blushed before rolling her eyes.

"You have got to be kidding me. I can take care of myself, thank you very much." Megan stood but tumbled back on the couch to avoid running into Jay. "Seriously? Can't you take your six pack somewhere else?"

"You know you like it." Jay stalked closer.

Megan glared at Kaylan. "Do military boys ever leave high school?"

"Boys? I am all man, baby."

"Jay, knock it off," Colt cut in. He looked at Kaylan and smiled. "We won't get in your way. The Feds have y'all covered right now anyway. We'll be around and available for our group's peace of mind. Since Jay, Titus, and I are on a different team from Logan, Hawk, Bulldog, and X, we aren't on the same training schedule."

"So we are at your beck and call." Jay flashed his most charming smile at Megan.

Megan's smile bordered on wicked. "You may regret that."

Kaylan sensed trouble ahead. She shot a look at Micah, who rolled his eyes.

"Jay, behave yourself while we're gone," Micah lectured. "She's off limits."

"I don't see you making a move."

"Jay, I mean it."

Jay waved a hand in Micah's direction. Colt grabbed Jay's arm and shoved him out the door. "Kayles, call us if you need us."

Kaylan released a breath, admitting defeat but comforted that she had someone she knew close at hand if necessary. "Thanks, Colt. I'll add you to speed dial." He flashed a pearly white smile as he closed the door behind him.

The room grew silent. Megan glanced between the three of them. "Well, I'll go first. I personally think this is overkill. But"—her voice quieted—"I admit I have no clue what is going on, and as long as those bozos stay out of my way, I can handle protection. And you said the Feds are still around?"

Micah nodded. "Keeping a low profile but there if something happens."

Megan stood and rubbed her hands together. "Well, that means I'm going home to sleep in my own bed tonight." She looked at Kaylan. "See you in a bit?"

"I'll be there soon."

As Megan left, Micah slipped from the room and Kaylan stood. "Guess I better go pack."

"Babe, wait. Talk to me."

Kaylan turned on Nick, eyes flashing. "I feel controlled and helpless. But worse than that, I'm scared."

"Kayles, I'm so sorry. I promise, we are ending this soon. Please bear with me a little longer. I'm not trying to control you. I just want to protect you."

He pulled her into his arms and lowered his lips inches from hers. Her frustration warred with her affection for him. "If anything, anything ever happened to you, Kaylan, I couldn't handle it. Especially if it was because of me." He tightened his arms around her until her anger lessened, and she leaned into him, responding to his desperation, needing comfort, wanting to support.

"You won't lose me."

His lips found hers, soft at first, then became more intense—as if kissing her enough could make the danger and everything else evaporate until nothing existed but the two of them. After a few moments she pulled back to rest in his arms. "You can't kiss this away. I'm fine."

He chuckled and rested his forehead on hers. She felt his chest rise and fall with a heavy sigh as if he carried the weight of the world. "Let's keep it that way, okay?" She nodded as he kissed her forehead. Despite his strength, she sensed an emotion he fought to keep at bay. She stroked his back, waiting for him to relax.

"Will you go with me to the hospital?" Nick mumbled against her hair.

"Oh, babe, Logan's surgery!" She pulled back to study his face. "How'd it go?"

"It's finished. I wish they had found an antibiotic that worked, but it is what it is. He's back in his room. I called Kim. She said it's okay if we drop in over the next couple days. He wants to see us."

Kaylan had never seen Nick so lost. The famous fixer couldn't fix anything, and lives were at stake. It terrified him.

She wrapped her arms around his neck. "I would love to go with you. Who has the kids tonight?"

"Logan's mom flew in to stay with them for a few weeks. I think Kim's mom will come out after that."

A low growl sounded behind them. "All right, you two, break it up." Micah used his arms to pry them apart and walked between them on the way to the living room. "I'm going to record the game tonight, and then I'm ready to hit the road."

Thirty minutes later they arrived at the hospital. Micah turned the car off and sat still. "I'm not ready for this."

Nick shook his head. "I still can't believe it came down to this. I thought the antibiotics would clear the infection, and after some therapy, he'd be back with us." The two exchanged a look, and Kaylan could feel their pain from her seat in the back.

Kaylan stuck her head between the seats. "Once a SEAL, always a SEAL. It's still Logan. You didn't lose the man, just some of the motor skills. Focus on him and all you can help him overcome now. This is your next mission as a team."

Nick met her eyes in the rearview mirror, and she saw a measure of peace mixed with the pain. "Now I remember why I'm dating you."

Kaylan snorted. "You forgot? I guess I need to remind you more often."

"Let's go, you two." Micah climbed from the car and slammed the door, Nick and Kaylan following suit.

Kaylan wove her fingers between Nick's, and he squeezed tight. After all he did to stand beside her after Sarah Beth passed away, she could and would do this and more for him.

She leaned in close as they walked to whisper, "I love you. You are not alone in this."

He stopped before they entered the doors and kissed her. "When can I marry you?"

She smiled. "Ask me later."

Within a few minutes they stood outside Logan's door, Micah joking with Kim and Logan inside. She squeezed Nick's hand as he took a deep breath. Ever the protector, it killed him when someone he loved was in pain and he couldn't change it.

They entered the room, and Kaylan struggled to keep her gaze from drifting to the end of the bed where two legs should lie under the sheets. Now one leg stopped short, the sheets abnormally flat next to his other leg. She focused on Kim's face and the beep of Logan's monitors.

Nick approached Logan's outstretched hand and clasped it tight. "Hey, man, how are you feeling?"

"Ready for another Hell Week. I could take on the world right now," he slurred, but his eyes held the humor they all knew and loved. Kaylan continued to be amazed by the strength of the SEALs and their occasional daredevil bents. Very little stopped them. If they couldn't accomplish a goal one way, they would try a million other options until they achieved success. To Logan and Kim, this surgery just became a challenge to conquer, not a hill to die on. Life remained to be lived.

"Does it hurt?" Micah asked as he came to stand at Logan's other side.

"It's weird. I still feel like the rest of my leg should be there, but it's not. I hear phantom pains are a possible issue. But so far I'm too drugged to care. I got to thinking though." His smile turned mischievous as his eyes drooped. "I need a new nickname: The Triple Threat, Tripod, Trey, something with three."

Micah chuckled. "How about you let us choose something less lame? Let's face it. You've never been good at choosing the nicknames."

Nick grinned. "I don't know. I kinda like Tripod. Or we could just go with something like Terminator."

"Oh, that's a good one. Even without a limb I can still whip most of the team."

Kaylan and Kim joined the laughter.

Logan's tired eyes turned serious. "How am I going to do this?"

Kaylan stepped forward to the end of the bed. "Did Nick ever tell you I was in Haiti during the earthquake?"

"He never shared details."

"Many lost limbs in the earthquake. Doctors volunteered and have fit many Haitians with prosthetics. This isn't over. If the Haitians can do it, I'm confident you can overcome this. One step at a time. And we're here to help with whatever you and Kim need. Besides"—she looped her arm through Kim's—"I've fallen in love with your kids."

Kim laughed. "You were an instant hit the moment you gave them ice cream."

"I might possibly have intended that to be a bribe. Apparently it worked."

Logan's eyes drooped more.

"I think we need to go. Don't worry about anything, Logan. We're here every step of the way." Nick reached for Kaylan's hand as they turned to follow Micah out the door. Nick kissed Kim's cheek. "Call when you need us."

"Thank you. All three of you. I can't tell you how much it means to know you are a call away." Kim teared up despite her smile. "We're going to get through this just fine."

Kaylan squeezed her hand. "Yes, you will. We're praying."

"She's a keeper, Hawk. Don't you mess this up, or I will climb out of this bed and beat you with my old leg," Logan croaked from the bed.

Nick's eyes twinkled. "Save your energy, Pops. I'm never letting this one go."

As they left the hospital, Kaylan thanked the Lord that their relationship hadn't been normal. In more ways than one they'd had to support one another in the darkest of times and learned to treasure the sweet moments. Life included the rough moments, and she knew with Nick by her side they could laugh or cry together, no matter the circumstance.

Chapter 24

KAYLAN KNEW SHE'D fallen in love when she went over to Nick and Micah's to clean just because she missed Nick and wanted things to be nice when he got home. She hated cleaning. The guys had been gone two weeks, two very busy weeks for them and two very uneventful weeks for Megan and Kaylan—unless they counted Jay's frequent and unexpected drop-bys.

At first, being alone set them both on edge. After a week of quiet they settled back into their old routine. Kaylan still couldn't quite figure out how to breach Megan's walls. But she figured a costume party might be fun. With Halloween a couple weeks away, she had time to plan a party with some of the team and their dates. It would be a fun way to laugh the night away and help Megan understand that not all military guys were like her dad. So far Kaylan had run out of luck convincing her.

"C'mon, Megan. You can be anything you want. Use your imagination."

Megan rolled her eyes from her slouched position in the love seat, a copy of *The Hobbit* in her hand. Kaylan liked to read, but the classics bored her. She didn't know how Megan managed to enjoy them. "The Grinch."

"That's Christmas. Try again."

"A vampire."

"Too cliché. Think out of the box, Meg."

"I'm cliché? Have you met you—Miss Perfect Life, Perfect Boyfriend, Perfect Family?"

Kaylan ignored the jab. "Are we really going there again?" Megan pushed people away to protect herself. Kaylan had decided to fight past that. A few bruises along the way were inevitable.

"Sorry. I'll drop that. Why can't I just go Goth?"

"You wear black all the time. Who did you want to be as a kid? Or who's your favorite literary character?"

"Juliet. She dies tragically with her stupid boyfriend."

"Seriously?"

"Fine." Megan grew quiet and thoughtful. When she finally spoke, she wouldn't meet Kaylan's eyes. "I always kind of liked Frodo and Sam from the *Lord of the Rings* trilogy. They left home and set out on this great adventure. And bad things happened, but they succeeded."

Kaylan struggled to maintain the seriousness of the moment while smothering a smile. "So...you want to dress up as a short person who likes to eat and has furry feet?"

Megan threw a pillow at Kaylan as Kaylan burst into laughter. "I'm sorry, Meg. I couldn't help it."

"See if I answer any of your questions again."

"Don't be that way. It was a joke. We can figure out a costume for that. You'll make a cute hobbit."

"I said that I like the characters, not that I wanted to be them. Let me guess; you were always a princess growing up."

"Not always. I did that more when I was little. Then Sarah Beth and I liked to pick something silly each year. One year we were salt and pepper. In college we dressed up like Google maps, complete with the location dots."

"What are you and Nick going as this year?"

"Well, he hasn't agreed yet, but we are going as Alice and the Mad Hatter. Maybe you and Micah should talk about this."

That got Megan's attention. She dropped the book in her lap and sat up to look at Kaylan. "Why do I need to talk to Sidekick about this?"

Kaylan hid behind a pillow as she spoke. "Because Micah is your date for this party?"

Another pillow flew across the sitting area, colliding with the top of Kaylan's head. "Hey. Are you out of pillows over there yet?"

"That depends. Are you out of stupid ideas and comments?"

"You're so tough. C'mon. It'll be fun, I promise."

A sly grin spread over Megan's face, and Kaylan wondered if she should warn Micah.

"I don't need to check with Micah. I have the perfect costume in mind."

"And what's that?"

"I'll be a superhero, and he'll be my sidekick. It will be perfect, especially at a party with all his macho friends. And I'm picking out the costume. I'm thinking tights."

Kaylan laughed so hard the armchair shook as she imagined her brother in tights and the looks on people's faces. It was bad enough that Nick would show up in full costume makeup.

Megan joined her laughter, and for the first time Kaylan believed they had achieved a breakthrough. Then a movement outside the window startled her. She stood quickly, pillows dropping to the floor as she searched for what had caught her attention. A woman lay crumpled in the yard across the street.

"Jenna!" Kaylan hit the floor running, throwing open the front door to their porch. Megan ran behind her.

Kaylan sprinted across the street and fell on her knees next to Jenna, who lay curled on her side, coughing uncontrollably. "Meg, can you get her some water?"

Jenna shook her head. "Inhaler. Red. Kitchen," she croaked.

"Meg, her inhaler. Hurry," Kaylan insisted. Megan took off into Jenna's house a few doors down.

"Jenna, let's sit up." Kaylan helped her into a sitting position as the woman struggled to breathe.

Meg arrived with the inhaler. Jenna's hands shook as she took a long tug on the inhaler before responding. "Couldn't catch my breath."

"Do you have asthma? Have you been taking your maintenance dose?" Megan took the inhaler back from her as Kaylan helped her to her feet.

Jenna glared at Megan. "I've taken that medicine my whole life. I'm tired of it."

Megan held up her hands in surrender. "Your funeral," she muttered under her breath, and Kaylan glared in her direction.

"All right. All right." Kaylan hovered at Jenna's side as they slowly walked inside her house. Megan trailed behind. "Jenna, can we help you in any way?"

"My couch. Please." She ground out the last word.

She helped Jenna to the couch, trying to ignore the tribal masks that seemed to glare at her from their position on the wall. "Can we get you some water?"

"Not yet."

Megan leaned against the wall, her eyes darting between Kaylan and Jenna as Kaylan sank into a couch across from their neighbor. Kaylan prayed for the right words, hesitant to leave until she knew Jenna was okay. "Jenna, have you seen a doctor lately?"

"I don't need to go to my doctor to hear that I need to take my medicine. Air pollution sometimes causes flare-ups." The corners of her mouth turned upward, but the smile didn't quite reach her eyes. "But I can beat this. After all, it hasn't kept me from doing marathons." She ran a hand over her chest. "Perhaps some water now, Megan?" Her contrite look set Megan into motion.

Kaylan took a deep breath, forcing herself to relax and fight the flashback that said she was trapped in a building, surrounded by a cloud of dust, and struggling to breathe. "I'm so sorry. Can I help you with anything?"

"No. I'll manage." She sank back in the couch as Megan handed her a cup of water and then stepped back to lean against the wall. "Truth is, I forgot to take my maintenance medication on my trip a few weeks ago, and can't seem to get back in the habit since." She took a sip and closed her eyes. "Thank goodness for emergency inhalers. I'll be fine soon."

Kaylan stood to leave, sensing the finality of the conversation. "At least let me bring your dinner."

"No. Thank you. I just need rest."

Kaylan moved to the door but came to halt at the two stairs leading from the living room to the entryway. For a moment she imagined Jenna collapsed on the floor, unable to breathe, and no one around to help. Terror gripped her at the thought of finding someone else dead. The blood drained from her face. She staggered away from the spot on the floor where her imagination created hallucinations of a lifeless body.

Megan came forward and steadied Kaylan. "You okay?"

Kaylan nodded, reminding herself that it was unrealistic to fear everyone near to her dropping dead. Taking a deep breath, she squared her shoulders, determined she would help whether Jenna wanted it or not. "I'm sorry your asthma has gotten worse, Jenna. Please let me know if I can help in any way."

A small smile played on Megan's face as she turned to Jenna. "I think you just found yourself a permanent caretaker."

Jenna's gaze darted back and forth between the two. "No. Not necessary." An edge tainted her voice as her British accent clipped through.

"Too bad." Stubbornness was a trait Kaylan came by honestly and used sparingly. But this situation called for it. She walked to the front door and opened it. "I'll bring some soup in an hour. Get some rest." Kaylan and Megan closed the door and stepped out into the dusky night.

The street lay quiet, porch lights twinkling as the sky turned from rosy red to navy with a slight glow on the horizon. Kaylan stared at her house across the street. Sarah Beth's life couldn't be spared—not by human hands. The Lord had a bigger purpose by taking her, although Kaylan and the Lord still argued about that from time to time. But He had placed a woman right across the street from her who didn't have family support and needed someone to look out for her, whether she acknowledged it or not.

Kaylan stepped into the empty street, staring down the road to the end of the block where the houses rounded a bend and the pavement slipped from sight. Death respected no person, and sickness never chose its victims with care. Unlike Jenna, Kaylan knew who held her future, and she wanted the opportunity to tell Jenna about Him, so no matter what happened, she was prepared.

With that commitment Kaylan entered her house and headed to the kitchen. Time to make soup for her neighbor.

Chapter 25

HALLOWEEN LURKED JUST around the corner, and Nick couldn't wait to get home to Kaylan. At one point she'd been a section of his life, one he had to lock up in order to concentrate during work. Now she'd become a fixture, a part of himself that he didn't need to isolate in order to concentrate. She'd become his reason to do his job, to focus in the field and then come home. He couldn't wait to get back home and make it permanent.

He'd talked to her parents, Scott and Marian, during his stay in Alabama. He'd never been so nervous or so sure of anything in all his life. Despite his past, the danger of his current job, and his lack of family to offer Kaylan, the Richards gladly welcomed him into their family and trusted him to love their daughter. He still couldn't wrap his mind around that reality.

Glancing at his watch, he grabbed his shoes, ready to track down dinner after a long day on the shooting range. His marksmanship had improved during this round of training. He hoped he had the opportunity to practice on Janus or her boss.

The phone rang, and Nick glanced at the caller ID as he left the room with his roommate to meet some of the other guys. It was Pap. He nodded at his roommate to keep going. "I'll catch up." After a moment, he answered the phone. "Yes, sir."

"Hey, son. I'm out in Georgia visiting some friends and heard you are nearby. Mind if we meet for dinner tonight?"

"I can make that happen. When and where?"

"Are you free now?"

"I just left my room to chase down dinner. How about Harriet's Diner a few blocks east of the mall in about fifteen minutes?"

"I know the one. I'll meet you there."

Nick hung up the phone wondering at the hidden urgency in Pap's voice and the need to meet in person. His mind wandered back to the information Pap had given him recently. Had he found out more in the two weeks he'd been gone?

Harriet's Diner took Nick to another decade. A bell rang every time someone entered. The red vinyl booths, jukebox in the corner, and milkshake machine all took him back to the 1950s when life was *Leave It to Beaver* perfect. Supposedly anyway. He enjoyed the retreat. And the burgers. The sweet potato fries cooked by Mrs. Harriet's granddaughter had no equal. He'd found the place on his first stint at sniper school and came back whenever he had a chance. He'd pay for the greasy burger in the weight room later, but nothing would stop him from enjoying it now.

"What can I help you with, honey?" A middle-aged woman in a pale yellow uniform and white apron gave him a once-over as she nibbled the pen cap. Her white smile, sparkling ebony eyes, and Southern drawl made Nick grin. No wonder Kaylan missed home. Maybe they would move back to the Deep South one day.

"How about a cheeseburger with everything on it, sweet potato fries, and a mint chocolate milkshake?"

"Mmm-hmm." She looked him up and down. "Honey, you're a big boy. You sure you don't need nothing else?"

"He doesn't, but I do." Pap sank into the booth seat across from Nick. "Give me the burger, regular fries, and a strawberry milkshake with a cherry on top."

"Pap, shouldn't you maybe go for the chicken sandwich? You know what Gran would say."

"Gran picks my diet the other six days of the week. Tonight it's my turn."

The waitress, Hilda according to her nametag, chuckled. "You got it. Two orders comin' right up."

Pap rested his cane against the side of the booth, and Nick recalled the conversation at the beginning of the year that consisted of that cane rapping his shin. He'd walked away from that meeting realizing he had tried to take the place of God in Kaylan's life, something he'd taken to heart since then. As her husband, he could never do that. He could only point her to Him.

"Well now, how's your training going?"

"Pretty good, Pap. My scores are up. Kinda makes me ready to deploy again."

"Any news when that will be?"

Nick waited to respond as Hilda brought two ice waters with lemon and placed them on the table. "About a year and half until I deploy with the team, give or take a little bit. Lots of school and training between now and then. With Support Activity 1," Nick chose his words carefully, "hopefully, it's sooner rather than later. We have a job we are itching to complete."

"Ah, yes. I understand that. Did Kaylan ever tell you I was in the Army for four years right after high school? I met Kaylan's gran when we were seventeen. I joined the Army right after that and was shipped off for the 1958 Lebanon crisis. Eisenhower initiated Operation Blue Bat as part of his plan to fight creeping Communism. The scuffle in Lebanon began because Christians and Muslims couldn't decide who to align with politically. Politics, religion, and money." Pap shook his head. "More like power, passion, and greed. Many wars begin because of wrong belief in a god made of human hands and intuition. Sad really. But the Bible says that wars and rumors of wars will continue 'til Jesus comes back and makes peace. Come quickly, Lord Jesus." Pap cast his eyes toward the ceiling.

Nick shook his head. "I didn't know any of that."

"Forgive the ramblings of an old man." Pap chuckled. "When I finished serving my country, I decided to dive into law, became a judge, and moved up to the state level. My Army days seemed far behind me at that point. But they taught me a lot about what to value."

"I get that. Facing a situation where you know you could depart for eternity definitely puts life into focus."

Nick's stomach rumbled just as Hilda arrived with their orders. "Perfect timing."

"Honey, I could hear your stomach from all the way over there." She cackled, pointing at the kitchen. "I told you that you should have ordered more."

"I'll already have to pay for this in the gym tomorrow."

She rolled her eyes and waved her hand in dismissal. "You're just fine. You two enjoy."

Pap bowed his head to thank God for the meal and for their time together, and then Nick dove into his plate, inhaling the food as Pap picked at his. Something didn't add up. Nick tossed a fry back on his plate.

"All right, Pap. Spill it. Why did you call?"

The vinyl booth squeaked as Pap shifted, then sighed. "Well, I told you I was looking into your parents with some of my contacts. Benefit of retirement and all that, lots of free time on my hands."

"Pap..."

"Right, sorry." He met Nick's eyes, and Nick recognized regret and compassion there. "It looks like you have a sister, based on other records I found from the US Mission in Berlin."

Nick sat back in the booth, his surroundings fading. He had a what? He couldn't think straight. "I'm sorry. I must have heard you wrong."

"Judging from your reaction, you heard me right. You have a sister. She tried to join the Air Force out there in California, but because of asthma, she was rejected. My contact said she still works on that base in an administrative capacity."

Nick couldn't think straight. All he'd wanted growing up was a sibling. He'd loved his parents, but since they'd adopted him in middle age, they didn't have much energy to keep up with a rambunctious boy. Now he learned he had a sister who had grown up in a different family, and because of his biological mother's choices, they'd never met.

He didn't know whether to be angry, thrilled, or terrified. He didn't know what to do, what to think. Would she want to meet him? Did she even know about him or their parents?

"Pap, I don't..."

Pap reached across the table and patted his arm. "I know this comes as a shock. And I'm sure there's some pain involved. Process through it. Do you want to know more about her?"

Nick could only nod.

Pap pulled a file folder from his folded jacket. "The name on her birth certificate is Natalia, but her parents called her Natalie Grace McMurray. Her dad is pretty high up in the Air Force. She grew up moving all over the place. She's your age. It looks like you may have a twin."

Nick groaned. "What do I do? Are you sure? This couldn't be a mistake?"

Pap shook his head. "They found records linking the two of you. It looks like your mom dropped you both off at U.S. Mission Berlin, which served as a type of embassy during the time of the

Berlin Wall. She was also adopted as a baby. She has a younger sister by her adoptive parents."

Nick only nodded, his food suddenly cold and unappealing.

"How could she do this?"

"Your mother?"

"Yeah. How can you just abandon your kids without even making sure they are okay?"

Pap reached over to grip Nick's arm, the pressure causing Nick to meet the old man's eyes so like Kaylan's. It put him at ease, settling his soul and making him feel at home. "Son, you will never, ever hear me defend your birth mother. However, I truly think that by giving you both up, she gave the two of you your best chance at life. You were both adopted and raised in homes with parents who were present. Don't doubt what God can do with our poor decisions. He works all things for the good of those who love Him. All things, son."

Tears threatened to overflow. Anger overrode the heart-wrenching pain of missing out on a sister his whole life. "But why? I missed so much with her."

"If you hadn't been with your parents, you may never have fallen in love with baseball, never gone to USC on a baseball scholarship, never met Micah, never given your life to Christ, never gone into the Navy, never met our family. That's a lot of nevers, son. This is the Lord's perfect timing for this information. I don't know why or what you should do now. But pray about it, Nick. Talk to Kaylan. Talk to Micah. And then move forward in faith."

Nick took the file and opened it to read the name at the top. Natalie Grace. He wanted, no, needed to find his sister. Life was too short not to make up for lost time. And now he knew exactly where to start.

Chapter 26

THE MINUTES COULDN'T tick by fast enough on the clock in Logan and Kim's living room. She'd helped the kids with homework, fixed dinner, and put them to bed. Candles burned on the mantel, a movie played on the television, and Kaylan dozed in and out of consciousness, waiting for the knock that meant Nick was finally home after four weeks away.

As the clock slipped past ten, screaming tore Kaylan from the couch.

"Molly!" Kaylan bolted down the hallway to Molly's bedroom and tore open the door. Molly sat board straight on her bed, her eyes fixed on her window. Tears streamed down her pale cheeks. Her blonde hair hung in tangles around her face.

She whimpered on the bed, and Kaylan couldn't bear it. She climbed in next to Molly and pulled her into her arms. "Ladybug, what's wrong?" She stroked her hair and looked in Molly's frightened eyes. "Talk to me, munchkin. What happened?"

"There was a shadow over there. And it came toward me and wouldn't stop. And I screamed, and it went away. Don't let it come back, Kaylan. Don't let it get me."

Kaylan looked to where Molly pointed. Her fairy night-light glowed in the dark room on the wall across from her bed just under the window. Shadows from her dolls and teddy bears on the floor flickered larger than life on the wall.

"Molly, it was just a bad dream. Just a bad dream."

Molly sobbed in Kaylan's arms, curling into a ball tight against her on the twin bed. Kaylan held her close, knowing that she would never let anything or anyone hurt her and wishing she could stop the dreams.

"They won't go away, Kaylan. Why won't the shadows go away?" Molly peeked over Kaylan to gaze at the wall again.

"It's just your toys." Kaylan loosened Molly's arms and crawled from the bed. She picked up the teddy bear on the floor and made him dance in midair so Molly could see his shadow move. Then she sat him down and stretched out on the floor, making finger puppets in the glow of the nightlight.

Slowly Molly sat up. "Rabbit." She giggled. "Worm." She cocked her head. "What is that one, Kaylan?"

"It's a giraffe, silly. Can't you tell?"

"Mmm, I think you need to work on that one a little more." Kaylan threw her hands in the air as Molly came to join her on the floor, her nightgown wrapping around her legs as she walked. She tugged her teddy bear in her lap and gazed at the shadows still looming on the wall. "How come they look smaller now?"

"Well, when we look at things clearly, they aren't as scary anymore."

"But where do shadows come from?" She huddled in a ball with her bear. "I don't like them very much."

Kaylan leaned close to her face. "I don't either," she whispered. She made claws with her hands, sending Molly into a giggling mess before she attacked her rib cage, tickling her until Molly rolled on the floor laughing.

After a few minutes they both lay on the floor looking up at the ceiling. Logan had stuck stars all over the ceiling that glowed a pale green. Molly rolled over and looked at Kaylan, smothering a yawn as her eyes drooped. "You didn't answer my question."

"Shadows come from a mixture of light and darkness, Molly."

"How do I make them go away?"

Kaylan stood up and crossed the room. She flipped on the light switch, causing Molly to squint in the sudden brightness. "Look at the wall now."

"They're gone! How did you do that?"

"By turning on the light. Shadows can't exist where the light is bright."

"Then never turn it off. Can I sleep with it on tonight?"

"Sure thing, sweet girl." Kaylan picked Molly up from the floor right as a breeze filtered through the window, causing the curtain to flutter. She stilled. She'd closed that window. She was sure of it.

Fear rippled through her as she tucked Molly in bed. As she turned to close the window, Molly clenched her arm, her nails digging into her skin. "Don't leave me. It will come back."

Kaylan sat down next to her on the bed, tugging the covers around her. "Molly, we turned the light on. The shadows can't come back, remember?"

"But the shadow wasn't like my bear. It moved."

"Well, sometimes curtains or something moves in my room and it scares me, but it can't hurt me."

She shook her head on the pillow, her eyes closing. "But it coughed," she mumbled as she drifted off, her fingers loosening from Kaylan's arm.

Kaylan froze. Her gaze raked the window, before she looked at Molly. The poor thing was completely exhausted. After laying Molly's limp hand on the covers, she tiptoed to the window, taking deep breaths to still her nerves.

"Nothing is going to jump out at you. It's all in your head," she whispered. Her hands shook as she lifted the curtain. A small, dusty shoe print visible on the ledge waged war with her calm. "No, no, no. Not possible."

She pulled the window down and latched it, knowing she had done this earlier. She gazed out into the dark night. If someone had been out there, they were long gone now. Something moved in the bush. Kaylan held her breath. With a screech, a tabby cat darted from underneath, a black and white one following in its wake. She exhaled, her hand going to her heart.

A knock sounded, and Kaylan jumped. Now who was jumping at shadows and noises?

She rushed from the room, pulling Molly's door shut in her wake. Running to the door, she opened it and flew into Nick's arms.

"You're here. You're home."

"When I'm with you, I'm always home, gorgeous." He picked her up, twirling her around on the porch. "Gosh, I missed you."

She held on tighter, wanting to flee back into the house but unsure whether it was safer outside or inside. She was sure of it now. Someone had been in Molly's room. Terror tore through her at the possibilities.

"Kaylan, your heart's racing." Nick grabbed her arms from around his neck and held her from him to look in her eyes. His smile immediately left. "What's wrong? What happened?" He looked past her into the house and then pulled her inside.

"Nick, I'm so sorry. This isn't how I wanted to welcome you home. I had this whole romantic night planned. And then Logan and Kim asked me to babysit so they could go out, but I still wanted to see you. So I planned something here, but then..." She rambled, fear taking hold. She didn't want to burden him. But if it was who she thought...

He cupped her face, calming her as their eyes met. "Kaylan, I don't care how I get to see you. I just wanted to be with you. Now, slow down and tell me what's wrong."

"Someone was in Molly's room."

"When?"

"About thirty minutes ago probably."

He let go and moved toward Molly's room, but Kaylan grabbed his arm, tugging him to a halt. "Be quiet. She's asleep again. I didn't figure it out until she was drifting off. And then you knocked."

"How'd they come in?"

"The window. But I know I closed it before I put her to bed. I remember doing it. She woke up screaming. Said she saw a shadow. I thought she was just seeing the shadows cast by her stuffed animals, but then she said the shadow coughed. There's a dusty partial footprint on the window ledge. Nick, what if..."

She couldn't finish, didn't want to think it, because if it were true, she'd placed these kids in danger.

"What if it's the same person who sent the notes and packages?" he finished for her.

She nodded.

He pulled her tight and whispered instructions in her hair. "I want you to call the number on that card we gave you for the FBI. I'm sure they are close by. Tell them what happened and that the person is gone and ask them to come quietly. I'll call Logan."

Where could she go that was safe? Where could she run to protect the ones she loved? She clung to him for a moment, feeding off his strength and his calm.

"Kayles, can you do that for me?"

"Absolutely. What are you going to do?"

His jaw tightened, and she knew there was something he couldn't or wouldn't tell her. "I'm going to see if our guest left a calling card before they show up."

She nodded and ran to grab her phone, resisting the urge to check on Molly again as Nick slipped from the house, silent as a panther.

Chapter 27

NICK FLIPPED OFF the porch light and gazed into the darkness around the house. Logan and Kim lived in a home much like his and Micah's; the neighborhood remained still and quiet with the occasional barking dog or car traveling down the street. Nothing seemed out of the ordinary. And yet it seemed that Janus may have invaded his world yet again.

She'd crossed a line entering Logan's home, terrorizing Molly. Rolling his eyes, he sighed. As if she hadn't already crossed a dozen lines. He stepped off the porch and tucked himself close to the stucco wall, creeping around the corner to where he knew he would find Molly's window. One thing concerned him. Janus hadn't demonstrated carelessness, and a shoeprint was just that. If it was her, had she done that on purpose? Or did she escape right before Kaylan came in the room and hadn't had time to erase the evidence? That thought chilled him. If Janus had been that close to Kaylan with an open window, she'd chosen not to act yet. Which meant she had a plan later if Nick and the SEALs didn't stop chasing her. They couldn't and wouldn't, but neither could they live with the repercussions to their families.

Nick stopped short of Molly's window and crouched low, searching for footprints in the dust. None, not even a broken branch or crushed leaf on the bush growing right next to the window. He was almost sure of it. It'd been Janus.

A flash of white caught his eye, tucked near the root of the bush. He reached for the paper, the beading sweat on his brow chilling at the familiar Russian scrawl. All doubt receded from his mind. A known terrorist stalking American families on American soil made his blood boil. Time to take this up a notch, lock Kaylan away or something. He inwardly groaned. Although if they did that, it would ruin the internship she'd worked so hard for, the one she had almost missed because of Haiti. But her life was far more valuable. He wished he could do something about it, but unless Janus left for overseas and he was tasked with the mission, he could do nothing. Unless…there *was* one other option. But his heart couldn't bear it.

He turned the card over. "I know where you live. I have easy access to those you love. Catch me if you can, little SEAL."

He called Micah. "I got another letter at Logan's."

"Is Kaylan all right? The kids?"

"I'm outside now. They're fine. I don't know what to do. If being close to Kaylan means I put her in danger, then…" He stopped short. He didn't want anyone who might be listening to know she'd rattled them. But if she'd lurked near the window as Kaylan calmed Molly, she knew enough.

"Don't go to the absolute extreme yet, Hawk. The Feds are on it. Let's talk this through before you do what I think you are thinking." The dial tone sounded.

Nick skirted the perimeter of the house, pausing to listen now and then. A car rolled up to the house, lights off and deadly quiet. He sent up a silent prayer of thanks. No use alerting the whole neighborhood. This was a one-time break-in arranged for one sole purpose—creating fear to gain control. She'd only shown interest in Logan's family because she knew Kaylan was there and most likely suspected Nick wouldn't be far behind. Logan couldn't chase her even if he wanted to.

Kaylan stepped from the house to meet the two federal agents coming up the sidewalk. Nick instantly appeared at her side, greeting them and filling them in. He wasn't sure of the next steps, but of one thing he was absolutely certain—his team was ready to make war.

Janus lurked in the shadows of the neighbor's house. Two men scanned the perimeter as Nick and Kaylan stood close, talking in the light streaming from inside.

She'd scared the little girl. She'd made just enough noise to wake her and stayed far enough out of the light to frighten her and make her doubt. That is until that nagging cough.

Nikolai had found her note. She chuckled quietly to herself. She hadn't had this much fun in years. She quite enjoyed this little game of cat and mouse. The cat always won. She relished the victory. Fear remained a worthy and effective tool in her arsenal. If she controlled their emotions, she controlled the chase.

Soon she would leave for a major deal that the boss had thought big enough to appear for. She wondered at the risk. He remained anonymous because he remained hidden. Her alias kept her hidden, and her clients feared to reveal her identity once business was complete. But this meeting had the potential to wreak havoc on everything they'd built. If only he trusted her.

She shivered in the evening air. Fear became a weapon against her, and she determined to double her efforts to make sure her boss was caught if she was. It seemed ironic that the thing that had almost ruined her life so many years ago had chased her down to try and ruin it again. She could run, leave well enough alone.

But they would chase her, and she couldn't let that go—not at the expense of her life, her freedom.

The Feds slipped into their car as Nick and Kaylan went back into the house. She shook her head. Her first impression had been right. He could do better. The meddlesome fool would get herself killed if she kept trying to help. The more Kaylan interfered, the less Janus cared what happened to her. At least that is what she would continue to tell herself. Feeling anything different was simply out of the question.

Her little game was all too real. If Nick wouldn't be intimidated, then the stakes rose. If he played to win, she would have no other choice.

Nick closed the door to the Feds, alone with Kaylan for the first time in weeks. His heart told him to take her in his arms and hold her until this mess ended. But logic told him they needed to address some things. He looked up to find Kaylan watching him and realized his hand rested over the lock on the door.

He dropped his hand and approached her, his lips finding hers. Some kisses made him ready for the wedding. Yesterday. But some, like this one, reassured him that he could spend a lifetime with this woman, not caught up in passion alone but because she symbolized home to him and all the things that lasted long after the fireworks faded.

"Welcome home." She pulled back and rested her hands on his arms. "I missed you."

"Missed you too. Looks like you couldn't stay out of trouble for a few weeks. What in the world am I going to do with you?"

"Me?" She stepped away, laughter and warmth filling her eyes as the threat of danger faded for the moment with him near. "It's not *my* fault."

He joined in her laughter but couldn't escape the gravity of the situation. "Kaylan, I can't leave you defenseless."

"So leave me your pistol next time you go out of town."

"What?"

"C'mon, darlin'." He grinned as her accent thickened. "I grew up in the South with three rowdy brothers, a dad, and a granddad close by, and you don't think I learned a thing or two about guns?"

Nick crossed his arms and tried to picture his sweet girlfriend staring down the barrel of a gun. "I can't see it."

"Well, I didn't say I actually shot at anything living. But I am a pro with old Coke bottles."

"Now that image makes more sense." He reached for her hand. "Seriously, though, Kaylan. If I gave you my gun, could you use it if you needed to? If you or someone else was in danger?"

Nick watched her wrestle with the reality of his words. Her eyes drifted to Molly's door and her grip tightened in his. When she looked him in the eye again, he saw no doubt, only a measure of sadness. "If there is no other option, then yes. I would pull the trigger."

"Kayles, anything around you can be a weapon. Look for a way to leverage your body and your environment to get the upper hand on someone. When adrenaline gets going, you will only have time to react, not think, so make your actions count."

She nodded. "Do me a favor?"

"Anything."

"Please don't let it come to that."

He crushed her to his chest, his fingers running through her hair. "I'll do my best."

But his heart sank to his feet. He was fighting a ghost and could only pray she made a mistake.

Chapter 28

X AND THE FIVE guys from the Ukraine mission reported to the War Room on Saturday morning. Titus had stopped at Starbucks, and everyone gripped cups of steaming coffee, the scent calming Nick's nerves and reminding him of mornings with Kaylan. With the FBI running the case on the home front, the SEALs kept waiting for something to break abroad so they could take the fight to her. Janus had managed to cost them an active member of the team. She had stalked Kaylan, sent threatening letters and tokens to Nick, and overall invaded their lives. She'd poked a beast that should never be riled, and now she would experience their wrath.

X made eye contact with every man. "I realize Janus has hit home for you in ways it hasn't for the rest of the Support Activity 1. That makes doing your jobs even more difficult. Because of the scope and delicacy of this situation, we will take a much larger team on the next mission. But because this is so personal for those in this room, I wanted you to learn what I know ahead of time to prepare yourselves. But if this leaves this room, I will personally throttle the tattle-tale."

Smirks greeted his threat. No one would leak info.

He tossed the photo they'd taken in Nicaragua down in front

of them. The grainy image of a woman in a bungalow felt all too familiar to Nick now. Too bad her features were still incomprehensible. "Meet Anya Petrov, aka Janus. Like I've said before, she works for a much bigger fish. No name for him or her. No photo. No ideas."

Micah elbowed Nick. "Hawk's started calling him the Big Kahuna. How do we catch her and this big fish?"

"Do we have a plan, X?" Nick crossed his arms to curb his anxious energy. He wanted to finish this, marry the girl of his dreams, and never worry about a terrorist invading their home. What if something happened when he deployed? He'd never know and wouldn't be close enough to help.

"Well, I'm stating the obvious, but we all know she has invaded our little community in some way. Now whether she is leaving us these love notes herself or through a courier is the question of the decade, but regardless, she or someone she works with is intimately aware of certain team members' routines and private lives."

All eyes shifted to Nick for a moment, but he kept his gaze centered on X. "So what does that mean? What can we do?"

"Hawk, you don't need me to tell you that we can't do anything. It isn't in our job description."

"So let's fit it in," Micah muttered through gritted teeth.

"Hold your horses there, Bulldog. We might get our chance. Intel came through that a big meeting is brewing between a group in Iran, Janus, and this Big Kahuna." X smirked at Nick. "Apparently it's big enough to bring her boss out of hiding. The top dogs are worried Iran has its sights set on disrupting Israel's new settlements, which is not okay with the administration. There's no love lost between Israeli and American leadership right now, but we want to make sure no fuel is added to the fire."

"Where is this shindig going down, X?" Jay chimed in, smacking on some gum as he rocked back in his chair. Nick could sense the energy radiating off him. He would go hard at the Halloween party that night. Nick caught Micah's eye and nodded. They would need to watch Jay, whose temper tended to flare under the influence of beer and a pending deployment.

"That remains unclear. It's possible that we are looking at another Yalta trip, or a little farther down the coast in Sevastopol. If not, we are looking at a very uncomfortable operation in the Iranian mountains."

"Bring it on." Colt rubbed his hands together in anticipation.

X sighed, and Nick knew the burden he carried weighed heavier in light of Logan's surgery. It had hit them all hard. "Look, guys, I know we signed up for this. But I don't think we ever sign up thinking the fight will physically invade our homes. I know you're angry. You're looking for revenge. You want to protect this team you care about, and you want to protect our families." He slapped the table. "But take this on board: don't be stupid. Logan is someone we can't replace, but at least he came home. We won't come home draped in a flag. We will have a larger team, more manpower, and more eyes."

Heads bobbed around the room in silent affirmation.

X waved his hand. "Now get out of here and get ready for that Halloween party you all have been yapping about for weeks."

The guys filed out of the room, somber, but eager for a night of laughter. This costume party would be epic, of that Nick had no doubt. He nearly groaned thinking about the costumes Kaylan had picked out. "Hawk, Bulldog, you got a sec?" X called.

Nick nodded to the rest of the team as they paused at the door.

"You guys don't need to hear this." X waved at the rest of the team. His Wisconsin nasal accent leaked through under pressure, and Nick grinned. So different from Kaylan and Micah's Southern drawl that stretched and deepened when they were tired. As Nick approached X, he noted black circles under his eyes. His shoulders slumped slightly as he leaned against the wall, an unusual pose for the military man.

X sighed and hung his head. "I don't know what to tell you two, and I'm not entirely sure what to do here. We are highly trained to take on all enemies, but we usually don't count on them terrorizing our domestic space." He looked up and met their gazes, his eyes carrying a new weight and a warning. Nick tensed.

The military bravado faded away, leaving only their friend. "Logan is one thing, but Kaylan...she hits you both at the heart. Can you handle what's coming without doing something stupid?"

"C'mon, X..."

He held up a hand silencing Micah. "Ever heard of Rudyard Kipling?" He didn't wait for an answer as he began to pace the small space in front of them. "He was a poet and writer in the late 1800s, early 1900s."

Micah snickered. "Man, seriously?"

"What are you laughing at, Bulldog? I may be a po' boy from Wisconsin, but I took several literature classes in college."

Micah choked back his laughter. Nick inwardly chuckled, loving the depth some people hid that emerged in unexpected situations. It astounded him that X could and chose to wax philosophical.

X continued as if Micah hadn't interrupted. "Kipling wrote this poem called 'The Law of the Jungle,' which reminds me a lot of the teams. One of the lines says, 'For the strength of the Pack is the Wolf, and the strength of the Wolf is the Pack.'" He came to a standstill in front of them again.

"That makes sense. We're trained to live or die together. As an individual, we can ring the bell in training and quit, but each man's success is largely determined by how well he can contribute and compel his team to greatness," Micah responded, his grin fading.

"So you're comparing us to a wolf pack?" Nick processed. "We're only as strong as our weakest member. Only as united as the least loyal man. That's why we all specialize in different skills and spend so much time traveling to schools all over the country."

X's voice dropped an octave, gravelly and insistent, passion and something else, almost desperation dripping from each word. "The strength of the team is the SEAL, and the strength of the SEAL is the men around him. This business with Janus hit home for you two more than anyone else on the team. But Janus is another target like anyone else, and we have a job to do, regardless of personal cost. We need you two to be one hundred percent."

Nick bit his tongue, frustration flooding every nerve and setting them on fire. To say that this pursuit wasn't personal was a lie. But he knew how to do his job, and he did it with pure focus, pure passion, and pure adrenaline.

"We've got this." Nick affirmed, and Micah followed with a nod.

Skepticism clouded X's eyes, and he ran a hand over his head. Lines ringed his face, whether from war or from two divorces and a third marriage, Nick didn't know. He couldn't miss this manhunt. They had to end this.

"Let's get it done." With a final swig of his coffee, X nodded and exited the room. Micah and Nick left the building without speaking. When they reached Nick's Jeep, they paused. The sun hung low in a blue sky smudged with a few cotton white clouds. Nick noticed the tension in Micah's shoulders, the way his hands clenched and unclenched, knuckles turning white. He knew the feeling. It felt like knives pricked his stomach, and every nerve in his body stood at high alert. A car door slammed in the parking lot, and he snapped his neck, following the sound.

Micah threw his arms over the car door. Top down and wind in their hair, Nick loved driving the beach in this ride. But not even a surfing trip could release the anxiety he felt.

"I don't know how to separate my heart and head from this, Hawk. I need to turn off the emotion, turn off caring. Forget everything happening here."

"Nah, man. You need to focus it. Your strength is your passion, Bulldog. Don't let her take that from you, but don't let it rule you either."

Micah growled and smacked the car with his palm.

"Hey, easy on the ride. She's my baby."

A smile played at the corner of Micah's mouth. Somewhere in the last couple of weeks they'd switched roles. Micah usually existed to cheer him up, be the life of the party, and lighten the mood. Nick reached in the back of the black Jeep and tossed a beach ball.

"C'mon. Your sister is dying to get us ready for the party."

Micah looked up at the sinking sun. "Think we'll get a full moon tonight?" He howled and laughed as they climbed in the car.

"If we do, it will only enhance your true nature."

"What, handsome beast?"

Nick chuckled as they peeled out of the parking lot and pulled off base. "Nope." He winked at Micah as he slipped on his shades and gunned the engine. "I was thinking more yappy mutt."

The wind sucked away Micah's loud protests, and Nick took a moment to let the sun, wind, and drive tear away the worry. They worked hard and played hard, and Janus would not control his life. Of that, he remained absolutely certain. X's words echoed in his ears as his mind settled in. His strength came from his belief in God, his country, and his new family. He couldn't separate that, but he could allow it to motivate him.

As they pulled into their driveway, the familiar gray paneling of their home welcomed him, Kaylan's car in front. His mind whirled with X's words. He knew he had to be ready. He muttered under his breath as they opened the door, "For the strength of the Pack is the Wolf, and the strength of the Wolf is the Pack."

Chapter 29

Nick would never be able to show his face around the team again. Already he felt emasculated, and he hadn't even changed clothes yet. True to her wish, Kaylan and Nick were going as Alice and the Mad Hatter. He didn't mind dressing up, but he loathed makeup. Nevertheless, his face cracked and tightened under layers of white face paint.

"Hold still, babe. You're making it crack." She ran a blush brush over his cheek and studied the picture of Johnny Depp as the Mad Hatter that she had printed and taped to the bathroom mirror.

"You may need to give me a list of what I can and can't do tonight. Because I will forget not to move and smile."

She shoved him. "Don't get smart," she said with a smile in her voice. "You can be still for me right now, though."

"Did you know it is near impossible to make a SEAL be still unless you stick us under a hide with a gun in our hands? That's life or death. This…" He gestured to the mirror where the painted face of a stranger stared back at him. "Well, actually, this might be a death wish."

She laughed. "Shut up and quit whining." She replaced the blush and picked up eye makeup. Before she could open it, he reached for her waist and pulled her onto his lap.

"Nick!" She giggled as he poked her ribs. "We don't have time for this."

He kissed her shoulder, resting his forehead there. "There's always time for this."

She grew still and slipped her arm around his neck. "Rough day?"

He shook his head, realizing the events of the day seemed distant with her in his arms. His world, his life was right here, no matter how many silly costumes he wore. He'd do anything for her. His gaze drifted to the long brown velvet coat hanging on the bathroom door and the purple and lime green scarf draped over it. He cringed. He really would do anything.

"Tell me why we are going in this getup again."

"I thought it would be fun and cute." Her green eyes seemed fathomless, like a forest that kept going forever—one he couldn't wait to explore. After the past eleven months they were as familiar to him as his own. Mascara dressed eyelashes he knew to be a shade darker than her auburn hair. Freckles dusted her pixy nose and cheeks, fading the less time they spent at the beach. Her auburn hair fell straight around her shoulders, ready to be tucked under a blonde wig she'd purchased to play the part of Alice.

"SEALs don't do cute."

"Well, then think of it as very macho. It takes a real man to play the Mad Hatter."

"Yeah, but we could have been anything."

Her eyes lowered, hiding under her lashes, and Nick's curiosity was piqued. "I'm guessing there is more to this than fun and games."

She shrugged and her fingers wound into the hair on the back of his head. "I think *Alice in Wonderland* reminds me to believe the smallest person can make the biggest difference. The impossible is always possible."

Her fingers drifted through his hair, sending shivers down his back. He leaned into her touch, gentle but firm, just like her. His Kaylan.

"I used to think we were impossible. That somehow our meeting each other was a mistake. Now I realize it wasn't the right time, and that if it is the Lord's perfect plan, all things are possible." A smile lit her lips. "Even a relationship between a California Navy SEAL and a Southern homebody. And ever when it seemed like no hope existed for us." A blush colored her cheeks, as a certain sadness wilted her expression. "Amazing what the Lord brought through the death of my best friend." Her fingers drifted to his face. His breath caught at her tenderness. "He gave me you."

He cradled her face in his hands, in awe that after the mistakes of his past, the Lord would grant him this precious gem. "You're amazing, you know that?" He lowered her face to his and whispered against her lips, "A virtuous woman, who can find? Her worth is far above rubies." Their lips met, and in their touch he felt all the longing for something more. He felt a future.

Pulling back, he rested his forehead on hers. "You'll mess up your makeup," she protested, standing up and opening the eye shadow case. "Good thing we didn't put your lipstick on yet."

"My what?"

Her lips curled over her teeth, hiding a smile. "Close your eyes."

He rolled his eyes and acquiesced. He'd humored her this much. Might as well take the full beating. He peeked at the picture taped on the mirror. Bright frizzy hair stuck out from a top hat with a bow tied around it. A white face stared back at him with pink ringing the eyes and lips. White mascara hung from the eye lashes. He snapped his eyes shut and groaned. This would either be really great, or he would never hear the end of it.

Kaylan's fingers cupped his face, tilting it up to the light as the brush made a smooth arc beneath his eyes. He could smell lavender perfume and her vanilla shampoo each time she moved or flung her hair. He reached for her legs, squeezing right behind her knee, causing her to squeal and laugh.

"Nick Carmichael, be still."

He opened his eyes and studied her, concentration etched in the muscles of her face and a smile curving her lips, her creative juices flowing as she transformed his face into a maniacal masterpiece.

"So anything's possible, hmm?"

She met his eyes for a moment and a faint blush colored her cheeks. "Anything's possible."

"Does that mean it just might be possible for me to ask you to marry me?"

She stilled at his words and met his eyes, curiosity clouding her face. "Are you asking?"

He grinned. "I'm planning on it. But not just yet. Not like this. I just want to make sure you actually believe what you're saying. We can make this work. You're willing to go where I go and be part of this patchwork family from all over the country."

She ran her fingers through his hair and her Southern drawl seeped through, causing his heart to leap. "Darlin', you're stuck with me."

"Perfect." He looked in the mirror and determined the job done. Without hesitating, he stood up and kissed her, her mouth moving perfectly with his.

"I don't think I've ever seen a guy kiss a girl and have more makeup on than she does," Micah observed from the door. He crunched down on an apple, his arms folded on his chest. Megan had decided to go with Jay, so Micah chose his own costume. He wore a skintight green tank top with a turtle shell resembling abs on the front. A red mask sat loosely around his eyes, and a thin bandana ringed his head.

Nick pulled back from Kaylan as she chuckled and turned to face her brother. "Check you out. You'll stop hearts at the party."

Nick did a doubletake. "Are you kidding me? He gets to go as one of the ninja turtles and I'm wearing a wig and makeup? Who are the other three?"

"Jay, Colt, and Titus. We decided not to tell you when we found out what Kaylan had in mind. Better to let you humiliate yourself than have you change your mind at the last minute."

Kaylan's hand rested over her mouth, but her eyes sparkled. Nick grabbed her around the waist. "I must really love you to put up with this."

"All right, all right. I give up." Kaylan laughed and ripped away from him, hurrying to her brother's side.

Micah stopped chewing for a moment, hearing such strong sentiment for the first time. A wicked grin spread across his face as Kaylan slipped out of the bathroom to change. "You better mean it too. I have a mean set of nunchucks tonight, and I'm not afraid to use them." With that he strutted from the room, leaving Nick to don the rest of his ensemble, secretly admiring his girlfriend's ingenuity and dreading his teammate's comments.

Kaylan tugged at the curly blonde wig on her head, already regretting the accessory. Her hair felt sweaty beneath the getup, but she was proud of their outfits for the character-themed Halloween party as they knocked on the door to Titus and Liza's place. The door opened with a burst of noise and light, and Kaylan, Nick, and Micah entered the fray amidst hugs, back pats, laughter, and wolf whistles. Carved pumpkins sat on each stair going to the second floor. Candy bowls sat out on every surface. Kaylan gave Liza a hug and followed her to the kitchen to make the punch she had brought from home. The atmosphere overwhelmed her.

"It's a lot, isn't it?" Liza leaned in to shout. Her plastic gold Cleopatra headdress brushed Kaylan's cheek as they pulled ginger ale and sherbet out of the grocery sacks. "Girl, this is nothing.

Last year it was at Logan and Kim's. Titus and I were just dating then. Talk about pranks and dangerous activity." She rolled her eyes. "I swore Titus to good behavior tonight. But"—she winked in Kaylan's direction as they watched Jay do a backflip off the couch through the living room door—"*behave* is a relative term to SEALs." She patted Kaylan's arm as they set about making the punch. "Don't worry, honey. You'll get used to it and come to love it."

Liza sauntered off, her caramel skin and sleek black hair enhanced by her floor-length cream gown. Normally a shy woman, Liza blossomed in her own home as she met Titus and walked into his waiting arms. Kaylan leaned against the door frame and smiled, taking in the action. Nick and Micah battled Jay and Colt in a vicious Ping-Pong battle in the corner of the living room. Nick's red wig and hat sat cockeyed on his head, his white face paint running a bit with his sweat. Despite her protests and Kaylan's coaxing her to be Micah's date, Megan had come with Jay to the party dressed as a mesmerizing evil pixy. Micah had agreed to keep an eye on the two of them. He and Kaylan both agreed that Jay and Megan would make a very pretty but highly volatile couple, which would be a bad idea.

The door opened with a loud bang and the sound of a goblin cackle as a very pregnant Kim wheeled Logan into the room. Other SEALs from SEAL teams 3 and 5 filtered in behind them with wives and girlfriends.

"Hey, hey. Let's get this party started!" Logan shouted into the room as Kim met Kaylan in the kitchen with a plate of cookies. The guys halted Ping-Pong as Logan rolled his wheelchair into the kitchen to help his wife unload.

"Party already started, Pops." Micah pounded Logan on the back, and Kaylan winced, her own body aching as she eyed Logan's limb, his bandage wrapped in crackly brown paper.

Nick tossed his arm around Kaylan while grinning at Logan. "What are you supposed to be?"

"Peg-Leg Jack, son." He coughed and looked between Nick and Kaylan. "Are you Raggedy Ann and Barbie?"

"C'mon, Logan. Mad Hatter and Alice in Wonderland." Kaylan giggled, trying to pull away from Nick's responding poke to her rib cage. "What's Kim supposed to be?"

Kim winced. "Please don't ask. Please…"

Logan winked at Kaylan and rubbed Kim's extended belly beneath her cotton shirt and black vintage-looking vest that didn't quite contain her stomach. "Kim's my wench."

Micah whistled and rolled his eyes. "So basically, the couples failed in the costume department this year, and it's ninja turtles for the win."

"You forgot the teenage part of that."

Jay grinned at Kaylan over his cup. "Nah. That was intentional. No one would mistake us for teenagers. I'm all man." He flexed his tan arm, his muscles popping.

"Hey, save the gun show for another time and not in front of my girlfriend."

Jay's smile turned wicked, and Kaylan wondered how many hearts he'd broken. "Scared you won't measure up, Hawk?" He dropped his arm around Megan as she rolled her eyes, unable to hide a grin.

Micah strode in between them, showing off his muscles. "Please. She grew up with the ultimate gun show. Ain't nothing better than this."

Kaylan chuckled, used to testosterone-driven performances, having grown up with three brothers. Leave it to Micah to diffuse a situation with humor and the proper perspective. She leaned into Nick, his red wig tickling her face.

"Oh." Kim bent near the cabinet with a hand on her stomach.

The room quieted as Kaylan moved to her side, placing a hand on Logan's shoulder to reassure him as she passed.

Kim's smile came out as more of a grimace. "Just baby making noise. I'm not so sure Molly is going to get her little sister. This feels like a little boy soccer player."

She leaned over a little more as she sagged against the counter. "That was a big one."

Kaylan noticed the sweat beading on Kim's brow, the way her body curled in around her baby bump, the strain creating tiny lines near her eyes.

"Kim, are you in labor?" she whispered.

"I'm sure it's just Braxton Hicks."

"You're due in two weeks, right?"

Kim nodded.

Logan wheeled his chair closer, careful to avoid hitting his leg. "Honey, do we need to go to the hospital?"

Kim put a hand on his shoulder and stood to her full height, all five foot two inches. "I don't think so. Go have fun with the guys." She smiled and Kaylan saw the strength in her stance, the courage that lay just beneath the surface, and the care she had for Logan. She envied their relationship and their home.

Her gaze drifted to Nick, where he stood watching her by the door. His smile warmed, and despite the face paint, his eyes spoke directly to her heart as he nodded. They could have that someday. The more she thought about it, the harder the wait became.

Chapter 30

THEIR SMALL CROWD had grown to over forty in one small house. Kaylan could barely move, but that wasn't what bothered her. A figure wandered in and out of the house, a figure in a black hooded robe, with a black half-mask, wielding a scythe. Hopefully plastic. But that still wasn't the problem. As she drifted in and out of the groups, sipping from a plastic cup, Kaylan had the odd feeling that the figure watched her. She shook her head, sure she was paranoid from all of Nick's gun and safety chats since he had returned. But she still couldn't shake her anxiety. Kaylan moved to a corner, searching for the flash of black garments in the crowd.

Every few minutes she saw the figure again, a slight frame just over five foot. But the angel of death never stayed in one place and never let Kaylan catch up with her, though she stopped occasionally to talk to others. Kaylan began to weave through the crowds, her eyes peeled. As the clock ticked toward midnight, Kaylan's dread grew.

Something felt wrong. Her nerves were on edge from all the notes and threats. That had to be it. She was in a home full of SEALs. Surely the terrorist they chased wouldn't be so dumb as to show up here.

She jumped as a hand wrapped around her wrist.

"Whoa, easy there, Jumpy. Where've you been?" Nick's fingers slipped through hers, slowing her heart rate.

She scanned the crowd again, her gaze colliding with the angel of death lurking near a window by the Ping-Pong table. She tightened her grip on his hand.

"Kaylan." He whirled her around to face him, but she twisted in his arms trying to find the figure. Gone again. She shook her head.

"Kaylan Richards, talk to me now. What's wrong?"

"Nothing. It's just…nothing. My imagination is playing tricks on me. It's Halloween, after all. I've always hated the creepy, scary parts of this day." She offered a small smile.

"Uh-huh." Nick saw right through the charade and immediately tugged her into the kitchen where the noise dialed down and only a few people lingered, drinking punch and eating snacks. Kim and Liza stood laughing by the sink as Liza washed dishes. "All right, spill it."

Kaylan took in his wig cocked the wrong way and his tan skin peeking through the white face paint. She bit her lip. "I'm sorry. I can't take you seriously right now."

"That's it. You are never choosing our costumes again." He grabbed the wig and top hat off his head and set it on the counter.

She laughed, the anxiety easing a bit. "We'll talk about it next year."

He crossed his arms over his chest, his sandy blond hair sticking out at odd angles on his head. "We'll talk about what we are dressing as together next year, but right now you are going to tell me why your face matches the color of the walls." He smirked. "Well, even more than usual."

"Ha, ha. Very funny." She glanced around again. "There's this person here, and I keep catching her staring at me. Only it's someone I don't know."

"Okay. You don't know about half of the people here. Care to explain that a bit more?"

Something black flashed out of the corner of her eye. She swiveled, catching a glimpse of the black-robed figure with a group outside on the patio. Kaylan's grip tightened on the cabinet as she strained to see where she had gone.

Nick's hand cupped her chin and brought her eyes to meet his. "I need you to slow down, focus, and talk to me."

"It's dumb."

"Kaylan, your instincts are not dumb. Talk to me." She could feel the energy he controlled in his touch, the frustration and desire to fix that he held at bay.

"There's someone creeping me out. Someone dressed as an angel of death. I keep finding her staring at me across the room but then she's gone before I can get close."

His grip on her chin tightened, and she pulled away. "Nick, you're hurting me."

"Sorry, babe." But now he scanned the crowd, setting her nerves on edge again. Normally calm, his now attentive demeanor scared her.

"Nick, I'm probably imagining things. Please don't worry about it. Let's just enjoy the party."

Nick caught Micah's eye across the room, and her brother immediately headed their direction. "What's up?"

"Kayles, describe this person to me."

Micah stiffened at her side. Something was happening she wasn't aware of, something they couldn't or wouldn't tell her. Was the person threatening her not a man, but a woman?

"She's in costume, Nick. Black hooded gown or cloak. Short. Probably just over five foot, maybe a little taller. Black half-mask, Phantom of the Opera style. Long black wig. Carrying a plastic silver scythe. And I keep feeling like she's watching me, but I can't get close. Last I saw she was outside on the patio."

A groan sounded from the sink. Kaylan's head snapped toward the sound. Kim's expression radiated pain. She darted to her friend's side.

"Kim?"

"I thought it was just indigestion or Braxton Hicks."

"After three babies you didn't recognize contractions? How far apart are they?"

Kim chuckled wearily. "I was in denial."

Liza put her hand on her hip. "Girl, I've been timing it every time you wince. They are about seven minutes apart now."

Titus entered the room in time to overhear his wife. "That's my girl." He kissed her on the lips before grabbing the keys from the counter. "I'll get the car. Bulldog, round up Logan, and Liza and I'll drive them to the hospital. You two"—he pointed to Kaylan and Nick—"are on house patrol along with Bulldog." He glanced at his watch. "It's midnight. Give 'em another hour, then kick 'em all out. We'll call you from the hospital. And maybe keep an eye on Jay. I think he had too much to drink."

Kaylan leaned past Titus to see Jay flirting with Megan in the corner, his laugh a little too wild and his motions a little too uncoordinated.

"We've got it. Call us, please." Nick pounded Logan on the back, and Kaylan kissed Kim's cheek. She remembered the night with Sarah Beth and Rhonda in the slums, watching a beautiful Haitian baby enter the world. Hope. He had signified hope and new life in the midst of destruction. And the new Carpenter baby? He or she spelled hope after loss too. She couldn't wait to meet the new addition. She put her hand on Kim's belly. "See you soon, baby." She hugged Kim and walked them to the door. Nick and Micah helped Kim and Logan into the car.

Within minutes Nick and Micah were back at her side as they rejoined the party. "Now about this angel of death character, sis. What'd she look like?"

Kaylan's head whipped around. She'd forgotten. She scanned the crowd, looking for a flash of all black. The party had thinned out some. "She's in a black robe, Micah. I don't know what else to tell you."

Micah met Nick's eyes. "With all the weird things going on lately, I'd like to check this out real quick. What do you think, Hawk?"

Nick nodded. "Let's just make sure it's nothing. Kaylan, you stay here." The two of them fanned out, while Kaylan fidgeted, her concern growing. Despite their attempt at nonchalance, Nick and Micah's attentiveness heightened her anxiety—and her frustration. Once again they were looking for a ghost. This one just happened to actually be in costume.

After twenty minutes of wandering around, they met back in the kitchen, admitting defeat. "She must have slipped out when everything happened with Kim," Nick said, rubbing Kaylan's shoulders.

"Now I know it was nothing. I'm sorry for making a big deal out of it."

"Kaylan, I think your instincts are better than that. But you're right. Let's just clean up." Nick grabbed a handful of trash bags from the pantry and handed one to Kaylan.

"I'll start shoving people out the door." Micah left the room, his voice carrying through the house. "All right, happy Halloween! Party's over, so it's time to go creep someone else out unless you want to stay and help pick up."

A few groans followed his announcement. Kaylan and Nick chuckled. "I knew your brother was the perfect man for that job."

"Never a dull moment with him."

"Has he always been like that?"

"Pretty much. You know Micah. He can be the life of the party or the most serious guy on the planet, but he's always there when you need him."

"His sister's kind of like that, too."

"Oh, yeah? Life of the party?"

Nick chuckled. "Well, maybe more the dependable part of that."

She smiled. "I'll take it."

Within minutes the house emptied, and the three of them collected plates and cups from every surface downstairs.

Kaylan stopped to catch her breath, then remembered her roommate. "Anyone see where Megan went?"

"I made sure Colt took her home before tucking Jay in bed," Micah hollered from the kitchen. She heard the faucet switch on in the kitchen.

"Perfect." She cast a glance into the dark hallway at the top of the landing. "I'll check upstairs." Kaylan dodged the jack-o-lanterns as she climbed, lugging the trash bag. Her feet ached, and she'd abandoned her wig. Bed sounded better and better as the clock neared 2:00 a.m. She opened and shut the two bedroom doors, noting everything seemed fine. She stepped into the bathroom, grabbing a couple of cups off the counter, and stopped cold. An envelope addressed to her sat on top of a bouquet of dead white lilies. Their petals and leaves lay shriveled on the counter. She reached for the envelope and slid her finger under the flap, withdrawing a piece of stationery.

Kaylan,

Tell your boyfriend and his friends he should have left well enough alone. He can no longer stop what is coming. It is your fate to end up like your friend.

Janus

Kaylan fought a scream as the image of Sarah Beth rose before her eyes. Who would taunt her using her best friend?

"Kaylan, they had the baby!" Micah shouted from downstairs. She made herself turn and follow his voice, the letter and bouquet now clutched in one hand and the trash bag dragging the floor behind her. Her mind raced. Who was Janus? Someone she was supposed to know? The person the team chased?

"It's a girl, Kayles. Molly is going to be stoked. Nadia Elaine Carpenter. Six pounds, twelve ounces, twenty-one inches long, and all her fingers and toes. Until y'all start giving me some nieces and nephews to entertain, I'm going to spoil the Carpenter kids rotten."

He stopped as he met her eyes, and then his gaze drifted to the flowers in her hand. "Kayles…"

"Micah, who's Janus?"

She heard a bag hit the floor in the kitchen, and Nick darted into view. "What did you just say?" He spotted the note and dead lilies in her hand. As the blood drained from his face, she knew. "Give it to me."

She descended the last few steps and stood in front of them. Fatigue made her eyes cross. She leaned into the banister behind her. "Answer my question, Nick."

"Give it to me. Now." She shrank back at the sharp edge in his voice and noticed Micah shoot him a glance.

She handed him the letter and flowers, the dry stems and petals crackling as they transferred hands. Wrapping her arms around herself, she fought to stay in the present. She needed air. She needed to clear the image of rubble and Sarah Beth from her head. And she was tired of the secrecy. Tired of not knowing who or what threatened her.

"I'll take the trash out." She shoved past them, grabbing a couple other bags from the kitchen and barreling out the door. She could almost taste the desire to run and hide. She gritted her teeth. New life. New start. New memories. "Lord, I'm tired. When will my memories stop shaking my present?"

She dropped the bags in the trash and slowly moved back to the house, thankful for the fresh breeze winging its way through the backyard. She sat on the patio and put her head in her hands, searching for the strength to let go.

Nick watched Kaylan head out of the house, her shoulders slumped and her hands shaking a bit. He'd messed that up, let his fear dominate his calm.

"Dude, what was that?"

"She was here. She left a note for Kaylan. And it freaked me out, Bulldog. What are we going to do?"

"Let's read the note first and take it one step at a time."

"Since when did you become the rational one?"

"Apparently since you lost your mind and your ability to keep your cool."

Nick glared. "What am I supposed to do?"

Micah snatched the note from his hand and held it in front of them both. "Like I said, one step at a time."

Together they read the short note. Nick noticed the paper was different. Same handwriting, just in English this time.

"You think the person Kaylan saw was Janus?"

"I don't know, Bulldog."

"Is there anyone close to her that could be Janus or a courier?"

Nick ran his hand over his face, wiping away makeup. "There are two women who moved to the neighborhood in the last few months. Both travel a lot with their jobs. Kaylan's met both of them and says they are nice. I've met one. But I don't know. It could be anyone. Someone at church. Someone who crossed paths with her during her internship."

Nick's hands grew sweaty. He rubbed them together as his gaze drifted toward the kitchen window. He could see Kaylan on the patio outside, her back rigid. "But a neighbor or friend at church would make sense. It would explain how she knew when we went to Alabama or when we were deployed and got back. It would explain how she knows where we live. She has the perfect stalking position since we are around Kaylan so much." He ran a hand over his face, chipping away at the remaining face paint. "There's only one way to find out."

Micah nodded. "Any of them resemble the woman we saw in Nicaragua?"

Nick ran a hand through his hair and sighed. "I don't know, man. It literally could be anyone. Either way, Janus just upped her game. This just got even more dangerous for Kaylan."

Micah nodded. "I'll call the FBI, let them know. Speaking of dangerous"—Micah motioned to the back door—"you might want to go clean up your mess."

Nick groaned. "I don't know what to do."

"Apologize. Explain as much as you can."

"You don't get it, Bulldog. They are targeting your sister because of me. Of us."

Micah's voice grew quiet and cold. "I get it, Hawk. Believe me, I get it. But I'm more worried what would happen now if we stepped out of the picture than if we stay close to her."

Nick shook his head and headed for the patio, leaving Micah to make his phone call. He could see Kaylan through the back door. His heart settled a bit knowing she was nearby and okay. Should he put space between them? Would Janus just target the team if he were out of Kaylan's life until they caught her? He couldn't bear the thought of someone harming Kaylan. He thought back to the note and understood why she'd been so rattled. She had no idea the danger she was in, but she did understand the reference to Sarah Beth. If he had to guess, her reaction had been based on that more than anything else.

He slammed his fist on the counter, unsure what to do or what this conversation would look like. Catching a glimpse of his reflection in the window, he paused. The face staring back looked frightened, haunted. He couldn't remember the last time he'd felt that way. Unless...he could. It was the last time he'd thought he'd lost Kaylan and couldn't do anything to stop it. Last January in Haiti.

He pushed past the reflection to study the woman outside. Her shoulders shook slightly. Her chin rested on her arms and her hair hung in a limp pony tail that stopped between her shoulder blades. He couldn't leave her. Didn't know how. She'd just reentered his life for good, moved to his city, integrated into his world. But was it best for her? With a ring box tucked away in his room at home, he needed to make up his mind quickly. The answer to all his questions lurked just out of reach in the shadows.

Chapter 31

KAYLAN KNEW THE sound of his footfalls as well as she knew her own heartbeat. Funny how more time with a person bred familiarity with the most basic habits. He sank down next to her on the patio.

They sat like that for what felt like hours. She heard every car that passed by, the sound of the wind whipping through the streets. But loudest of all seemed to be the roar in her head, dark memories still fighting for prominence. Tears pricked her eyes, but she refused to let them win, let an unknown force scare her back to the cave she'd made inside herself months before. It had almost cost her the man she loved.

Loved. The commitment bound her to him regardless of a ring. As certainly as she knew life had not ended with Sarah Beth's death, she knew life had only just begun with Nick Carmichael. She couldn't turn her back on that. If only she could be as strong as Kim.

Nick's arm settled around her, and she gave into his embrace, resting her head on his shoulder. He'd always been her rock. But the man she'd seen in the entryway had somehow snapped. What if she was in danger that even he couldn't protect her from?

"Kayles, I'm sorry for letting my temper get the better of me.

You asked a question I couldn't answer, and it scared me." His fingers traced patterns down her arm. She shivered, leaning in closer to him. "Please forgive me?"

She sighed and nodded. Closing her eyes, she pressed into him, imagining everything was okay, remembering the bliss of Labor Day weekend when he had told her he loved her and everything seemed right in the world. Now fear and uncertainty filled her. "Can we talk it out before you snap, next time?"

He groaned. "I told you I have some anger issues occasionally."

"Can you tell me anything?"

"Kaylan, please don't make this more difficult than it needs to be. All I can tell you is that hopefully we will wrap this up in one more mission."

Knowing this was the price for dating a SEAL, she swallowed the urge to ask more. Demanding answers wouldn't change the reality anyway. They could do nothing but wait. For now, she was safe.

The quiet stretched between them again, and she forced herself to relax. She wondered if it would be like this fifty years from now when time had bonded their souls so much that they could say as much in the quiet as in conversation. It had been like that with Sarah Beth, although that bubbly blonde had rarely shut up for a moment. Kaylan smiled at the memory, thankful Nick had met her.

Nick's deep voice broke through her reverie. "You know, growing up, Mom hated Halloween. Since I was an only child, our house was always full of the neighborhood guys, and they loved my mom. She never let us dress up as anything scary for Halloween. When I was really little, she dressed me up as the Cookie Monster."

Kaylan laughed. "Still got those pictures?"

"Somewhere. Buried in a box. Where you can never use them for blackmail."

"C'mon." She could hear her Alabama twang emerging more as the night wore on. "I'm sure you looked cute."

"I think we've covered this. Me and cute do not mix." He squeezed her knee playfully.

She shrieked and tried to pull away, but his arm tightened around her. "All right, all right, I give. I'm sure even at three you looked very tough." She rolled her eyes but slowly quieted, sensing he had more on his mind than costumes.

"When I was ten, I decided I wanted to be G.I. Joe. Dad helped me go all out with my costume. Toy guns, camo, patches on my uniform, the whole nine yards. When the other guys came over to go trick-or-treating, I felt tough and in charge. I barked orders all night."

He shook his head, his sigh carrying in the quiet breeze. "Oh, Kaylan, if only I'd known then." He turned to face her. She could barely discern his features in the dim glow of the bulb hanging next to the screen door. "I don't know how to keep you safe right now. Even in a house full of Navy SEALs, this woman still had the nerve to come in and this time leave you a direct threat. I have no idea what she'll do."

His eyes were wild, and for the first time Kaylan feared his next words. "I'm wondering if it is best for us to spend some time apart. Maybe if she thinks we broke up, she'll leave you alone."

Emotions roared through her, filling her ears. His words stung in places where scars from Haiti hadn't quite calloused. She couldn't, wouldn't be abandoned. And she wouldn't walk away from this. She'd lost one best friend. She refused to lose another to something outside her control.

"Are you kidding me?"

"Kaylan, I…"

"No, shut up and listen."

He pulled back, his eyes regarding her, uncertain.

"Don't you dare break up with me or pull away. You aren't

199

allowed to do that. You want me to let you leave, to fight for your country. You want me to support you like Kim does for Logan. You want to raise a family with me. But you want to walk away now? I think it's pretty clear that we are better together, stronger together. And I refuse to let something shake our relationship. No more earthquakes, Nick. Do you understand?" Tears rolled down her cheeks, but anger overrode the fear. "I will not lose you too. You got it?"

A small smile lit his face, but uncertainty clouded his eyes. "Kaylan, you aren't losing me. This is temporary. Just so she thinks…"

"I don't care what she thinks. What happens if this comes up when we get married? We won't separate then. No." She shook her head, determined to fight this, determined to never hide or cower again. "We fight this. We figure it out together. And we do what we need to."

He pulled her tight against him, his hands running through her tangled hair. "I don't know what I would do if I lost you."

"That's usually my line. You trust the Lord. And we do this together."

"Kaylan, you don't get it. If I can't protect you, if something happened to you while I'm gone…"

"Stop. That's not your job, Nick."

"It is my job to protect you, to love you, to keep you safe."

She knew he would pack her in a bubble and send her to Antarctica if he could. She traced the hard cut of his jaw, the stubble growing there, the faint traces of white left over from where he had scrubbed his face. She loved the safety she felt in his presence. But too often he tried to play God for her.

She'd wanted that after Haiti, wanted it more than anything because she'd thought God wasn't a safe place for her. He had allowed the earthquake. But as she saw hundreds rise up after the earthquake to follow "the best way," as so many Haitians referred to it, she couldn't help but acknowledge that even in the moments that shook her faith, God remained good and in control. Of all things. Even if things weren't her version of "good."

"Babe, you can't protect me from the world."

"Kaylan, if you agree to marry me that will be a big part of the 'husband' job description."

"That's not what I meant. Nick, ultimately that job belongs to the Lord. He gives you that position in my life, but He alone can truly protect me. Don't take on yourself what isn't yours. Trust Him with this, with me, with whatever comes."

He rested his forehead on hers. "When did you get so smart?"

"Some guy shared that with me early this year. He can be my knight in shining armor, but not my King."

"Sounds pretty smart. Whatever happened to him?"

"He forgets from time to time. But thankfully he has someone pretty awesome around to remind him."

She could feel his grin charge the air even though she couldn't see it. He placed a gentle kiss on her lips before pulling her to her feet and wrapping his arms around her. "Well, I guess he better keep her around then, hmm? No matter what comes."

Kaylan wrapped her arms around his neck, loving the fact that for once she could help him. She kissed him this time, reassuring, trusting him. "No matter what," she whispered against his lips.

They returned to help Micah finish with the house. In the morning they would see the baby, she would ask more questions about Janus, and they would determine a plan. Together. No matter what, their relationship was worth fighting for.

Chapter 32

Nick had promised her one day of no worries, a date. Really the first one they'd had with just the two of them since she had moved to California several months before. Between the move, a deployment, Logan's injury, taking care of his family, the threats from Janus, Nick's training, and her internship they had very little quality time alone.

Nothing could ruin what lay ahead. Church had been sweet that morning, especially after their tough conversation at Titus and Liza's. Despite Kaylan's adamant declaration to stay together no matter what, she could feel his distance, the way his eyes shifted through the restaurant patrons as they sat down under an umbrella at their favorite café in Coronado.

"Have I told you lately how thankful I am that you're a burger girl?" Nick grinned as he glanced through the short menu.

"Have I told you that it's a product of growing up in a family of mostly guys? No 'chick food,' as Seth likes to call it."

"There's a definite difference in chick food and eating healthy. But every once in a while it is really nice to have a burger."

A chair scraped the cement behind them as another couple sat down. She watched his attention revert slightly, his eyes subtly studying the woman. Kaylan knew she should be nervous, but she'd meant what she said. The Lord was in control. If she doubted that, then the earthquake, Sarah Beth's death, and her relationship with Nick were all freak accidents of chance and not worth the pain or effort.

She reached across the table and entwined their fingers, bringing his attention back to her. His gray V-neck T-shirt only enhanced the gray blue of his eyes, and the sun made the golden strands in his hair pop today. His slow, lazy smile responded to her touch, warming her and bringing a blush. Not for the first time, she cursed the reaction. Why couldn't she stay as cool as he did?

"Let's play twenty questions again today," Nick suggested. He paused to give their orders to the waitress and then focused on her again. Kaylan appreciated the effort.

"That game got a little heated last time."

"Heated in a good way, babe." He winked. "Besides, I like the fact that you have to answer."

She shot him a look that drew a laugh. "Don't press your luck, mister. I still reserve the right to pass."

"That's not in the rules, gorgeous."

"Since when did we make rules?"

"Since I decided to." Every once in a while that arrogance emerged, and right now it blossomed as he sat back and crossed his arms. "I'll even let you ask the first question."

She sat back in the patio chair and tapped her fingers on the glass table top. "All right. Tell me something I don't know about you."

"That's not a question."

"Pretend it is."

"Fine." He leaned forward, and his expression grew serious. "I have a sister."

Kaylan didn't quite know how to take that one. She'd expected him to tell her a new interest, hobby, secret about work, or an embarrassing story. Never did she expect that revelation. She rejected a stab of betrayal at the revelation of a secret so big.

"You have a what?"

He linked both of their hands again. "A sister. I know. It's a big deal."

"Just a little. Why didn't I know this before? Where is she? Who is she?"

"Babe, I just found out. When I was in Georgia, Pap called. He was nearby and wanted to meet for dinner. He's been looking into my family. I guess it gives him something to do right now."

She squeezed his hands. "No, he does it because he loves you. Even if he were the busiest man in the world, he would still make time. You are family now. It's what we do."

He smiled. "It just takes some getting used to. It's been a while since I had a real family. And now I have family I've never met. Blood, Kaylan. Pap gave me some info on her." His voice dropped. "And a picture. She's beautiful."

The waitress came back with their orders, and both of them dug into their hamburgers and fries. Kaylan often forgot that Nick had never known his blood family. As long as she had known him, he'd had a desire to find his birth parents. And now he had a sister. She couldn't imagine never knowing David, Micah, or Seth. They were her whole world and shaped so much of who she was today. As she watched Nick, she knew he grieved the years he'd lost with his sister.

"Well, I know I spent my turn, but I'm writing a rule that I get to ask more questions on this one."

He chuckled. "I'll allow it. Just this once."

"What's her name? Have you met her? Older or younger?"

"She goes by Natalie. She works at an Air Force base here in California." He smirked. "I'll forgive her that little oversight. She should've gone Navy. And apparently she's my age."

"A twin? You've got to be kidding."

Nick shook his head. "I wish I were. We were adopted separately. Two different homes, two different lives. We've lived in the same state and have never met."

"Well, I think it's time to fix that."

"Kaylan, I think the last thing we need to do is add that to our life. I don't want to disrupt her until we catch Janus." He lowered his voice and leaned forward, his gaze raking the people nearby. "I think it's better if we don't put her in the line of fire. For some reason this chick has a fascination with the women in my life. Let's not give her ammo."

"Then catch her and let's meet your sister."

Nick studied her, and Kaylan let him see every part of her heart, her eagerness for him to have a family, her willingness to support him, even that she would lead the charge with this new information.

"You're pretty amazing, you know that?"

Kaylan put her hand over her heart. "Was that your question? I'm shocked it took you this long to notice."

"Sometimes I can be a little slow."

"Sometimes?"

He dropped money on the table and stood up, stealing a kiss in the process. His smile spelled danger. "Watch it, gorgeous. You may get more than you bargained for. Or I may decide to take back my surprise."

She stood up and slipped her hand in his. "You planned a surprise?"

"I'm a man of many secrets."

She elbowed him in the ribs. "Better not be too many."

He met her eyes and held them, all joking aside. "Only when I have to, Kaylan. But never something that could hurt our relationship."

"I understand. And you still won't tell me who this mysterious letter writer is?"

He laughed as they walked down a row of shops and restaurants. "It's my turn for the questions. Speaking of, you up for ice cream?"

She rolled her eyes. "Now that was a dumb question."

"How can I ever make it up to you?"

"Spring for two scoops."

The ice cream store smelled of sugar and happiness to Kaylan. She could remember many trips to get ice cream with her parents and Seth in particular after school.

Kaylan loved sampling the flavors. She chose a waffle cone and requested two scoops of cheesecake while Nick chose two scoops of double chocolate chip with what looked like marshmallows in it.

He swung his arm over her shoulder as they left the shop and wandered down to the beach. "Why do you get cheesecake flavor? We could just go get cheesecake instead."

"First of all, no one makes cheesecake as good as Gran. Second, this way I get two desserts in one. Don't knock it 'til you try it."

He kissed her hair as they walked, her feet sinking into the sand. "You're missing your family today, aren't you?"

"I always miss them. What was your first clue?"

"I know you. But you've mentioned them a lot. You tend to get this distant look in those gorgeous green eyes."

"I guess I'm feeling a little nostalgic today."

"Why is that?"

"It's our first day to really put aside the busyness of life and just be together. I guess with that comes a break from routine and a chance to feel everything I've pushed away. I miss Alabama, the trees, the weather, the people. With the holidays creeping up, I miss Sarah Beth. It's almost been a year since we graduated. I miss being able to watch Seth's games and be around Dave on the weekends to fish or watch a movie with him. I miss decorating with Mom, cooking with Gran, playing games with Pap, helping Dad build those model ships in his office. I miss mornings on the lake. I miss college. I guess things were simpler last year." She gazed up at him. "Who would have thought what the past year would bring?"

He stopped walking and faced her, brushing a strand of hair behind her ear. His fingers stroked her cheek. "Do you regret coming here?"

"Never." She stood on her tip toes and kissed him, tasting the lingering chocolate from his ice cream. She could feel his smile.

"You're right. That cheesecake doesn't taste half bad."

She giggled and pulled back. "Nick, I wouldn't trade this time with you. As much as I miss them, this is my life now. When I finish this internship, I can take that awful test, get licensed, and hopefully add a voice for improvement when natural disasters strike. I think you told me once that Sarah Beth will always be part of me. I can't erase that living here. But this, Nick"—she gestured to the ocean and people milling around on the beach, enjoying the last day of their weekend—"this fits, too. You are my world now."

His face lit up, and her heart warmed that she was the reason. Never could she have prayed for a man like Nick Carmichael. His past was his past. She couldn't change it any more than she could change her own. But they could build a beautiful future on the rubble of past mistakes, and she couldn't wait to make that happen.

"It's time for your surprise." He grabbed her hand, tugging her back to the car. Already she loved this day of escape.

Chapter 33

NICK NEVER FELT this nervous. Not when facing down locals with guns in the desert of the Middle East. Not when training. Not when caught in the middle of a brawl in college. Not when boarding Janus's boat in Ukraine. But now his hands felt slick with sweat. His heart pounded as if it could burst from his chest. He took a deep breath, steadying his heart and fighting the nerves.

He'd blindfolded Kaylan and now led her to where Jay had docked his boat. He prayed for the perfect evening. He glanced at the orange tint in the sky, guessing they had about an hour before the sun set.

"Nick, where are you taking me?"

"I lied about the note. I wrote it. I'm kidnapping you. Next stop Hawaii."

She giggled. "I think I can handle that. You can take the blindfold off now. I'll go willingly. I wouldn't want you charged with kidnapping."

"Not a chance, babe. We're almost there."

He checked his shorts pocket again, the edges of the box reassuring him as he walked the last few steps and stopped. Megan had outdone herself decorating and, true to his request, had avoided using black. He'd thank her later.

He came around Kaylan and unfastened the blindfold, his fingers brushing her wavy auburn locks. She'd changed into a knit sweater and linen pants, perfect for the weather as the November evening dipped into the sixties and a small breeze teased their skin.

"Oh, Nick. No way." She turned and flew into his arms, placing a kiss on his lips before turning back to the scene before them.

Luck B A Lady, Jay's speedboat, sat before them. Jay had cleaned her, and Megan had set a picnic basket and blankets on the deck, where a couple of padded bench seats sat ready and waiting for dinner.

"She's ours for the evening." Nick helped her climb on board and started the engine; it roared to life then purred, waiting for his command. He navigated past the surf and out into the still water, gunning the engine for full effect. Kaylan squealed as sea spray lighted on her face, dotting her eyelashes like diamonds in the setting sun. Nick chuckled, relaxing in his natural habitat. The sea, the sunset, and the coming darkness, a Frogman at home.

As they hit a cove of smoother water, he cut the engine and threw anchor, letting them bob in the gentle current. A light cloud cover smeared the sky, and he hoped it wouldn't obscure their view. The lap of water against the boat cooled his nerves. The world receded. The only thing that mattered was her laughter and his fingers wound through hers.

He spread the blanket on the floor of the boat, facing the setting sun. She quickly unpacked the picnic—gourmet sandwiches, chips, fruit, and chocolate cake dripping with a cherry glaze awaited. "Who in the world made all this?"

Nick grinned, ecstatic that the details had come together without her knowledge. "Turns out your roommate is a fantastic cook."

"Clearly she missed her calling." She tossed him a sandwich and then curled up next to him, pulling a plaid blanket over both of their legs. "I'm not usually a sunset girl, but this is pretty amazing. Thanks for today."

"My pleasure. I gotta say, I think my California sunsets rival your Alabama sunrises."

"Blasphemy. Don't ever say that again."

"It's true. I've requested a poll, and I won."

"I demand a recount. But I have to say..." She set her sandwich aside and curled into his chest as her voice lowered in awe. "This one is pulling out all the stops."

Nick couldn't have agreed more. He'd grown up watching the sunsets over the water, but this one seemed unlike any he'd seen. Pink and orange tinted the gray clouds as if lava built in the heights. At the skyline a fiery orange and yellow spilled over the water and shot rays into the sky, slicing into the clouds and coloring the water. In the stillness the water directly reflected the sky above. Beauty surrounded them on all sides.

"Whose turn is it for a question?" Kaylan mumbled against his chest.

"My turn, I think." He swallowed hard, his hands slipping as he reached into his pocket and grasped the box. "But I want you to look at me for this one."

She moved to sit cross-legged next to him, her gaze wary. "Are you going to ask me to do the Macarena again for you? Because like I said earlier, that is not a valid question."

He threw his head back in a laugh, letting the nerves bleed away for a moment. He loved the humor that returned the more she healed. He'd missed this Kaylan in the past months. He reached for her hands, tasting the words he wanted to say, feeling them well within him like the ocean he loved so much. He feared she would say no, that a part of her remained terrified of his past, of his job, of making a life here. But as she'd challenged him, what they did, they would now do together.

210

"You've changed a lot this year, you know. I've watched you go from a broken woman to a woman who refuses to back down, who doesn't just need support but who desires to support others. Kaylan, if I could have picked the woman I wanted to spend my life with I never could have dreamed you up. You're beautiful, fun, talented. Your love for the Lord is infectious and pure. You love others and put them before yourself, no matter the circumstance. Even today, the fact that you would help me find my family, unite with my sister, no questions asked, meant the world to me." He tucked a strand of hair behind her ear, watching the flickering emotions pass across her face. Emotion tore at his throat, causing his voice to become husky.

"I love you, Kaylan Lee Richards. I want to spend the rest of my life with you. I want to grow old with you, have babies with you. Your family will be my family. I want to love you as Christ loved the church, and I would give my life to protect you." His fingers caressed her face, causing her breath to catch. "I want to support you in your dreams, fight for your heart, and wake up to a beautiful sunrise with you for the rest of our lives. I don't know where this journey will take us. I don't know what states or countries we may live in. I can't promise ease and comfort. I can't promise full disclosure. But I can promise to partner with you and do my best to point you to Christ, no matter what."

He pulled himself onto his knee and reached for the box, tugging it open. Her breath caught as another spike of light shot through the sky, and the horizon line glowed a dusky pink.

He smiled, all hint of nerves gone. He'd never been so sure of anything in his life. "So for my last question of the day." His eyes locked with hers. "Kaylan, will you marry me?"

Tears coursed down her face as she rose up on her knees and threw her arms around his neck. Her lips met his, and he had his answer. This girl belonged to him, a gift from God in every way.

He knew without a doubt that he would treasure her the rest of his days.

He chuckled. "Is that a yes?"

"Yes. Yes. A thousand times yes."

His lips met hers again. He didn't think he would ever tire of her kisses or her arms around his neck. He cupped her face in his hands, drowning in the hope rekindled in her eyes, hope he hadn't seen in a year. Hope for a future. He pulled back and removed the ring from the box, reaching for her finger.

His whisper carried in the gentle breeze as he recited Proverbs 31. "'A wife of noble character who can find? She is worth far more than rubies. Her husband has full confidence in her and lacks nothing of value.' You are my treasure, Kayles."

Her eyes shone in the darkness. "That was the best question of the day." She ran her fingers through his hair. "I love you, Nick Carmichael. And I can't wait to spend the rest of my life with you."

He pulled her close as the last of the light slipped beneath the water line and shadows descended on the boat. As Nick pointed the boat back to port, he couldn't help but think that the sunset had been appropriate. It was the end of one stage and the dawn of another, one he couldn't wait to begin.

Chapter 34

KAYLAN AWOKE WITH a start and looked at her hand. She hadn't dreamed it. A pear-shaped diamond adorned her finger, evidence of a sunset proposal the night before. She fell back against her pillow. It had happened, really happened.

A party had awaited them when they got back. Megan and Micah pulled out all the stops. Despite being miles away from Alabama and the rest of her family, she felt more loved than she could hope for. Every day California felt more and more like home.

She jumped up to shower and get ready for work, just in time to read her Bible and watch the sunrise too. She had much to be thankful for this morning. Yet a small twinge of sadness stole across her heart. Sarah Beth wasn't here to celebrate, and she wouldn't be there to stand next to her on her big day.

Kaylan knew it would always be this way, big moments of celebration followed by quiet moments of grieving. She knew one day she would rock away on a front porch in heaven and tell Sarah Beth all about it. They had eternity to enjoy their friendship. For now she would carry on and celebrate, knowing that's exactly what Sarah Beth would want her to do.

Her phone rang as she left the porch after reading her Bible.

Nick. Her smile nearly slipped off her face as she hurried to her room. "Morning, babe."

"Kayles, we need to talk."

Her smile froze, and she stopped in the middle of her room, her eyes darting around. The serious tone of his voice set her nerves on edge. "Everything okay?"

"We're leaving, Kayles. We got the call a couple of hours ago. They're briefing us when we get there. We're loading the plane within the hour. I'm not going to see you, and I'm not sure when I'll be back. Could you…"

"Yeah, I'll take care of the house and check in on Kim and Logan. Don't worry. Please be safe." Her heart sank. She'd had a brief break from reality, but she realized this is the life she would marry into. Moments of celebration and fun, followed by long absences. If she wanted Nick, she would learn to embrace both.

"Kayles, I'm sorry. This isn't how I wanted to spend the next few days."

"Don't apologize. Go do what you need to do and then come home to me."

She could hear his smile, even though she couldn't see it. "Have I told you lately that you're amazing?"

"Keep telling me. I love you."

"I love you too. Hold down the home front. I'll call when I can."

"It's a deal. Bye." She hid her cracking voice as she ended the call, her emotions riding a roller coaster.

"Lover boy leaving again?"

Kaylan jumped and turned to find Megan leaning in her doorway. She'd donned shorts and a T-shirt for her work at the aquatic center and nursed a mug of coffee in her hand. "You scared me."

Megan smiled. "I guess with everything going on around here you have the right to be a little jumpy."

214

Kaylan shuffled through a pile of clothes to grab a light jacket and her keys. "Guess so."

"So Nick's leaving to avoid wedding planning." She shook her head. "Typical."

Kaylan laughed. "Thanks for planning the party last night. It was incredible."

A shyness crept over Megan. "I liked hanging out with your friends."

"Well, how about you come with me to see Logan and Kim tomorrow night? I don't think you spent time with them at Halloween."

"I'm game. What do you have in mind?"

Kaylan slipped past Megan in the doorway, talking as she moved toward her car. "Kim is back from the hospital with her baby. I want to check in on her. I would love for you to get to know her. I'm taking dinner over."

"Babies, Kaylan? I'm not so good with kids."

Kaylan stopped at the door and flipped a strand of Megan's hair, grinning at her roommate's cringe. "Just one baby. And three kids. Trust me, these are the best-behaved kids on the planet."

"Fine. Sign me up. You've got me helping neighbors and kissing babies. Maybe you'll have me believing in Jesus soon too." Megan rolled her eyes.

"That's the plan." With a wave she walked out the door, praying for her roommate and the SEAL team heading to who knew where. She planned to watch the news constantly until the guys came back.

Nick's head buzzed from lack of sleep, too little caffeine, and the drone of a plane. They taxied onto the runway at the navy base in Sevastopol, Ukraine. Back again to the country where his buddy had lost a leg. Back to chasing a terrorist that haunted their daily lives. He glanced around at the faces of the men around them. It was payback time.

They unloaded their gear and moved to a room awarded them by the base commander. X took charge as soon as they dropped their gear.

"Titus, round up coffee. Jay, get the white board set up. Hawk, check the gear. Micah, see about sleeping arrangements. Hopefully we will only be here a few hours. Colt, unscrew the paperwork. Let's make a plan, ladies." He bit down on a fresh toothpick while he paced the room, muttering under his breath.

Within minutes the room evolved. X spread a city map out over a table. "All right, listen up. Our friend Janus is back at it again for a huge meeting that goes down Wednesday night. Intel says our Big Kahuna will be there too, along with a leader from Iran to negotiate the terms of a big weapons deal. We think the intended target for weapons use is Israel."

"Perfect. Got a plan?" Nick was chomping at the bit to end this. And he wanted answers. Why was Janus targeting him and his girl-friend? How did she know his full name? As much as he wanted to catch her for the greater good, he had his own agenda as well.

"We will be stationed at a warehouse where the meeting is sup-posed to take place. We're partnering with one of our buddies in the Agency, so once we get the go-ahead, we will move in and cap-ture those involved. Notice I said capture, not kill." X made eye contact with every one of them. "I know this has turned personal for all of us. But we have to keep cool heads and get the job done." He laid out the plan, and then sent them to crash. Nick grabbed his gear and followed Micah and the guys to the bunks they'd been granted for a short R and R session.

Despite his desire to catch Janus, Nick felt weary. He'd asked Kaylan to marry him, honored her request to fight together. But if they didn't catch Janus?

He stretched out on a bunk, Micah to his right. "Stop it, Hawk."

"Stop what?"

"You did the right thing with Kaylan. Don't second-guess."

Nick studied the metal underwire holding the mattress above his head. "I haven't second-guessed Kaylan. Not since we've been back together."

"Maybe not. But you're second-guessing not walking away for a season. I know you."

Nick sighed and closed his eyes. "What if we don't catch Janus this time? What do I tell Kaylan? What happens if Janus ups her game with our families at home?"

"We'll catch her this time, brah. Don't even worry." Colt's voice rang out in the dim room.

Nick normally felt invincible, but a feeling of dread he couldn't shake continued to weed into his mind. "But if we don't?"

"Stop thinking that way, man. We will," Jay added, his voice groggy.

"How can you be so sure?"

Titus leaned over the side of the bed to look at Nick, his dark face and dark eyes in shadow against the light streaming in behind him. "Because we want it more. Because she's fighting for her twisted, selfish empire, and we're fighting for people we love."

"Get your head in the game, Hawk. We need you." Micah rolled over on his side and shut his eyes. "Sleep. It will help your perspective."

Nick closed his eyes, readying his mind to face down a killer, but instead his dreams revolved around the one he desired to protect the most.

Chapter 35

KAYLAN MADE A mental note to teach Megan how to hold a baby by practicing with a sack of potatoes. She'd never seen her roommate so out of her comfort zone. Nadia Elaine Carpenter had Megan wrapped around her finger, and Megan couldn't figure out how to hold her.

"Here, Megan." Kim helped Megan balance the tiny newborn, supporting her bald head that was dusted with tufts of blonde.

"I'm not sure who she looks more like, you or Logan," Kaylan marveled, her heart stolen by this new addition to her SEAL family.

"Isn't she beautiful, Miss Kaylan? I got my sister." Molly plunked down in Kaylan's lap, her eyes trained on the newborn. Kaylan had no doubt that this baby would be the most fiercely protected child on the block. Her brothers already hovered over her. Molly barely let her out of her sight.

"I'm going to teach her how to play dolls and have tea parties and play dress up." Molly clasped her hands in excitement. "I just can't wait."

Kaylan hugged her close, tickling her in the process. "You're going to be the best big sister ever. It takes a special kind of love to be a big sister."

"Are you a big sister, Miss Kaylan?"

She nodded. "I have a baby brother, Seth. But he's not a baby anymore. He's taller than Uncle Nick. When we were your age, I wouldn't let Seth out of my sight. I took care of him, but he changed pretty quickly, and soon I was chasing after him and my two older brothers."

Molly rolled her eyes. "I know all about chasing after those older brothers."

Megan chuckled at Molly's drama queen antics.

Logan entered the room in his wheelchair. "All right, Molly baby. Time to get ready for bed. It's Tuesday night, which means you have preschool tomorrow."

"Ah, Dad, do I have to?" She slipped from Kaylan's lap and gingerly climbed onto Logan's, balancing on his good leg. Kaylan loved that Molly didn't see her dad any differently. He remained her hero.

"Pretty please, Daddy?" She batted her blonde lashes, and Kaylan watched Logan hide a smile.

He tweaked her little nose. "Bedtime. Now. Hop to, Molly baby."

With a groan, she hopped to the floor and stomped down the hallway. Moments later Kaylan heard the faucet turn on.

Kim entered the room with a burping cloth slung over her shoulder. "Honey, if you'll get the kids to bed, I'll feed Nadia and chat with the girls."

"You got it, love," Logan responded. Kim bent to kiss Logan, smiling near his face.

Kaylan turned away from the moment, tears pricking her eyes. How quick they all were to think a lost limb signified the end of the world. This family couldn't be happier.

Kim settled on the couch next to Kaylan, and Megan passed Nadia to her. "How long have you two been together?" Megan leaned into the couch and wrapped her arms around her legs.

Kim patted Nadia's back. "Seems like forever. We started dating when we were nineteen. Got married when we were twenty-one, so coming up on twelve years."

"Whoa." Megan shifted in her chair, clearly curious about this couple. Kaylan could think of no better example of a healthy, Christ-centered relationship than the Carpenters.

Kim held out her hand. "Now let me see your ring, Kaylan."

Kaylan grinned as Kim examined the ring. News traveled fast. Kim had heard of the engagement almost before it was a done deal.

"It's beautiful, Kaylan. Tell me how he proposed."

Kaylan recounted the story, still feeling the anticipation and surprise. "It was tough having him leave yesterday after all the excitement."

"Get used to it. Logan was away when both of the boys were born. Thankfully he was back for Molly and now Nadia."

"I know all about absentee parents," Megan intoned, a hint of bitterness in her voice. "My dad was in the military."

"I'm so sorry your dad wasn't around, Megan. I've never seen Logan as an absentee parent, though. I've always seen him as a very active one, active when he's here and active in prayer when he isn't. Even when he was gone, I knew he was actively protecting our family. We believed the sacrifice was worth it. I've always been thankful that when Logan couldn't be here, I knew my kids had a heavenly Father watching over them."

"Yeah, but He doesn't really do much, does He?"

"I guess that depends on how you look at it. I believe that even though God isn't physically present with us, He is providing, protecting, and working all things for the good of those who love Him."

"And even when bad things happen, you still see God as good?"

Kim smiled. "My husband is alive and still active. But even if he had died"—Kim paused to blink back tears—"the Bible says God is a Father to the fatherless. Even when life is hard, you can trust Him."

Megan sat chewing her lip, watching Kim and Nadia.

"Kim, how did you handle Logan missing the big moments?"

Kim shifted Nadia in her arms and looked at Kaylan. "I knew I found a fighter when Logan and I started dating. When he came to my room to tell me he wanted to join, it was never a question of him doing it alone. I knew we would go together. When you marry a fighter, part of loving them is having the strength to let them go, take care of things while they are gone, and still submit to their leadership when they get back, knowing they probably saw things that you will never be able to understand. You comfort, you help them adjust to normal life, and you send them off and welcome them home with your head up."

"I don't know how to do that. I wish I were as strong as you."

"Kaylan, you are."

Kaylan glanced at Megan, knowing she was about to share things her roommate had never heard. "Last January, during the earthquake, I broke. I lost my best friend. I became angry and bitter toward God and my family. And Nick, Nick was the strong one. He pointed me back. I'm still not fully myself. I still have nightmares. The fact that he might not come back makes me panic. I don't know how to let him go without losing it or begging him to stay. I don't feel strong, Kim. I'm not sure how to do this."

"It's not about me feeling that way, Kaylan. It's about making a daily decision to be strong for my husband, knowing that some day I'll need him to hold me together," Kim said.

"Doesn't all the stuff going on terrify you? The fact that this person was so close to Molly?"

Kim lifted Nadia on her shoulder to burp her, the baby nuzzling into the cloth. Kim's face tightened at Kaylan's question.

"It terrifies me and makes my mama bear instincts kick into high gear. With Logan's leg still healing, I'm trying not to worry about that. I can take extra precautions, but that's it. Kaylan, strength isn't the absence of struggle or chaos or fear. It's choosing not to let it beat you and knowing who is bigger than fear. I'm strong because I trust my husband, I know who my God is, and I know He is in control. Before you can let Nick go and be strong for him, you've got to remember the One who supplies that strength for both of you in your relationship. Let God be who He is."

Megan shook her head. "Whoa. Kaylan isn't the only one who buys into all this. You believe it too. I mean, you really believe it." She stood abruptly, signaling the end of the conversation. "I'd like to see Molly before she goes to bed."

Kim smiled and nodded. "Feel free to read her a story or play with the dolls for a few minutes. It will help her wind down."

Kaylan cleaned the kitchen while Kim put the baby down and finished helping the kids get ready for bed. She mulled over Kim's words. She could feel herself getting stronger, but it was so much more than a feeling. She wasn't the same girl who had graduated last December or the same girl who had returned from a second trip to Haiti in July. She wasn't even the same girl who jumped at fireworks at the Labor Day party.

She was somehow more herself and a stranger all at once, growing into a new role and stage she never dreamed or planned. In that came the necessity to trust the Lord for each new step, and in that process came strength.

Kim entered the kitchen and stopped. "Kaylan, thank you. This looks great."

Kaylan chuckled as she dried the last pan and returned it to the correct cabinet. "If you can't find something, give me a call. I tried to put it all back in the right place."

"Will do." Kim's brown eyes turned thoughtful. "Kaylan, you know Nick wouldn't have asked you to marry him if he didn't think you could handle this."

"I know. And I think I can. I just have moments of wondering how in the world I'm going to do this."

"Baby steps. You'll develop a rhythm, and it will get easier over time. And you'll have all of us to help you. We've got a pretty great community."

Kaylan leaned on the cabinet and studied her friend. "How are you handling all this?"

As Kim sighed, Kaylan caught a small glimpse of the weight she shouldered so well. "Little by little. Logan is already talking about a prosthetic lower leg. He's thinking through jobs that can combine his knowledge of the military with his passion for justice. We might be looking at law school and then JAG. We'll see."

"I hope you know we're here for you too. Anything you need, just call."

"You're stronger than you give yourself credit for, Kaylan."

Kaylan smiled. "I'm getting there. I better find Megan and get home. Congratulations again on Nadia. She's beautiful. I can't wait to baby-sit."

"Believe me, we'll take you up on it."

"How did you choose her name anyway?"

Kim bowed her head. When she once again met Kaylan's eyes, tears glistened. "Nadia means hope. She came at a time when we needed to remember that gift the most. Kaylan, that's a major component to strength—hope when all else seems hopeless. Don't lose that."

Kaylan nodded. She'd experienced the strength of that hope already, a hope in something eternal, something Janus and the earthquake could never take away.

Chapter 36

THE CAR RIDE home seemed quiet, broken only by the country music playing on the radio. Kaylan knew her roommate had a lot to think about.

"How'd it happen?"

"How did what happen?

"Logan's leg. I didn't want to ask."

Kaylan turned the car into their driveway and cut the engine. "It's one of those things I'll never know, Meg. But whatever happened, it really shook the guys."

"And they still went back out there."

Kaylan nodded, resting her head on the headrest. "It's their job."

"I don't know how they do that. It's so thankless. I mean, people like me mock them or bash war all the time, but I've never heard them complain, even though it affects them the most. They just go to work, and leave for God knows where, and come home and don't say anything, live life, and do it all over again. No one will ever know about Logan's leg"—she sniffed—"or that he's a hero."

Kaylan risked getting slapped and put her hand on her roommate's leg. "We know. His family knows. His kids know. That's enough for him."

"I just don't get it. My family fell apart when my mom left, but Logan and Kim? What have they got that we didn't?"

Kaylan knew the simplified answer. Jesus. They had faith and hope in something much bigger than themselves. "What do you think they have that your family didn't?"

Megan grew quiet, so quiet they could hear the road traffic a block over. She sniffed again. "Peace," she whispered. "They have peace." She shifted in her seat to face Kaylan. "Thanks for letting me into your world. For sharing your friends. I've never had girl-friends, not like Kim anyway."

Kaylan reached for her hand and squeezed, holding on when Megan flinched. "My friends are your friends. If you think they're great, you should have met Sarah Beth."

"How come you never talk about her?"

Kaylan shook her head. "I guess sometimes the memories are just too hard. She would have been my maid of honor at my wedding. I can't imagine that day without her, but I have to. She was my sister in every sense of the word."

"But she wasn't blood?"

"The ties that bind don't always include blood, Megan. My family adopted Nick long before he and I started dating, purely because of what he meant to Micah."

"Your family sounds pretty great."

"Why don't you come home with me next time? You can spend a weekend at my parents' lake house and meet all of them."

"That I might be able to do as long as you promise me one thing."

They climbed from the car and slammed the doors shut. "And what's that?"

"Do not try to convert me to your Southern ways. I refuse to say 'yall,' eat fried animals and roadkill, and watch football all day."

Kaylan threw her arm around Megan's shoulder as she unlocked the door. "We may not convert you, but we at least need to educate you. And for the record, my gran makes the best fried chicken in the state of Alabama."

"I don't eat meat."

"You might change your mind if you…"

A scream tore through the air and Kaylan whirled to the sound, her gaze sweeping the street. Nina stood at her front door shouting, "Kaylan, Megan, a man just ran from the back of your house. He had a knife in his hand."

Kaylan bolted from the porch, pulling Megan with her. They sprinted across the yard to Nina. "Get inside now, girls." She shooed them indoors. Through the window Kaylan saw two men running around the side of their house having exited a car she now knew housed the FBI. Nina grabbed her phone, and Kaylan stopped her.

"Nina, don't call the police. It's under control." No one else needed to get involved.

"Don't be silly. We have to call the police."

Kaylan covered Nina's phone with her hand and lowered her voice. "Nina, because of Nick's job, the FBI have been hanging around lately, keeping an eye on things. They'll take care of this, I promise."

Nina's look bore a hole in Kaylan, the look that demanded the truth from lying children. Kaylan met it head-on. "I promise."

Nina tossed her hands up in the air, her floral robe gaping to reveal silky pajamas. "Good grief. I'll make some tea. You aren't leaving here until I say so."

Head spinning, Kaylan gripped her own phone, knowing she needed to talk to someone. Who could she call? Not Logan and Kim. Nick and Micah were out of town.

"Kaylan, what is going on?" Megan muttered as Nina fussed over the kettle on the stove.

"I have no idea."

"Can we call someone?"

"All the guys are out of town."

"Call Logan."

"I can't. They've got too much going on in their lives."

"Kaylan, quit being independent and call the family that just told you to call if you needed anything," Megan gritted under her breath.

"Pot meet kettle." Kaylan stepped into the living room and dialed Logan.

"Carpenter residence."

"Logan, it's Kaylan."

"Kaylan, what's wrong? Did y'all make it home okay?" His voice went stiff, and Kaylan remembered that it would take more than losing a leg to slow down this Navy SEAL.

"Someone was at our house. Our neighbor saw him. She said he was holding a knife. What do I do? All the guys are out of town."

"What am I, chopped liver? Hang tight and don't tell your neighbor any details. I'll check in with the Feds. But I would expect they will tighten their leash with you. And, Kaylan, you did the right thing calling me. It may be totally unrelated, but I don't believe in coincidence."

"Logan, I can't..."

"Yes, you can. Take a deep breath and do what you need to. And make sure Megan stays quiet."

Kaylan took a deep breath, reaching for reserves she didn't feel like she could muster. But it wasn't about what she felt. She could and would do this.

"Let me know what you find out."

"Hang in there. We got your back." He hung up as a knock sounded on Nina's front door. Time to talk to the FBI.

Home. Even for a loner like Janus the thought of being back on Ukrainian soil, hearing her own language, seeing familiar sights, brought a hint of nostalgia. But she usually drowned that out with vodka. She stared out over the Sevastopol city center from her roost in a luxury suite. Her contacts back in Coronado didn't know if the SEALs had left or not. They vacated the house a little earlier than the usual time.

The eyes on Kaylan said she went about business as usual. No word if the SEAL team had caught her scent. If they had, well, a lot more was at stake besides this deal. If her boss were caught before she made her getaway…she didn't even want to think about the ramifications. They all ended with her six feet under in an unmarked location.

She took a long drag on a cigarette, and coughing seized her. No one would miss her anyway. She glanced at her watch. Her boss and the Iranian would knock on her door only hours from now. And if her contacts in California didn't hear from her after that, they had orders to take the girls, both of them. She'd given Nick every opportunity. A girl with hair like Kaylan's would get a good price on the international market. It was her last resort. The only option. The men were on standby. The SEALs should have left her alone.

Despite the expansive windows, she felt like a hamster trapped in a cage. Even gilded rooms made prisoners of their occupants when subject to the whims of greedy men. She would not be taken alive. Orange would not look good on her, and a cell wouldn't suit. She took another drag on her cigarette before pouring a drink. Yes, it was a good day to die.

Chapter 37

WHAT WAS IT with these people and boats? Nick shuddered in his wet suit, hunched down in a shipping yard after his swim to shore. The workers had long since gone home for the day. The scent of fish and trash wafted his way in the still night. From what he understood, the meeting had taken place, and the takedown was only minutes away. Or at least he hoped so. Something didn't feel right.

Janus and her boss were supposed to rendezvous back on his yacht after the meeting. But first they would show proof of weapons to the Iranian liaison, proof that remained hidden in the warehouse where Nick, Micah, Titus, and Colt crouched. Nick's job was to secure the weapons, but so far they weren't sure which set of crates contained the right shipment.

Row upon row of crates filled with machine parts and delivery items sat in the dank, dark warehouse. Nick shuffled from station to station, checking the arrival date and location. At this rate he might as well wait for Janus to point him to the right shipment, something that was highly unlikely.

A rusty door slid open, and voices sounded in Arabic. The team stilled, fading into the shadows with barely a sound. Nick hunkered behind boxes, readying his gun in case an "imminent threat" arose—the two words that always stood out in their briefs.

Titus breathed over his microphone. "They're discussing the weather. This isn't helpful. Sure we have the right rendezvous?"

Nick gazed through his scope, his eyes stilling on a slight woman, blonde hair, icy blue eyes, immaculate clothes, and gloved hands. His pulse accelerated. He recognized her. Only now her hair was shorter, her eyes icier, her expression determined, hostile. No longer sweet and inviting. No longer matronly. Cathryn.

"That's Kaylan's neighbor," he breathed. No time to process that. At least now they knew where she had been getting her information.

"I've got eyes on the Kahuna," Bulldog whispered over the radio. They would finally have a picture to help with a name.

Nick analyzed the man approaching his hiding place—tall with a pudgy belly, glasses on his nose, and graying brown hair. His angular facial features were classic Eastern European. Nick froze.

"We've got a problem. That's Sasha Baryshev, one of the biggest oil moguls in Russia and nearly untouchable because of his influence in government. Taking him would be a political nightmare. We may need to stick to intel here."

"Stick to the plan, Hawk. Capture only. We'll let the guys back in DC deal with the political red tape. At least we have a name and identification," X whispered over the intercom. Nick knew Jay would radio it back to HQ from his overwatch position nearby.

The three targets stopped near Nick's hiding place. He could hear the Arabic cadence and watched as Sasha gestured to a large crate in front of them.

"Seven males incoming. Look to be European. All armed," Titus warned, his voice remaining as bland as if he were commenting on the weather. Nick smirked. Sometimes he wondered if they were trained too well.

"They're blocking the entrances," Micah muttered.

Nick's finger hovered near the trigger, ready to respond if things escalated. Two of the goonies walked forward with crowbars and attacked the crate with gusto. Built like tanks, the men tore the top off with ease, revealing a layer of multicolored silk scarves resting on straw.

Sasha leaned forward and brushed aside the layers, and Nick caught a glimpse of AK-47s and RPGs.

Titus swore over his intercom, and Nick tensed. "Sasha is telling the Iranian he can get him uranium for a nuclear warhead if the price is right. They are negotiating a meeting next month. This shipment is chump change. They met to discuss a bomb."

Colt's deep voice hissed in Nick's ear. "Trouble on my six. Might have to step this up."

Nick heard shouting in Russian and shots fired just as all hell broke loose. "Grenade!" Colt shouted as an explosion rocked the air a hundred feet from where Nick crouched, shattering crates and boxes in its wake. Nick ducked, trying to keep his eyes on their three targets, but they'd slipped away in the chaos.

"Colt?"

"Fine. Go!"

Nick left his position and took off in pursuit of the three targets, radioing his plans as he ran.

A man stepped out in front of him, the barrel of his gun coming even with Nick's chest. Nick couldn't slow down. He slammed into him, grunting with the impact. The gun fired into the air. Twisting free, Nick aimed and fired, sending the man sprawling backward. He paused long enough to confirm the fight was over before he took off again.

"Right behind you, Hawk." Nick heard Micah's feet pounding in perfect rhythm behind him as the rest of the team secured the warehouse while the two of them pursued Janus. He didn't care about anyone else. Just catching her, ending the threats, the worry. Ending her career and reign of terror. Ending, or at least slowing, the slaughter of American soldiers fighting on foreign soil.

They spilled out the door into an industrial shipyard hugging the bank of a water channel that flowed out into the Black Sea. Nothing moved, and he and Micah slipped back into the shadows, guns ready, their black wet suits blending into the night.

A crane hovered above Nick's head and smaller boats with glowing lights sat silent, their owners in bed. A shot pinged the building behind his head. He ducked, and his senses sharpened. He scanned the dimness to determine direction. Another shot whizzed past, and Micah inhaled sharply. Nick shifted to look at his best friend. Micah's wet suit hung split open, and a slim gash bled from where the bullet grazed his arm before embedding in the side of the warehouse.

"I'm good. Keep moving."

Another shot hit the building. Either the person lacked marksmanship or he was shooting blind. This time Nick guessed the direction to be an old industrial fishing boat of some sort about one hundred yards to their right. He signaled to Micah to go around the side while he slipped up onto the deck.

A click sounded over the radio as Colt slithered into view, rounding the boat and disappearing to cover the other side. Three-on-three. Nick liked their odds. He was thankful for more men on this mission taking care of the rest of the guys inside the warehouse. But right now all he cared about was Janus. He wasn't sure who fired at them or if the other two lay in wait or fled the scene. But he swore that at least one of them would fly back to California with his team. And he knew which one he wanted.

He crept across the deck, his footfalls silent in the murky night. The moon hid behind clouds, the light muted for a moment. He scanned the deck. A small figure shifted, leaning over the railing, gun aimed and trained.

"*Do svidaniya.*" She whispered just as Micah entered her line of sight. Nick reacted and launched himself forward, regretting his directive to capture and not kill. Her shot went wild. Micah yelled over the intercom.

Nick tackled the slight frame, rolling on the deck in a mess of arms and legs. Blonde hair tangled in his fingers, obscuring his view of Janus's face. Although she was wiry and strong, he heard a slight wheeze in her breathing. Taking advantage of the weakness, he punched her in the stomach, enough to stall her breathing for a moment, then flipped her over and bound her hands behind her back with lightning movements.

Nick's breathing slowed as he radioed his team. "Female jackpot apprehended on fishing boat near warehouse. Radio HQ. Any sign of the other two?"

"None, Hawk. Searching now," Titus's voice sounded over the intercom.

"Coming up, Hawk." Micah pulled himself up just as Janus regained her breath.

"We're going to take a little trip, Janus. I hear you've taken a liking to my town."

"It suffices if you like tacky American culture."

"What I like is you staying away from my girlfriend. What I like is you in American hands."

She squirmed beneath him. In one swift movement he stood, hauling her to her feet.

"But the games were so fun. And you are so gullible. Face it, little SEAL. I infiltrated your world all too easily, and you could do nothing to stop me."

Nick towered over her, his temper fighting his good sense.

"I should have shot you when I had the chance." He grabbed her arm and tugged her with him.

"The game's not over yet."

Micah stalled next to Nick, studying their adversary. "What do you mean?"

"Exactly what I said. The game does not end until I say it does."
Her eerie chuckle turned to coughing as she doubled over.

Nick gritted his teeth, unsure what to do. Colt radioed that the
Iranian and Big Kahuna were gone. Jay responded with confirmation that the sniper and remaining men in the warehouse had been
taken care of. The helicopter would pick them up in five minutes.

Despite the victory chatter in his ear, Nick could only focus on
Janus. His head spun. "You're crazy."

"What you call crazy, others call brilliant. It is all a matter of
perception, is it not?" she wheezed, a smirk twisting her lips. Gone
was the polite, affluent, proper neighbor. Instead, a calculated,
cold-blooded killer stood before him.

Micah grabbed Janus's arm and hauled her from the boat.
"Listen, lady, I've had about enough of you, your games, and your
threats to my family. I don't care if they lock you up and throw
away the key. You are getting on that helicopter. You lost, you got
that?"

Between the two of them they half-carried, half-dragged Janus
to a waiting helicopter, hovering above an empty dock. Colt and
Titus pulled her in as Micah and Nick jumped on.

"I expect we are flying home?" All eyes turned to Janus, who
stared back with icy blue eyes, her cherry red lipstick still perfectly
painted on thin lips that grinned triumphantly. "Perfect. I still
have a few tricks up my sleeve."

Nick's heart stalled. He had a sinking feeling that Janus spoke
the truth. This game wasn't over yet.

Chapter 38

EGAN DIDN'T COME home after work Friday night. That wasn't too unusual, but when Kaylan tried to call, she couldn't reach her. After dealing with news of the intruder Tuesday night, Kaylan couldn't believe Megan wouldn't let her know her plans. The FBI had found no signs of a break-in and no indications that someone had tampered with the door, and they reassured Kaylan that they were watching the house 24/7. Still, Kaylan couldn't shake the feeling that something didn't add up.

Thankfully the rest of the week had gone by without incident. On Wednesday Megan brought by her latest flame, Jackson. On Thursday Nick called to say they were fine and hoped to be back by late Friday night or early Saturday morning, but he would be out of pocket until then. Now it was Friday evening, and no sign of Megan. She was probably spending the night at Jackson's, but then why hadn't she called or texted? Should she tell the Feds? With the events of the past few weeks, Megan's lack of communication rattled her. She tried Megan's cell again, but it immediately rolled to voicemail.

At eight o'clock Liza came over for a movie, bringing popcorn and chocolate-covered almonds to snack on. Kaylan immediately unloaded her anxiety, hoping it was another case of overactive imagination.

"I'm sure she's fine, Kaylan. Isn't she dating someone again? That girl's a firecracker. I bet the guys just line up." Liza popped in a DVD and curled up on the couch.

"Yeah, she brought a new guy around a few days ago. I just wish I could tell her that it's going to end in a lot of heartache."

"Honey, they don't all end bad. Look at Titus and me. We lived together for six months before we finally got married. My parents threw a fit, but when it's meant to be, why wait? I mean, I'm sure you and Nick get that."

Kaylan smiled and shook her head. "We're waiting. Nothing's happened between us."

Liza's eyes grew wide. "Girl, are you serious? That man is hot. What are you waiting on?"

Kaylan settled into the couch and thought of Nick. She never felt cheap or used with him. Every touch demonstrated care and affection, every look showed attentiveness and love. He honored her. She'd seen the way Jay looked at women, like a lion on the prowl. But with Nick, it had always been pure innocence. They were both attracted, but they hadn't made a covenant yet, so he didn't belong to her.

"I guess I believe there are two ways to do this. A way that feels good and a way that is best."

"What do you mean?"

Music on the home movie screen filled the room as Kaylan prayed for the right words. "I think that God intended one man and one woman for life within the confines of a marriage. I think it is supposed to feel amazing within the commitment. But we love what feels good now and in our own way. I think we settle for immediate pleasure over God's best, which would be a committed, devoted, and loving life partner. I think you two got lucky.

Not everyone who lives together ends up getting married. That 'try before you buy' mentality usually ends with a lot of pain."

Liza waved her hand in Kaylan's direction. "I'm glad you're a good church girl. I was that way once. But Titus and I were in love. It all worked out in the end."

Kaylan smiled. "I'm so glad it did. But these guys Megan spends time with, they like her because she's feisty and gorgeous in her own tart way. No commitment. Just a night purely for their own pleasure. And that makes me angry for her because God says she is worth more."

Liza pursed her lips. "I see the way Hawk looks at you. It's different from some of the other guys. Almost like he worships you."

Kaylan chuckled. "Believe me, Nick would like to shake me sometimes. I can frustrate the heck out of that man. He doesn't worship me. Nick treasures me because we both belong to Christ, and he wants to honor me. That's what you see. Respect. Love. Honor."

"Not too bad. Maybe Titus and I need to get back in church. I want our kids growing up that way. I'd kill my daughter if she followed my example and moved in with a guy."

"I'd love for you to come with Nick and me, Liza. But it's not about the church. A changed life is a direct result of a relationship with Jesus."

Liza popped an almond in her mouth. 'Yeah, I thought I had that once. It's about time I got back to it. You keep fighting for Megan. One day she'll realize how much you love her, and she'll start fighting for herself. She's lucky to have you."

'Someone fought for me once when I was in that dark place, and it changed my life."

"Well, you sure are shaking up ours. Now let's watch this movie."

Kaylan and Liza enjoyed a few hours of pure laughter. By the time Liza left a little before 11:00 p.m., Kaylan had almost forgotten her roommate. Almost.

She walked down the hall to Megan's bedroom and flipped on the light. Her room decorated in navy and white held a feminine grace most people would never see behind Megan's tough exterior. Kaylan glanced around at art on the walls and photos of the whales and dolphins from Megan's work, enjoying the glimpse into her roommate's world. They'd made major strides the last week. She not only liked her roommate, but she'd come to enjoy her as well.

Kaylan sat down on the navy bed spread and noticed a dark smudge. Looking closer, her heart stopped. She knew that sight anywhere. Blood. Not just a streak or a dot like with a paper cut, but almost as if someone had wiped a scrape or cut on the hem of the bed spread.

She jumped from the bed, stumbling over a shoe lying in the floor. The smell of dust and blood assailed her nose as her mind flew back to Haiti and days under tents, her hands stained a brownish red. Tears pricked her eyes, and she fought to steady her breathing.

"You aren't in Haiti. You're in California. You're in your home. Everything's okay."

But nothing was okay. Her home had been violated. Now she wondered if her roommate was missing.

"Megan?" she breathed.

She flashed back to panicked moments looking for Sarah Beth. She pivoted in the room, and her gaze stopped on the closet. No. She wouldn't be in there. She wouldn't find another friend dead.

"Megan!"

She sank onto the floor in a heap. "Think, Kaylan." Taking a deep breath, she focused on the room around her. Megan had stayed away multiple nights before. Really, there was no reason to be alarmed. Kaylan picked up her phone to call again just as the screen lit up.

Megan.

"Hey, where are you? I was just about to call."

Heavy breathing filled the line.

"Megan?"

"We have your friend." A thick accent assailed her senses. Eastern European with a hint of Middle Eastern mixed in.

"Who are you? Where's Megan?"

"It does not matter who I am. It only matters that we have a mutual friend in common. And she has sold you to the highest bidder. I'm here to collect."

The man's cavalier tone sent her over the edge. Rage unlike anything she'd ever known filled her. She would not lose someone else. "I asked you a question. Where's my friend?"

"Temper. Temper. You want to see your friend? Meet us on Imperial Beach Pier at midnight tonight. Come alone, and do not tell any of your little SEAL friends. I would hate for something to happen to Megan."

Kaylan heard a scream in the background. "Kaylan, don't!"

"Megan!"

But the phone went dead. Kaylan stared at the blank screen. She wouldn't leave Megan alone. She wouldn't lose someone else, not when she could stop it.

Glancing at the clock, she stood. Less than an hour to figure out a plan. If only she could talk to Nick. But he had said she wouldn't be able to reach him. She could call Logan, but she didn't want to risk these men killing Megan. No FBI either. She had to do it alone.

The lamps cast an eerie glow in the house as her feet pounded a track on the hard wood floor, thinking. Finally she grabbed paper and scribbled two letters. At a quarter past eleven she changed, dressing in a lightweight jacket, yoga pants, and tennis shoes. She had a plan, and no one could stop her. But she'd have to speed. She took the letters, folded them, and palmed her keys. Praying for whatever came next, she took one last look at her house, unsure where she would wake up the next morning. She knew the risk. To get her friend back, she would hand herself over.

Nick would kill her.

She slipped out the back door and across to Nina's, keeping to the shadows to avoid any detection from the agents who watched the house. She prayed they were otherwise occupied.

A dim light glowed in Nina's kitchen as Kaylan silently approached the back door. A figure leaned over the stove. Kaylan paused, her heart jumping in her throat before she recognized Nina's robe and unusually flat gray hair. She rapped on the glass.

Nina whirled, her hand going to her throat. Rushing to the door, she flung it open. "Kaylan Richards, what on earth?"

Kaylan nearly bowled her over as she slid inside and closed the door, hushing Nina's protests. "Please, I need you to be quiet."

Nina's brown eyes grew wary. "What is going on, young lady?"

She nearly rolled her eyes at the motherly tone. Time was precious, and she had to make two stops before arriving at her destination.

"Nina, I need your car keys and no questions."

The woman crossed her arms over her chest. "Why?"

"Please, no questions. Megan's in trouble. It's bad, Nina. I have to go get her."

"Well, just go tell the FBI. Their car is right outside, isn't it? I see everything that happens on this block, you know."

"I can't tell the FBI. No cops, no SEALs, or Megan gets hurt. Please. Your keys." Kaylan held out her hand, trying not to panic.

Nina's gaze darted from Kaylan's face to the dark window where the FBI silently watched from somewhere down the street. "No." She covered her mouth. "You both could get hurt. I can't let you do that." She moved toward the front door, but Kaylan darted in front of her.

"Nina, I promise you can tell the FBI. Just let me borrow your car and give me a thirty-minute head start. I need them to come.

They just can't get there at the same time. I'm begging." Megan's face flashed before her eyes.

Nina shook her head, and Kaylan held her breath. A tear tracked down her cheek. "Oh, honey." She pulled Kaylan to her chest in a hug, then reached for her keys and shoved Kaylan toward the garage. "Go. You have twenty minutes before I run hollering out of this house. You got it?"

It would have to do. With a quick thank-you Kaylan slipped into the garage, opened the door, and started the engine. Keeping her head down, she pulled out and pointed the car away from where she knew agents waited. Everything moved in slow motion, as if she were driving through jello. She hit the highway and sped to Nick and Micah's, now racing the clock and outrunning the FBI.

The key scratched in the lock as Kaylan opened the door to Nick and Micah's and hurried inside. The lingering scent of Nick's cologne and the faint scent of sweaty clothes almost made her change her plan. Almost.

Keeping the lights off, she felt her way to Nick's bedroom and placed a note on his pillow. Moonlight from the window glinted off the glass shielding a picture of the two of them, Nick kissing her cheek, his arms wrapped around her shoulders. They were happy. Together. A tear drifted down her cheek, and she bit back a sob.

She couldn't let Megan go through this alone. Her fingers found the ring decorating her left hand, and she slowly slipped it from her finger to place it on the letter. No matter what happened, she didn't want these men to have the pleasure of confiscating it. She prayed she would get it back from Nick. Placing one foot in front of the other, she ran from the house and back to Nina's car.

Eleven thirty-eight. One more stop. She was almost out of time.

Minutes later she pulled up in front of the Carpenters' house.

Everything looked quiet, but she knew Kim could be up feeding Nadia.

She tiptoed up to the house and placed the letter against the door. A light flipped on and she stumbled, turning to jog down the three steps. A creak behind her made her freeze.

"Kaylan? What are you doing here so late?"

Logan. The last person she needed to see. She slowly turned to face him as he bent in his wheelchair to pick up the letter.

"What's this?"

"Just a note. Read it when I leave."

His alert eyes scanned her, and he held her gaze as he opened it. "Logan, please. Wait to read it."

She guessed he didn't make it past the first line. "Kaylan, why didn't you call?"

This couldn't happen. He couldn't stop her. She turned and sprinted to the car, calling over her shoulder, "I've got to do this. I included the location in Nick's letter. I've got to go."

"Kaylan!"

She slammed her car door and peeled out of his driveway. Clearly she would make a terrible SEAL. No points for stealth or subtlety. She couldn't even lie well. Pointing her car toward the beach, she prayed she reached Megan in time, before Logan alerted other SEALs in the area. Before it again became too late to save her friend. An image of Sarah Beth's chalky face, blood coloring her lips, popped into her mind. She slammed her eyes shut for a moment, jerking the car to avoid a collision. Not again. Not this time.

Eleven fifty-nine p.m.

Kaylan spun into the parking lot and climbed from the car, her shaking hands hidden in the black night. She hit the beach running, her feet sinking deeper and deeper as she beat a path toward the unknown.

Chapter 39

NICK THREW THE door open with a bang and dropped his bag on the floor, glad to be home even if it was 1:00 a.m. California time, and his body clock was all jacked up. Micah entered right behind him and headed straight for the refrigerator. They hadn't slept much since taking Janus Wednesday night. They were anxious to get home, waiting for approval while they wrapped up mission specifics. Something lurked in Janus's eyes as they flew her back to the States. He wondered what she had up her sleeve and dreaded finding out. Nick doubted he would truly be able to rest until he held Kaylan in his arms and knew she was safe.

Nick trudged to his room and flipped the light on. Something shiny glinted on his pillow. His heart stopped.

Slowly Nick walked to his bed. He picked up Kaylan's engagement ring and noticed the letter beneath it. He tore into the envelope.

Nick,

Please know that if I had any other option I would have taken it. The men have Megan. They said no police and no SEALs, and I can't lose another friend. I'm to meet them at Imperial Beach Pier at midnight Friday. I left a letter with Logan. I also asked Nina to give me thirty minutes before she called the FBI. Know that I love you. Know that I want a lifetime with you. And know that I couldn't live with myself or with you if I didn't do what I see you do every day— fight for someone else. I pray that you will be able to place this ring on my finger again, but I would rather you have it than the men I go to meet. I don't know what will happen. I can only pray you get home in time. Find me, Nick. Please.

Love,

Kaylan

She left an hour ago. They could find her. The trail would still be fresh.

He sprinted to the kitchen, tossing the letter to Micah. "Janus got to the girls. I don't know how, but she did."

Micah scanned the letter quickly, then reached for his cell and dialed Logan. Nick heard a heated exchange and rapid-fire instructions as he ran to his room and reached under his bed for the box containing his pistol.

Micah appeared in his doorway. "Logan already called the FBI. They found Nina's car and Kaylan's phone in the sand before the trail ends near Imperial Beach Pier. I told Logan to call the rest of the team and tell them to meet us at the base."

Nick listened while loading his gun.

Micah continued. "We can't do this. Legally we can't chase down these terrorists on American soil. We can't shoot them or harm them, and if we do, it better be in self-defense. This is FBI territory. But if they hurt my sister or Megan..." Micah shook his head. "I won't care about the consequences at that point. I'll kill them."

Nick met Micah's eyes. Even in Haiti he'd never seen Micah so wound tight or angry.

"Me first." He shoved past his best friend, grabbed his keys, and moved to the door.

Micah followed, still filling Nick in on his phone conversation. "Logan says the Feds are looking for abandoned houses or boat docks in the area that might be used as a holding cell. We need to get back to the base and Janus before her flight leaves. If she knows something or even the girls' exact location, we will be able to find them faster."

Micah stopped at the door to Nick's Jeep. "You know this could end our career if it goes south, right?"

Nick didn't look at Micah. "Let's make sure it doesn't go south."

"Good, then. As long as we're clear."

They climbed into the Jeep, and the engine roared to life. Nick peeled out of the driveway.

Normally the wind cooled Nick's mood. It made him think of days on the ocean, surfing, sailing, throwing the baseball and Frisbee with his dad. But today it pushed him along. *Hurry. Hurry.*

He swerved into a parking spot and jumped from the Jeep, his feet landing on gritty cement. Micah appeared at his side, his face etched with controlled rage. Janus had done the unthinkable from captivity. She'd taken one of their own.

Seconds later Colt, Titus, and Jay climbed from their cars on either side, and together they entered the base, a solid wall of enraged SEALs.

Chapter 40

KAYLAN'S HEAD THROBBED, the cadence of her heart mixing with the rush of waves not far away. She groaned and grasped her head. The room felt is if it were rocking. She stilled, ignoring the pounding. She could almost feel the waves lapping beneath her.

A sharp pain shot through her, causing her stomach to churn. She sat up and emptied her stomach on rough wood planks, dizziness assailing her with the quick movement.

"Drugged," she heard someone croak to her right.

She lay back down and turned her head slowly. Megan. She could barely make out her form in the darkness. Her heart settled. They were together.

"Are you okay?"

"I've been kidnapped, drugged, and locked in a boat shed. No, I'm not okay."

At least she hadn't lost her attitude. As if in déjà vu, Kaylan took stock of her prison. Water lapped beneath the floor, indicating they were at a marina on the ocean. A speedboat sat six feet to her right. Doors resembling those found on a barn barred their exit and any escape to the sea. But at least they weren't tied up. If only they were both in a condition to swim, but without an understanding of what lay below the boat where water sloshed, venturing out into the ocean seemed unwise.

"What's going on? Who put us in here?" Kaylan fought to sit upright.

Megan seemed to have a clearer head as she pushed herself up on her elbow. "Don't know. Haven't seen him since he threw you in here a while ago. I've been waiting for you to wake up."

"The last thing I remember is climbing out of my car and heading for Imperial Beach Pier. Then this sweet smell."

"What are we going to do when they come back?"

A sinking feeling filled Kaylan's stomach, and she shook her head, trying to dispel the fog. "I left a message with Logan for the FBI to start looking for us at Imperial Beach Pier. The rest of the SEAL team is supposed to arrive home tonight. Let's figure out a plan and pray the Feds or the SEAL guys get here in time."

"Pray for both of us. If we get out of this, I just might start talking to this God of yours."

Kaylan stood and offered her hand to Megan. "Let's look around, see what we can find that could act as a weapon." They split up and began to survey their prison, groping in the darkness as Kaylan silently prayed for a miracle.

They found tools on the boat—a wrench and a screwdriver. But Kaylan didn't care about the size of the weapon as much as the strength of her swing. "Did you get a look at the guy who took you?" she asked Megan.

"Did I ever. Good-lucking guy, blond, about five-eleven. Sexy accent. He knocked on the door and asked if he could borrow some tools to fix his broken-down car. I let him in, we wound up in my bedroom, and I woke up here."

Kaylan looked at her.

"You can drop the judgmental look. Mark this as the day I acknowledged I have a serious guy problem."

"If we get out of here, I'll remind you."

Kaylan and Megan huddled at the back of the boat shed behind the boat, wrench and screwdriver in hand, listening for any sounds of their kidnapper returning. The drugs had worn off, leaving Kaylan with a splitting headache and really bad temper. She doubted their assailant would return alone and feared what more manpower would mean for her and Megan's escape plan.

"Have I ever told you that I'm claustrophobic?" Megan's alto voice broke the silence.

Kaylan chuckled. "No, I don't think I knew that."

"It's bad. I start hyperventilating. Then drooling all over myself. Then talking really fast."

"I think you're just doing the last one."

Megan hit her head against the wall of the boat shed. "Man, it must be getting worse. I'm doing it all out of order."

"Save your energy, Meg."

Silence descended again. Kaylan gripped the wrench. They'd be in for the fight of her life if she had anything to say about it. Exhaustion threatened to break her focus. "Have I ever told you that you're the best friend I ever had?"

Kaylan turned to look at her roommate. In the dim light from the moon, Megan's porcelain skin looked even paler. She wouldn't look at Kaylan, but Kaylan reached for her hand and squeezed.

"You aren't so bad yourself."

"I mean it, Kaylan. I don't know anyone that would have come after me like you did."

Kaylan tasted fear creeping over her. In a way, this moment reminded her of her last minutes with Sarah Beth. She gripped Megan's hand tighter. "You know we're getting out of here, right?"

Megan shifted to face Kaylan, her legs curling beneath her on the boards. "I want you to promise me something. If it comes to a fight and one of us has the chance to get away, I want you to run and not look back."

"No way."

"Kayles, I'm serious. You have a life, a family who loves you, a man who would die for you."

Her fingers dug into Megan's skin, and Kaylan's gaze never wavered from Megan's eyes. "Listen very closely. I will not leave you. We are going to fight, and we are going to get out of here. Logan will send someone."

Megan shook her head. "I know you believe that. But just promise me. I've been through this before. I can handle it."

Kaylan's heart sank. There it was, the secret Megan guarded with sarcasm. "Megan, what do you mean...?"

Scuffling sounded from outside the doors, and Kaylan heard the shifting of a metal chain sliding free. She stood to her feet, fighting the dizziness. If they came in, she would not be lying down. She would take this fighting. Megan stumbled up behind her. They scurried to the back of the shed, flattening themselves to the wall. The metal tool seemed to heat in her hand. Time to fight.

Chapter 41

NICK HAD FAILED to protect Kaylan, and he was going out of his mind with worry. Surrounded by other SEALs, he beat a path toward Janus, caring little about the repercussions. If she wouldn't talk, someone would have to restrain him from killing her. They had reached a dead end. Their last hope for quickly identifying Kaylan's location remained in the hands of a psychopathic terrorist.

"Hawk, chill, brah. You're not thinking clearly." Colt grabbed at his arm, but Nick swung away, barreling across the landing field and toward a waiting plane. They'd only been back from Ukraine a few hours, but he knew they didn't want to wait long to transport Janus to a safe place for questioning. The plane sat gassed and ready to load.

He spotted her walking across the tarmac. All five foot one of her, head held high, nose almost stuck in the air. Right now he didn't care if this woman was the pope; he wanted to punch the smug look off her face and keep going until she told him Kaylan's location.

Micah stepped in front of him, and Nick stopped short, coming nose to nose with his best friend. "Move."

Nick watched Micah's jaw flex, could almost see his mind

whirring, choosing his words carefully. "I want to find my sister as much as you do. But you will not help things if you take that woman out, wanted murderer and terrorist or not." Micah reached in his pocket and tossed Nick a piece of Juicy Fruit gum. "Now pop that in your mouth, shut up, and let me talk since you clearly can't control yourself right now."

"Bulldog, get out of my way." He attempted to shove past Micah, but he stood firm, his mouth tightening slightly as Nick jarred his injured arm. Nick would care about that. Later.

"Hawk!" Nick flinched at the sound of X's gruff voice. He stiffened and refused to turn around, his gaze glued on Janus's progress. The team around her had stopped, taking in the action.

X moved past Nick and popped the back of his head. "What are ya thinking, you idiot? Let me handle this." He moved toward the head of Janus's security, his hands on his hips as they talked.

Nick held his breath, straining to hear across the tarmac, but the sounds of base life ruined his chances. He took a step, but Micah and Colt stepped in front of him again. "Cool it. It's under control." Nick refused to meet Micah's eyes, knowing the concern and caution he would find there. He didn't want to be the controlled man. Irrational, in love, terrified, and pumped full of adrenaline with no direction all defined him right now. He'd temporarily deleted *calm* from his vocabulary.

But he knew if he were to get anything accomplished, he would have to remember to stuff his emotions and call on his training to do what was necessary, even when his world crashed around him.

X motioned them forward to join the party. "Carmichael, they are having trouble with the preflight check. They are giving you ten minutes with her in the hangar. But I don't trust you or Bulldog alone with her. Colt and I will stay in the room. You keep your hands to yourself, you understand me?" He pointed a finger in Nick's face. Nick choked down his anger at feeling like a child under the administration of a disapproving parent.

"Got it."

"Great, now that we've got that out of the way, let's go find your girl."

X led the four of them into the hangar where Janus's security detail stood waiting for them. At a nod from X, they moved a few feet away and began to whisper.

Nick clenched his fist and furiously chewed his gum, trying to find the inward calm he usually achieved in the heat of a mission. Somehow, making it personal stripped any semblance of normalcy.

Janus smirked. "Come to gloat?"

"No. There's no point."

She flexed her hands, the handcuffs rattling. "These aren't the prettiest bracelets I've ever worn, but far from the worst." Her smirk went slack, and a deadly cold filled her face. "Even in custody, American hospitality is better than anything under the Iron Curtain."

He didn't have time for her mind games. He took a measured step. "Where's Kaylan?"

A wicked smile blossomed on her face, and he forced himself to stay put. "When they didn't hear from me, they took her."

"Who's 'they'?"

"Men you never want to meet. They live for money, and they are very good at what they do. You will not find her unless I give the word."

Nick advanced a step, Micah tensing at his side. He held his phone out for her to take. "Then give the word."

She held her hands out in front of her face, checking her now cracked nail polish. "And why should I?"

"Because it might make things a lot easier for you."

"*Might* is not a promise I am willing to cash in on. I speak in currency. And in comfort."

"Two things I can promise you will never see again if you don't help me."

"Again, you haven't given me a reason to."

"What do you want?" Nick shouted. Micah took a step closer to him.

A wicked grin spread across Janus's face. "I want to tell you a story."

"We don't have time for that."

"Oh, I think you will make time for this one," she snapped. "About twenty-eight years ago a young Stasi officer received an assignment to make contact with American military personnel in strategic locations on the other side of the Berlin Wall. Sometimes she posed as a young student, other times she just slipped past the guards. Quite an accomplishment, I might add. She met a young man in the United States Air Force. He was young and handsome enough. Full of life and naivety. The perfect candidate."

"Does this story have a point?" Micah gritted through clenched teeth.

Her cold blues eyes fastened on him. "In fact it does. And that point is standing next to you."

A roar filled Nick's ears as her gaze shifted to him. Her eyes, icy blue. Lifeless. And entertained. He felt sick.

"And how am I the point? I need to know where my girlfriend is. Now."

Janus seemed to tire of the charade. The smirk dropped from her voice, and the ice in her eyes laced her voice. "I left you wrapped in a blue blanket with a brown rabbit for the Americans to find. Your name is Nikolai Sebastian." She shrugged. "I am not the motherly type. It was even worse when I found out I was having twins. I got rid of you as soon as I could. Now do you really want to turn me over to your government?"

Nick smirked. "You have really done your homework. I'm impressed."

"Man, I said she was crazy." Micah shook his head.

"In my business that is possible, but it is more than likely that

I know what I am talking about. I never had to research you, Nikolai."

Nick's head spun. Mother. Janus was claiming to be his mother. It seemed impossible. He didn't have time to think about it now.

"You're lying."

"Now is that any way to talk to your mother?" She took a step closer and spoke in Russian. "I know you understand me. I know your name. I know who you are. And I know where your sister, Natalia, is. I can make life very difficult for her as well."

Nick responded in English, fighting the fear that clawed its way through his entire body, threatening to paralyze him. "If you have a motherly bone in your body, you will tell me where Kaylan is."

"Do you not realize I never had that trait? I gave you up when you were only days old and never looked back." She grinned. "Kaylan and her annoying friend will be put to good use. She will make many men happy. Cheer up, my son. You will find someone else to warm your bed."

Nick snapped. He lunged forward, his fists raised, but X yanked him back. Colt struggled to restrain Micah on his left. "You sold her into the sex trade? Tell me where my fiancée is!"

"Temper, temper. I am sure she is awaiting transfer at this very moment. You should have left well enough alone."

Nick took a deep breath and tugged free of X's grip. He straightened his shirt and imagined himself under a hide on one of his missions, his finger massaging the trigger as he scanned the area through his scope. Another deep breath. His senses honed in. A plane taxied down the runway. A gnat buzzed near his ear. His knuckles ached from his wadded fists. The gum in his mouth sent bursts of flavor down his throat with every movement of his jaw. He could smell gasoline and exhaust and the faint scent of body odor mixed with liquor. His heart rate settled.

Janus studied him, her blue eyes growing wary. "You could have done better, you know. Kaylan is just one of many."

Nick blew a bubble with his gum, ignoring her jab. It popped and he chewed some more, folding his arms over his chest. "Here's how this is going to go." His voice adopted a deadly calm, back in control and back in his element. The predator instead of the prey. Micah settled next to him, his posture relaxed but his hands balled into fists.

"I'm going to ask you one more time for any shred of information. You then are going to tell me something. The more you share, the more I will work with these guys"—he nodded to the security that had come nearer during his episode—"to negotiate a deal. Your help in exchange for a more comfortable prison sentence."

He took a step closer, towering over her, his shadow a giant on the wall behind her. His teammates flinched but held back. "But if you don't, I'll make sure your life is a living hell, and every man in Gitmo that you ever cheated in business will know exactly who you are and what cell you cower in. Got it?"

"You have searched for me long and hard." Her smug smile made his blood boil. "I have watched you with those you care about. Your threats are empty. You wouldn't do that to your mother."

Nick finally fully appreciated the home he'd grown up in, the love of a woman who hadn't shared his blood but had spent nights awake when he was sick, hours at the hospital after every major accident, and made dozens of cookies for every kid in the neighborhood. "My mother died. I only see a woman who will die alone."

If her eyes could freeze him in place, he would have been a block of ice. But Nick noticed that her hands began to shake.

"I can give you a name." Her nose remained tipped firmly upward, but there was a slight crack in her voice.

"You'll give me more than that."

"In a card game it is not good to show your hand. I think I will still keep some cards close to the vest, as you Americans like to say."

Nick could feel his calm slipping away again. They were losing time. He dug his ringing phone out of his pocket. Logan. The Feds had a possible location. At least it was something.

"The name, Janus?" He took another step, his face towering over her, and the only place she had to point her nose was up at him. "My offer stands this last time. Name and location."

He could almost feel the war rage in her. For the first time he saw her face flinch in fear. He wondered how many people she had double-crossed or left in her wake as she slipped into the shadows. If he won this battle, what others could he win on the hunt to capture her boss and end a major arms operation?

"And what if I said it is too late? She cannot be saved?"

"Then your boss and all your former clients will know where you are kept. I'll make sure of it." He turned his back on her and began to walk away.

"Dmitri Novechek," she nearly shouted.

Nick breathed a sigh of relief that she hadn't called his bluff. He slowly turned around. "Location. Now," he gritted.

Her hands shifted, the metal cuffs jingling with the movement. "I do not know a location, but you will be lucky to find him. He is ruthless, cunning, and knows how to hide. I do know where he is going but not when." She spat an address before a small smile of triumph twisted her bitter features. "It may already be too late for your nosy girlfriend and her terrible friend."

Nick took a step back, fighting the urge to run in her presence. "Fiancée. She's my fiancée. And she's tougher than you give her credit for."

"I would not count on that if I were you."

This time it was Nick's turn to smirk as he turned to walk away. "Oh, I like my odds. You see, she's marrying a United States Navy SEAL."

Chapter 42

THE DOORS OPENED outward, the beams of a flashlight streaming into the dimness. They had a direct view of the moonlit ocean from what appeared to be a quiet inlet. A man entered, but Kaylan couldn't make out his features behind the glow of the orb.

"Come out, come out, my beauties. There are few places to hide, and I am not in the mood for games."

Kaylan bit down on her tongue, fighting a sarcastic reply. Better to learn what he wanted and try to play her cards right. She needed to buy time. Squaring her shoulders, she skirted the edge of the boat to stand before him. Tall and stylish, his blond hair fell across his forehead in a boy-band style. Gorgeous didn't quite describe him. Neither did ruthless. His eyes were as fathomless as a pit, and she tensed as his gaze raked her body.

He laughed. "Anya did not do you justice. My clients will be very pleased with you."

He closed the space between them with a few steps. Kaylan spotted two more men entering behind him, both Arab in appearance, both impassive. Two on three. She wasn't thrilled with those odds.

The blond man reached behind her head, pulling her hair loose from the band and fluffing it around her shoulders. His fingers drifted down her jawline to her neck, and he stepped even closer, shining the light into her face. Kaylan fought the urge to cringe and run, but she refused to show fear.

"If I didn't want the money, I would be tempted to keep you for myself."

Kaylan inwardly curled away from his leering gaze as his hands settled on her waist and pulled her close to his body.

"Oh, please." Megan broke in, shouldering her way between them. "Why does Kaylan get all the hot guys? Can't a girl get a little appreciation around here?" Megan threw a hand on her hip, her dark sultry gaze raking the man before them.

Kaylan almost grabbed her friend when the man threw his head back and roared with laughter. "Janus did not tell me she sent a comedian. We will have to identify just the right buyer for you." His smile fell away immediately, and his hand cracked across Megan's face, sending her to the floor. "But you will learn to control your mouth, my flower. These men like their women seen, not heard."

Kaylan fought the urge to kneel down next to her friend, but her gaze remained unwavering on their assailant. She anchored her feet, preparing to defend herself if necessary, but his smooth smile had returned. "You may call me Dmitri. I think I will have some fun with you. I promised two beauties, but I did not say when."

Grabbing Kaylan's chin, he placed a rough kiss on her mouth. She yanked away, running the back of her hand over her lips, and spitting on the rough boards beneath her feet. His grin made her blood run cold.

One of the Arabs began preparing the boat, the other standing off to the side while Dmitri stood watch. Kaylan eyed any means for escape. They could slip out the doors into the shallow water and up the slight sandy embankment she could barely see in the darkness. Shadows of other boat docks sat what seemed like miles away in the moonlight. If she could make it to one of those... The grind of a crank caught her attention. The Arab man lowered the speedboat into the shallow water below. If they got on that boat, they would lose their ability to escape. If only...

Dmitri motioned to the deck. "Climb aboard, lovelies. Time to leave."

Kaylan placed her hand on Megan's arm, and neither of them budged. The smile slipped from Dmitri's face, and he maneuvered around the sinking boat to stand in front of them.

"Let us establish a few ground rules, *da?* When I give you a command, you will obey immediately." He gripped Kaylan's chin again. "Or I will make life very difficult." His gaze drifted to Megan. "Do we understand one another?"

While his gaze focused on Megan, Kaylan let the wrench slide down her sleeve and into her waiting hand. She swung with all the strength she could muster, clobbering Dmitri on the side of his head. He stumbled backward, falling onto the deck of the descending boat.

"Megan, run!"

The two bolted out the open doors, Kaylan splashing into water that came up to her waist. They fought through it and hit the sand. Another splash sounded behind her, and she knew they didn't have long before the Arab and Dmitri caught up. She forced herself to run as fast as she could. Her long legs kicked up sand in the cove, but she kept pace with Megan's shorter strides. They would get out of this together. She would accept no other alternative.

Kaylan glanced behind her. The guy who had stood watch was in close pursuit.

"Faster, Meg!" Kaylan wasn't sure where they were running. She aimed for the closest boat dock, but it was too far down the beach. She realized for the first time how isolated their hiding place seemed. She didn't know if they were still in Imperial Beach or

Coronado or farther up the coast, but one thing seemed certain: they needed to get to civilization quickly.

The man lunged and grabbed Megan around her waist. She tumbled to the ground under his weight, crying out as she fell. With one hard slap of his hand, Megan went limp, groaning as she lay in the sand.

Kaylan turned around, facing off with Megan's attacker. Her hands itched to still hold the wrench, and she regretted that she'd lost it after hitting Dmitri. Her eyes darted around the beach near her feet. She spotted a rock the size of her palm lying a foot away. Keeping her eyes on the man before her, she snatched it from the sand, suddenly feeling stronger with a weapon in her possession.

The man remained expressionless. His fingers twitched, and his eyes studied her every move. Kaylan doubted he spoke English.

"Just let us go, and I won't say a word." She shifted the rock in her hand as she moved toward Megan, who struggled to sit up.

Down the beach, Dmitri screamed instructions in a language she didn't understand as he advanced on their position. She reached for Megan.

"Go, Kayles." Megan shoved at her hand, trying to push herself up.

Kaylan could run. She could attack the man, hope to knock him out with some of the moves Nick had taught her and then get help. But she knew she would never find Megan again, and she wouldn't leave her friend behind.

Too late; the decision was made for her. Dmitri appeared and yanked Megan from the sand, gripping her arms in his thin hands. His white teeth glistened in the moonlight as he reached behind his back and retrieved a gun. He raked the barrel down Megan's cheek, and she whimpered in response.

Kaylan's heart sank.

"You have spirit, my flower. But I will beat it out of you yet. That was stupid." He spat and nodded to his companion. "Take her."

The man standing before Kaylan took a step closer, his eyes on the rock in her hand. She could tell by his movements he didn't fear her, and her heart sank. She dropped the rock and raised her hands, but the man lunged forward and gripped the back of her neck in his hands, tossing her forward.

Kaylan fought to stay on her feet, but she went down hard, feeling the impact as her knees hit the sand first. Her hands stung from the bite of the tiny grains. She pushed herself to her feet, just as a booted foot made impact with her ribs. Her body jerked as she flew onto her back. A groan slipped through her lips, betraying her pain.

"Enough." Dmitri barked. "Get her on her feet."

The Arab yanked her up. Pain rippled through her body. Her ribs ached as she forced herself to walk in front of the man back to the boat shed, her heart heavy at what lay ahead. Dmitri shoved Megan along in front of her.

As her feet hit the wood of the shed, her gaze found Dmitri glaring at her, the gash above his eyes running with blood. She fought the fear welling inside her. He looked mad enough to kill. Dmitri grabbed Kaylan's arm in an iron grip and tossed her to the boarded floor. Megan cried out, but remained powerless as the Arab shoved her into the boat. The other Arab had stayed with the boat, and at Dmitri's nod he started the engine.

Kaylan tried to stand, but Dmitri's hand flew, colliding with her cheek and sending her head smacking into the floor. She tasted blood and spat, refusing the tears.

The cold feel of metal at her neck paralyzed her as Dmitri crouched over her, pressing his body to hers. A knife dug into her throat, and she fought the urge to swallow, despite her cotton mouth.

"I think I will have some fun with you, my beauty. Teach you some manners, hmm? I like my women feisty, but I do not tolerate disobedience."

261

The knife dug into her skin, and something warm and wet trickled down to meet her collar.

His finger traced down her face, and she recoiled as his eyes studied her as one would a deer they had just killed. He let the knife tip drift down her chest and hover over her heart, his face inches from hers. She fought the urge to turn away and instead glared, anger burning away every passive bone in her body.

"What a pity to waste something so unique, so beautiful." He leaned closer and smelled her hair. His breath tickled her ear as he whispered, "Do not defy me again, or your friend will taste the bitterness of this blade."

He placed a long, harsh kiss on her mouth, and Kaylan thrashed beneath him. When he finally lifted his head, her lips tingled and burned where he'd made contact.

He pushed off her, towering over her crumpled frame as she shoved up on her elbows. "You will learn respect before I am through with you." He yanked her up and dragged her on the boat.

Despite the weakness in her knees, Kaylan fought to stand. She tore away from his grip and took a seat next to Megan. The two huddled together, shivering and holding hands as the boat maneuvered into the bay. With each passing second Kaylan fought hopelessness. It was an emotion she couldn't afford. Not now. Not ever.

Chapter 43

KAYLAN GRIPPED THE seat as the boat rocketed out to sea. She studied the water skidding by beneath them and swallowed. Jumping would feel like hitting a sheet of cement. She remembered being thrown from the jet skis one too many times going forty miles an hour. She needed a different plan, but nothing came to mind.

Nothing but prayer. She'd sacrificed her peace with the Lord for her anger over what He allowed with the earthquake and Sarah Beth's death. This time she refused to question Him. But somehow none of this seemed fair. Just when she'd found a rhythm with Nick and the beginning of a beautiful future together, all hell broke loose.

Again she struggled to trust God in a new way. She knew none of this would have happened if she weren't dating Nick. But regardless of where this situation led, she wouldn't trade one day with Nick for a thousand days of safety.

Megan leaned in close to be heard over the engine and thrashing waves. "Got any bright ideas?"

"Prayer." Kaylan smiled at her roommate.

"What is it with you and thinking some invisible man in the sky is going to get us out of this? You have no idea what's coming."

Inwardly Kaylan groaned. "I have a good guess."

The boat turned quickly, tossing Kaylan and Megan to the floor. The driver yelled gibberish over the noise and banked the other way, adding another burst of speed. Kaylan could almost hear the engine groan in response. Dmitri pulled a gun and stalked toward them. Bracing his feet, he pointed the gun at Megan's head and looked to Kaylan.

"Who did you notify?" he yelled, a vein popping at his temple.

Kaylan stared back, her hands forming fists.

He pressed the barrel into Megan's head. "Who did you tell? How?" he screamed. Kaylan wondered if he would sacrifice money to kill them before reaching their destination.

He shoved Megan out of the way and squatted next to Kaylan, the gun pointed at her chest. "I have an itchy trigger finger. Now tell me who is following us."

Kaylan's head snapped up, and she strained to see around him. He yelled and yanked her up with him, pulling her back against him and pointing the gun at her head. "I know the SEALs are challenging target practice. But I'm an excellent marksman. And I have bested one before."

Kaylan saw the glint of moonlight on the side of a boat before it disappeared in the darkness. She strained to listen. Another speedboat perhaps.

Dmitri whirled her around and ran his hands up and down her body, patting her pockets. "How did you tell them, huh? How did they know?" His face turned purple when he found nothing on her, and he pushed her back to the deck.

"Maybe your precious Anya sold you out," she spat. "Did you really think you could take us without retribution? You just ticked off an entire community of Navy SEALs."

His foot connected with her already sore ribs, and she bit back a cry. Wincing, she rolled out of his way as he thundered back to the wheel and shouted instructions.

Megan helped her back onto the seat, the sea spray drenching them. "Do you think it's them?"

Kaylan squinted in the darkness, unable to make out anything. "He thinks it is. Maybe they made it back. Maybe it's the Feds. I don't know."

Megan stared at Kaylan in awe. "Maybe there is something to this praying thing."

"True. But we're not out of this yet." Her mind began ticking again with possibilities. "Still have that screwdriver?"

Megan lifted her shirt slightly to show Kaylan the tool. "You thinking what I'm thinking?"

Kaylan nodded. "One of them comes close again, you use it."

Megan's eyes glowed black. "Nothing like a kidnapping to turn a pacifist into a fighter."

The boat behind them veered into sight, moonlight glinting off its white sides. Kaylan's heart jumped as she recognized Jay's boat. Relief flooded her. They were going to get out of this.

"Woohoo, Lover Boy and his sidekicks arrive to save the day," Megan cheered, the sight of the SEAL team bolstering her spirits.

Dmitri let loose a string of expletives before motioning one of the men to take care of Megan and Kaylan while he joined the driver and began yelling over the sound of wind and waves. Megan tensed and slipped her hand beneath her shirt, retrieving the screwdriver. Kaylan moved closer to her as Megan hid the weapon in the space between them on the seat. Kaylan felt her trembling.

Lord, please, help.

The man grabbed a piece of rope from the deck and reached for Kaylan's hands, binding them together with lightning speed. Kaylan winced as the ropes dug and chaffed her tender skin. Glancing at Megan out of the corner of her eye, she mouthed one word, "Now."

Megan threw her body forward, shoving the screwdriver into the man's leg. He let out a cry of rage as he lost his balance.

Without waiting, Kaylan grabbed his shirt and propelled him forward, Megan helping as they shoved him into the sea. He tumbled once on top of the water before disappearing. The boat behind them swerved to miss him. One down. Two to go.

Dmitri cried in rage, glancing behind him at Megan and Kaylan. With a jerk of his hand the driver forced the boat to pick up speed.

Megan tugged at the ropes binding Kaylan's hands, pulling them free. Just as the rope slipped from Kaylan's hands, Megan screamed and jerked backward. Kaylan's heart stopped.

"You are more trouble than you're worth," Dmitri screamed over the wind. He held Megan tight against him, his hand yanking a handful of her hair. Megan whimpered as Dmitri pulled his knife free from his belt and brought it to her throat.

"Say good-bye."

Just as Dmitri tightened his grip on the knife, a shot fired. Kaylan hit the deck. She heard a scream and a splash. Megan and Dmitri were gone.

Her brain felt like a foggy mess as she stumbled to her knees. Jay's boat slowed, and the distance lengthened between them. In the moonlight Kaylan watched two bodies dive overboard. She stifled a sob. Would they find Megan? Had she been shot?

The distance and the darkness made it impossible to see the events unfolding behind her. She forced herself to focus on escape. She whipped her gaze back to the man driving the boat. They'd maneuvered closer to the coast, and Kaylan caught a glimpse of a mansion embedded in a cove.

The drop-off. If she entered that house, she might never come out. She could no longer discern a boat behind them. She was on her own. Even if the SEALs came, she didn't have time to wait.

She clenched her fists, still feeling the rope gripped in her fingers. Goosebumps danced up and down her arms, and her hair whipped in her face. Her fingers felt stiff from the cold and nerves.

Could she overpower this guy and take over the boat? He glanced warily back at her, a gun within reach.

She had to try. She wouldn't disappear without a fight.

She remembered Nick's instruction that anything and everything could be a weapon. Wrapping the rope around her fists, she pulled it taut and studied the man. About five foot ten. Wiry build. Cagey eyes. No emotion. She'd have a fight on her hands for sure, but Nick had taught her to leverage what she could. Praying for strength, she began to crawl toward the front of the boat, trying to balance against the speed of the boat and the wind ripping past her.

Taking a deep breath, she shot to her feet and charged the last few steps, throwing her arms around the man's neck, the rope pulled tight. He gagged, struggling to hold his balance. She jumped on his back, wrapping her legs around his waist and pulling back on the rope with all her strength. The rough strands bit at her hands, but she held on.

His hand flew backward, grabbing a handful of hair and yanking. She screamed but tightened her grip. She had too much to lose. The boat careened into the cove and Kaylan panicked, worried they would crash. The man gurgled and whipped the wheel, sending the boat back into the waves in the open sea. A wave rocked over the side of the boat, sending shivers of fear over Kaylan. If they didn't crash, they might capsize. She wasn't sure which she preferred.

Kaylan doubled her efforts as the man grabbed his gun. Though he choked, she couldn't seem to leverage her weight enough to knock him out. A boat zipped into view and pulled even. Micah stood at the wheel with Nick leaning over the side.

Nick. Kaylan realized her grip had slipped a second too late. The man yanked her head to the side again, his gun tilted backward. It fired close to her head, and she dropped from his back. Her head rang. Her stomach heaved. Everything moved in slow motion. And somewhere nearby Nick yelled.

A pair of dark eyes closed in on her face. His breath smelled like liquor. He said something indiscernible, raised the butt of the gun, and connected with her head.

Pain shot through her skull as the world faded to black. The last thing she heard was the sound of gunfire. Then nothing.

Chapter 44

NICK WATCHED THE scuffle from Jay's boat, his blood boiling as he fought the urge to have target practice with the man on board, but he couldn't get a clean shot. When Kaylan jumped the man, he bit back the urge to cheer. Now they had a fight.

"Bulldog, get us close to that boat."

His best friend gunned the engine and brought them even with the boat. Nick leaned over the side. The water splashed and frothed, trails from both boats winding behind them and disappearing into darkness. He dug his boots into the boat, trying to find traction.

"Hawk, you can't jump!" Micah shouted over the wind. The sea grew choppier the longer they stayed out, and Micah fought to keep the boat straight.

A gun fired, and Kaylan fell backward.

"Kaylan!"

Their boat rocketed past as the other boat slowed, their speed decreased in the scuffle. The man turned and smashed Kaylan's head.

"Hawk, jump now," Micah yelled as he pulled even to the other boat again.

Nick didn't think twice. He leaped right as the other boat accelerated. His gun tumbled loose and into the water as he hit the deck and rolled, slamming into the back of the boat. Nick pulled himself onto his knees, taking stock of anything close to him and hating himself for losing the pistol.

The man driving the boat turned and caught sight of Nick. Nick heard a string of Arabic before the man pointed the boat to the beach and accelerated. He turned and pointed his gun down at Kaylan, never transferring his gaze from Nick's. Beads of sweat formed on the man's forehead. His left hand shook, but his right hand gripped the gun without hesitation.

The man knew he'd been beaten. He closed his eyes, and dread filled Nick. A martyr.

Nick crouched, took a deep breath, then rushed. Even with a few inches on the man, he felt like he hit a solid wall. The man's eyes flew open, and he fired a wild shot. Nick didn't even have time to make sure it missed Kaylan. He used all his strength, shoved the man through the partial glass windshield, and sent him plummeting over the side of the boat.

Nick grabbed the wheel and jerked with all his might, but it refused to budge. He fought the accelerator, but the man had jammed the track, making it impossible for Nick to slow their speed. He yelled as they narrowly missed a rock. They were going to hit shore in a matter of moments, and this boat would blow. He was tired of exploding boats. He signaled to Micah they would need to jump.

Micah maneuvered his boat away, giving them space and slowing in preparation for removing them. Nick worried about hitting the water at this speed, but they had no choice. He knelt next to Kaylan.

"Kaylan, baby. Wake up. We gotta jump." She groaned, blood pulsing from her head, but her eyes remained closed. Nick glanced up. Four hundred yards from shore and closing. No time.

He swung Kaylan over his shoulder, her long legs dangling. He shoved himself onto his feet, fighting the motion of the boat. Digging his feet into the deck with all his might, he ran and jumped.

His head plunged under water, and he lost his breath. The icy current seized his body. Kaylan slipped off his shoulder, and he grabbed her around the waist. Kicking with his remaining energy, he pushed them to the surface, breaking just as an explosion rocked the beach. He covered her head, shielding her with his body.

Heat seared his back even as the waves carried him farther away from the shore. Kaylan moaned in his arms, and Nick's stomach dropped. He needed to get her out of the water. Now.

He scanned the darkness, finally spotting the boat. With a wave and shout, he caught Micah's gaze and waited as his friend maneuvered closer.

As soon as Micah pulled even, he cut the engine and reached for Kaylan. Nick shoved her upward into her brother's waiting arms.

Waves lapped at Nick's face, and he spat salt water. Grabbing the side of the boat, he pulled himself on deck. He landed and rolled, for a moment too tired to move.

"C'mon, sis. You are not allowed to go out on me like this."

At the strain in Micah's voice, new adrenaline spiked through him. Nick crawled to where Micah bent over Kaylan on the deck, pumping her chest and blowing air into her lungs. Her face was deathly pale, and a gash leaked blood on her forehead. He reached for her fingers. Ice cold.

"Kaylan Lee Richards, you are not leaving me like this." He pushed Micah out of the way and began to pump her chest, stopping to breathe into her mouth. *Lord, please don't take her. Not like this. Not yet.*

With a shudder she gagged. Nick uttered a cry of relief as he rolled her over. Gasping and coughing, she threw up seawater.

"Thank You, God," Micah croaked.

Nick pulled Kaylan into his arms as they shivered on deck. "I love you." He kissed her forehead. "I love you so much. Don't you ever do that to me again. The only one allowed to have near-death experiences from now on is me, got it?"

Kaylan laughed weakly, her voice scratchy from swallowing salt water. "I thought we were supposed to share everything."

Nick kissed her forehead. "Not that."

The sound of another boat engine broke through the slosh of water. "The Feds are here, Hawk. Looks like they picked up the others."

"Megan?"

"Jay, Colt, and Titus have her. She's fine. Looks like they caught Dmitri too."

Kaylan wilted in his arms, tears streaming down her face in relief. "I can't believe you're here. I can't believe you found us."

Nick rose up on his elbows to look at Kaylan. He studied every part of her face. A bruise blossomed on her cheek, and he touched the spot gingerly, anger filling him at whoever had hit his girl.

"I'm okay, babe. But I never thought I would see you again."

He cupped her face and kissed her bruise, her cut, then settled on her lips. He kissed away the terror and a long night of wondering. He kissed away the possibility of never seeing her or holding her again. They'd made it. And he would never let her go again.

"Break it up, you two. Save it for the honeymoon."

Micah grabbed Nick and pulled him off Kaylan. Then he reached for his sister, wrapping her in a blanket as he pulled her into his arms. She nuzzled into her brother's chest, her tears flowing unchecked. "We better call home. And just get ready for Mom and Dad to give you the lecture of your life," Micah grumbled.

Nick hung his head in relief. Justice at last. They had Janus in custody, had caught the head of a major human trafficking ring, and hadn't lost the girls in the process. Regardless of the struggle, he could live with the results.

Chapter 45

AFTER A KIDNAPPING and near-death experience, Kaylan had spent time taking a hard look at her life. The truth was she missed a lot of things. Kaylan missed the colors of fall in Alabama. She missed the cool, crisp air, the need for sweaters, family game nights, making s'mores in the fireplace with her brothers. She missed her parents, grandparents, and brothers. She missed Sarah Beth. She missed her quiet, sheltered life in Alabama. But she didn't miss missing Nick, and as much as nostalgia overcame her at times, she wouldn't trade her life now for anything.

She curled tighter around the throw pillow on the couch, thankful to let her body rest after the harrowing events of last Saturday and a week back at her internship. With the mundane events of each passing day, she relaxed a little more. Even Megan had begun to unwind a bit.

Megan padded into the living area and flopped down in the armchair, yawning. Her short, dark hair twisted haphazardly around her face. "Thank goodness it's Friday."

"Mmm-hmm. And it's almost Thanksgiving."

"You headed home?"

"Yeah, Nick, Micah, and I are flying back to Alabama for a few days."

"Must be nice."

Kaylan pushed up on the couch so she could look at her roommate. "What are your plans?"

"I have a date with a really cute new guy."

"Not another one, Meg."

Megan held up her hands. "Trust me. You'll like this one. He's handsome, has a beautiful fin, and a smile that lights up my world."

Kaylan grinned. "New dolphin at the aquatic center?"

Megan smiled. "He's a beauty. And so much fun."

Kaylan noted the bruises healing on Megan's head and face and the way her eyes didn't light up with her smile. "Meg, why don't you come home with us for Thanksgiving?"

"You don't want me with your family."

"I wouldn't have it any other way."

Megan fell silent and nodded, looking down at her lap. "I prayed, by the way."

"What did you pray for?"

"That if I'm wrong, God will show me who He is." She rolled her eyes. "Better move, though. I might get struck by lightning for questioning the Big Guy."

Kaylan laughed. "If that actually happened, you never would have met me. I can't even count the number of times I've asked Him 'why' this year."

"But you don't doubt Him? Even after losing your best friend, getting kidnapped, and almost getting shot?"

"Believe me, I've wondered about that. But I finally stopped asking Him 'why' and started focusing on my response. When you understand that God is good not because of but in spite of circumstances, you stop questioning His character every time something bad happens."

"He's big, though. He could've stopped all that."

"Yes, but He chose not to."

"Why?"

Kaylan stood and tossed her pillow at Megan. "Maybe so you would ask Him the tough questions." She tousled her roommate's hair as she walked by. "He can handle them. Keep asking. He's not afraid of the questions."

"Well, you may convert me yet."

"If I can get you to a relationship with Jesus, I can live with that. Now c'mon. Let's go book you a plane ticket to Alabama before Nick picks me up for our date."

Nick wrapped Kaylan in his arms as soon as she stepped from the house. "How's my girl?"

"Fine, Nick. Stop worrying about me."

He held her away from him and checked the gash on her head. "It's healing well. I'm so sorry he did this to you."

Kaylan buried her head in his chest. "I'm sorry too."

"For what, gorgeous?"

He felt her hold her breath and made himself wait her out, fearing the answer.

Finally she exhaled. "He kissed me. A couple times. And I couldn't stop him." Her soft voice broke his heart.

Nick ran his fingers through her hair wishing he could have pulled the trigger on Dmitri. Wishing the man experienced worse than what he put the kidnapped women through, and then hating himself for wishing that. *Lord, forgive my vengeful heart.*

"Kaylan, look at me."

She slowly raised her head to meet his gaze. He brushed his fingers down her cheeks and over her lips. "Allow me to erase that memory."

He took his time, kissing her forehead, her cheek, whispering his love. When his lips finally met hers, he worked to erase her hesitations, reassuring her that he would love her no matter what, and no evil person could erase that. He let his hands drift down to her waist, holding her close as if to reassure her that nothing could ever steal her away or hurt her again.

After minutes they were both breathless. "I love you, Kaylan Lee Richards. Nothing can change that. And it is not your fault. He was sick and twisted."

He tugged her toward the Jeep. "Come take a drive with me."

A gentle wind whipped through their hair as they drove along the beach. Her fingers were wrapped in his, and he refused to let go the whole ride, letting the miles bleed away the stress, worry, and pain of the last week.

He'd asked for a blood test to determine if Janus really was his mother—but for now he'd only told Kaylan that her neighbor, Cathryn, had been the one threatening her and had been apprehended. She'd rightly been enraged, but they were working through it. Dmitri was facing massive charges. The two Arabs had died, their bodies recovered the next day. The Big Kahuna had slipped back into his shoes as a high-ranking businessman in Russia, but Nick knew he was being watched. They would catch him in due time. The weapons were confiscated before they made it to Iran, but Nick guessed his team might head to the Middle East in the future, possibly on his next deployment. But none of that mattered. For today, he had Kaylan, he was home, and life was good. Everything in the shadows had been brought to light.

He pulled into a sandy lot and parked. Grabbing a couple of blankets from the backseat, he jumped from the car and spread one out on the hood overlooking the ocean.

"Hop on."

Kaylan clambered up beside him and tugged a blanket over her legs. Together they watched the sky change color to a blood red as the sun sank.

Kaylan broke the silence first. "You might change my mind. Sunsets are pretty good here."

"I'm sorry. What?"

Kaylan giggled and curled up under his arm. "I'm not repeating that twice. I will not cheat on sunrises or my lake house."

"It's not cheating if it's truth."

"Loyalty, Nick. Loyalty."

"For you, always. For my team, without question. To Alabama, well…"

She punched his chest, drawing a laugh from him. "Okay, okay. Alabama's not so bad. But we'll have to agree to disagree on sunsets and sunrises. By the way, I have something for you."

He sat up and pulled something from his pocket. It glistened in the failing light.

"My ring. I was starting to wonder if you changed your mind."

She reached for the ring, but Nick closed his fingers over it. "On second thought, since we can't agree on this whole sunrise, sunset thing, I don't know what we can agree on. Maybe it isn't meant to be."

Kaylan gestured to the sinking sun and the pinks and oranges now mixing with the red. "It's amazingly beautiful. Better than sunrises. In California," she added under her breath.

'Well, I guess that will have to do. Conflict resolution at its finest. May I?" He reached for her hand and slipped the ring on her finger. "Promise me something?"

She leaned close to his face, her green eyes glowing in the dimming light. "Anything."

"Don't ever take this off again."

Her fingers drifted over the scruff on his chin. He loved her gentle touch. "Never."

He clasped her hand and kissed her fingers. "Great. I have one more surprise." He reached into his pocket again and withdrew a box.

"What's this?"

She opened the lid and her breath caught. On the top of a sheet of cotton he'd placed a chain with dog tags. He removed the chain from the box.

"Kaylan Lee Carmichael," he read as he slipped the chain over her head.

Tears filled her eyes. "Nick, I can't believe you did this." She turned the tag over in her hand. "'Charm is deceptive and beauty is fleeting, but a woman who fears the Lord is to be praised.' Nick." Her eyes met his.

He brushed her cheek, thankful for the depth of love that now radiated from her eyes. Her walls had dropped. She trusted him completely, loved him fully, and depended on the Lord whole-heartedly. In that she found strength, the heart of a warrior the size of any SEAL he knew.

"You amazed me out there. You fought hard for your friend. I could kill you for not getting help. But your courage is undeniable."

She laughed. "There had to be proof I was strong enough to marry a SEAL."

His fingers drifted down her cheek and into her hair, pulling her face to his. "No, Kayles. I never needed any proof. You had it in you all along. Your strength comes purely from your relation-ship with the Lord and who He made you to be. God is faithful, and I'm honored to call you mine."

His lips met hers as the sun sank lower, colors dimming in the light of his love for her. He deepened his kiss, his fingers weaving through her hair. His Kaylan. His gift. Something he would never deserve but God had given. He silently thanked his Savior.

Kaylan drew back and rested her forehead on his. The colors were gone. A turquoise sky hovered above them as stars began to appear. "So what's next?"

He leaned back against the windshield, pulling her against his chest. "Now? I guess it's time to plan a wedding. And I can't wait to marry you, Kaylan Richards."

"Soon to be Carmichael, mister."

He kissed her forehead, thankful that no matter what came their way, he'd found a woman capable and willing to stand by him forever. In her he'd found an invaluable treasure.

COMING FROM KARISS LYNCH WINTER 2016

BOOK 3, HEART OF A WARRIOR

SURRENDERED

Chapter 1

THE BATTLEFIELD, POCKMARKED with old cars and metal remains, yawned before Nick Carmichael and his team of SEALs. He'd never fought a battle quite like this before, nor faced a more formidable opponent. He crouched behind a beat-up red pickup truck. The insides had disappeared at some point, leaving the shell to the mercy of enemy fire. Nick dug his boots deeper into the mud, evidence of rain the night before, although the deceptively blue sky showed no trace of it now. Despite the slightly cooler January temperature, moisture seeped from beneath his armor. He hated feeling stuck and sweaty.

He folded his body behind the tire to avoid the peppered shots coming from the other side and glanced down the line to Micah Richards, his best friend and the brother of his fiancée, Kaylan. The enemy had them penned for now, but Nick grew tired of waiting.

"I thought you said she knew how to shoot," Nick shouted over the cacophony of paintballs striking the truck bumper.

Micah lifted his face mask and rolled his eyes. Yellow paint splattered above his head, causing him to duck.

"Masks on!" shouted the referee from across the field, and

Micah slapped his mask down again just as a pink paintball splattered near his feet.

"I said we taught her. Not that she was good." He shrugged, his voice muffled beneath the plastic. "At least they are hitting somewhat close to us."

Across the field their SEAL buddies Titus, Jay, and Colt crept from obstacle to obstacle, avoiding fire until they finally huddled with Nick and Micah. David and Seth Richards—Micah's brothers visiting for the week—joined from the other end of the metal line.

The San Diego paintball course affectionately named "The Fuel Depot" stretched the length of half a football field. It reminded Nick of a deserted old gas depot in some podunk Southern town. Nick peeked from behind the tire to get a better lay of the land. Old cars, painted to look rusted, long since retired, sat scattered in something resembling a horizontal line formation from one end of the field to the other. Barrel obstacles sat stacked two tall and two wide throughout the course, providing the perfect cover for their wives and girlfriends regaling them with colored paint. The girls had insisted on playing with one fewer teammate, convinced they could still dominate.

They could shoot. They just couldn't aim.

"Come on out, fellas!" Titus's wife, Liza, yelled as another barrage of fire peppered the air.

"Yeah, don't be chicken." Megan, Kaylan's roommate, hollered from behind a barrel.

"Says the girl at the back of the course," Jay shouted back. He spat in the mud and crouched behind the truck with Nick. Self-titled "team prankster," he clearly didn't see the current predicament as challenge enough for his skills.

Nick pulled a piece of Juicy Fruit from his pocket and popped it in his mouth. "Colt, you got eyes on all the girls?"

Colt's grin sparked beneath his mask. As team daredevil, taking on the ladies seemed the perfect job for him. He'd even brought a date, Jia, a leggy redhead more skater girl than hipster. Where most of the guys dreaded the repercussions of shooting the girls and hearing about it later, Colt didn't carry that emotional stake just yet. "Jia is to our right about fifteen yards behind the brown Chevy. Liza is the closest behind that jacked-up blue bug."

"My sister is hiding out behind a couple of barrels off to our right and back about twenty yards," Seth huffed beneath his mask. A University of Alabama linebacker, his shoulders barely fit behind the single barrel he crouched behind.

"Anyone else?"

At their silence Nick rolled over again, trying to gauge the direction of the paintballs with the locations he now knew. His sniper skill served him well in moments like these. Melody, David's girlfriend, popped from behind a single barrel at the back right of the field to fire a shot. He grinned at her shoot-and-hide approach. That left one more.

"Jay, where's your date, man?"

"My what?"

Micah bent next to him and slapped him across the chest. "Gorgeous blonde, successful lawyer, way out of your league, responds to Bree. Ringing any bells?"

"Oh, right." His bored expression caused Nick to chuckle. "She's got guts. She's behind the car right next to Liza and sneaking pretty close to our line."

A movement caught Nick's eye, and he fired. A frustrated cry met his ears as Bree stood tall with her hands over her head. "I'm out. You happy?"

"Well, one down." Nick rolled and sat up, swiping the drying mud from his cargo shorts. "Jay, if you don't like her, why'd you bring her?"

"Because Megan won't go out with me. Now, for the love of everything sacred, can we please put them out of their misery?" Jay begged as he readied his gun. "Whose idea was it to play paintball with a bunch of women anyway?"

"I can't take much more of this. They think they're winning," Colt huffed.

"They have to be about out of ammo," Titus said as he swiped a bead of sweat rolling down his neck.

The sun hovered in the California sky, heating the metal around them. Nick sighed. "Kaylan bruises like a peach. I'm going to hear about it for the next two weeks."

Jay flipped his mask up, his blue eyes incredulous. "That's what's holding us back? Man, forget this!" With a whistle the men took off in twos and threes, taking cover behind the obstacles. Gunfire erupted in earnest. The SEALs were out to win.

Micah slapped Nick's back, chuckling as he scurried off. "She's your problem now, my friend. No refunds or exchanges."

"I haven't married her yet," Nick muttered as feminine cries filled the air. He might as well help end this quickly. He rolled onto his belly beneath the truck and took aim. He watched Kaylan creep closer and take cover behind two metal barrels fifteen yards away. She took aim facing away from him, her green eyes intent beneath her mask. Nick grinned. Why not up the stakes a bit?

"Yo, Seth! Feel like picking on your big sister?"

Seth shuffled closer and leaned down to hear as the carnage continued, the SEALs now fully engaged and decimating the enemy. "What do you have in mind?"

Nick's smile spread wider in anticipation, his breath heating the air in his face mask. "How 'bout a game of catch? Keep her distracted while I sneak up behind her. I'll take her hostage, and we'll force the girls to surrender."

Seth smirked. "You do remember this is paintball and not BUD/S, right?"

Nick remembered well his days training to be a SEAL, but it's what made this faux war even more fun. "You're playing with

SEALs, son." He slapped Seth on the back and crouched low to take up his position before Seth could toss another jab his way. He needn't have worried. Seth trained his sights on his sister instead.

"Hey, Kayles, we taught you to shoot better than that."

His taunt worked like a charm. Kaylan fired and the shot went wide, causing Seth to momentarily duck and snicker. His head popped up as he continued his teasing, fulfilling his role of younger brother. Nick ran to the next barrel. A shot came from his right. He swiveled, aimed, and fired in a fluid movement, taking out Megan, who lost her balance and fell rear first into the mud in surprise.

"Seriously?" Megan shrieked. She swiped at paint on her protective vest as she stood to her feet and stalked off the field. "I hate pink."

Nick smirked, imagining her in the pink bridesmaids dresses Kaylan was thinking about choosing in honor of Sarah Beth, her best friend who had died in the Haiti earthquake almost a year before. He shook his head. Only two barrels remained between Kaylan and him, but Kaylan had eyes only for Seth.

His shoes squeaked in the mud as he ran to the next barrel, assessing the scene. Bree, Megan, and Jia slumped off to the side, watching as the guys cleaned shop. Jay stood fuming next to them, paint on the center of his mask and covering his thigh. "Let's end this, men," he shouted. Only Kaylan, Liza, and Melody remained in the game. Nick knew just how to force their hand.

With a final sprint he pounced on Kaylan, forcing a squeal as she tried to swivel around.

"Nuh-uh, gorgeous. Just drop the gun nice and easy."

"Nick Carmichael, this is paintball, not war games, and I am trying to shoot my smart-mouth little brother."

"I'm afraid I can't let you do that. He may be a smart-mouth, but he's on my team."

"I heard that, traitor!" Seth shouted.

Nick pulled Kaylan to her feet in front of him with his arm wrapped around her and his gun held at the ready in his other hand.

"All right, all right. Game's over, ladies. Time to give it up," Nick called across the field to Liza and Melody.

"Don't think because Kaylan is in front, we won't still shoot," Liza hollered. Titus had married a spitfire, a spitfire he was about to take out from the looks of it.

"Liza, look out," Melody and Kaylan yelled from different sides of the field as Titus crept up.

Liza spun and fired at Titus just as Colt let loose a round that splattered against her back. She howled, and her eyes shot daggers at her husband. David put a quick end to Melody with a shot to her toes peeking out from beneath an old, dented Cadillac, and the game ended.

Kaylan swung around in Nick's arms, her green eyes sparkling. "That, my dear fiancé, was world-class cheating."

Nick bit back a chuckle. He pulled her face mask off, placed a finger under her chin, and murmured, "When you learn how to actually shoot, we might call it a game."

"You jerk," she squealed. "I grew up in the South. I can outride and outshoot most other people."

Nick crossed his arms over his chest as Kaylan's brothers and Melody joined them at the barrels in the center of the field. "First of all, not everyone in the South rides a horse, so don't perpetuate the stereotype. Second, you are playing with Navy SEALs. You will never outshoot us. And third, your brothers epically failed to teach you how to shoot at anything."

"Hey there, don't blame us. We tried." Micah popped Nick on the back of the head.

"She finally shot a coke bottle a couple of years ago," David said as he threw his arm around Melody. The petite blonde folded her arms and leaned into him, her smile evidence of her familiarity with Richards' family banter.

"Actually," Seth interrupted, "I kind of shot that bottle and let her take the credit." His sheepish expression almost made Nick feel sorry for Kaylan. Almost.

"Seth Richards, I really am going to kill you." Kaylan's face went red as she took off after her brother. She was no match for the sophomore collegiate football star. He let her chase him before turning around and flipping her over his shoulder. He trundled back to his family as she screamed.

"Shall we?" he motioned to the parking lot where the rest of the guys and their wives and girlfriends were gathering to leave.

"I'll take her," Nick responded, bracing himself as Seth dumped Kaylan into his arms. Nick swung her into a cradle position as David, Micah, Seth, and Melody walked ahead of them to the gravel parking lot. Laughter drifted on the breeze, and Nick thanked God for the family he would join in just a short time.

He gently placed Kaylan on the ground and they hung back for some alone time, Kaylan gazing after her brothers. "You know, sometimes I hate that my brothers are all much stronger and taller than I am. I think God made a mistake by not giving me a sister." A sadness stole across her eyes, tugging at Nick's heart.

He pulled her into a hug. "You had one, babe," he murmured, thinking of Sarah Beth, Kaylan's childhood best friend. Joy. That word always came to mind when he remembered her.

"I know."

They walked in companionable silence and climbed in his Jeep. Nick allowed the silence to linger as he pulled onto the road behind his friends and headed back toward Coronado and the house he lived in with Micah. Gravel crunched beneath his tires, and a thin layer of trees lined the back road as they pulled away from the pop of other paintball games behind them.

"Speaking of sisters..."

"No, Kaylan."

He felt her eyes on his profile as he kept his gaze glued to the road. He added pressure to the gas pedal.

"Nick, we've got to talk about it. You've got to talk about it. It's already been a couple of months since you learned of her existence. I know you've been busy with work and then Christmas and now my brothers visiting, but you need to meet her."

He met her eyes. "I thought we were talking about Sarah Beth. When are we going to talk about her?"

"That's not fair, Nick."

He gripped the steering wheel, regretting the low blow. "I know. I'm sorry."

"January tenth is a week away. I can't believe it's been a year since the Haiti earthquake. A year since she…you know. I'll figure out something. It's just hard. No one here knew her."

"Your brothers are here, and they did. Let's do something to remember her while they are in town."

The wind grew louder in her silence, and he glanced over. She sat rigid, her jaw tight, her eyes moist. She swung her gaze to meet his, and the fierce look surprised him.

"I promise I will figure out a way to grieve and celebrate Sarah Beth, if you promise to plan a time to go meet your sister."

"Kaylan…"

"Promise."

He gripped the steering wheel harder, the hot rubber uncomfortable beneath his sweaty palm. "I promise."

"I want her at our wedding, Nick."

His heart leapt at her quiet statement, the highway symphony almost drowning her out. He ground his teeth and punched the button to turn on the radio.

A cloud drifted over the sun and a cool breeze chilled his skin. He didn't want to deal with this. He didn't want to deal with any of it.

But he no longer had a choice.

Be Empowered

Be Encouraged

Be Inspired

Be Spirit Led

FREE NEWSLETTERS

Empowering Women for Life in the Spirit

SPIRITLED WOMAN
Amazing stories, testimonies, and articles on marriage, family, prayer, and more.

POWER UP! FOR WOMEN
Receive encouraging teachings that will empower you for a Spirit-filled life.

CHARISMA MAGAZINE
Get top-trending articles, Christian teachings, entertainment reviews, videos, and more.

CHARISMA NEWS DAILY
Get the latest breaking news from an evangelical perspective. Sent Monday–Friday.

SIGN UP AT: nl.charismamag.com

CHARISMA MEDIA

P0780